"An irresistible hook, an unlikely (bu. the winsome voice of author Angela Ruth Strong come together in *Husband Auditions* to form a sweet and funny love story readers will adore. Simultaneously an homage to and a lampoon of old-fashioned pursuits of matrimony, inspirational romance fans will gobble up this thoroughly modern tale. I was completely charmed from aloha to aloha."

BETHANY TURNER, award-winning author of *Plot Twist* and
The Secret Life of Sarah Hollenbeck

"*Husband Auditions* is as hilarious as it is charming! Angela Ruth Strong once again brings her unique voice and quirky sense of humor to create memorable, laugh-out-loud characters that subtly teach important lessons in love—and not so subtly linger in our minds long after the final page is devoured."

BETSY ST. AMANT, author of *The Key to Love*

"Original and fun! *Husband Auditions* is a wonderful staycation of a book. Grab your latte and prepare to giggle."

KRISTIN BILLERBECK, author of *Room at the Top*

"A sweet, warmhearted love story that encourages the soul and draws plenty of smiles. Readers of Christian romance will enjoy this fun, modern tale of a list that, when used as intended, just might snag you a husband."

MELISSA FERGUSON, author of *The Dating Charade*

"To say I enjoyed *Husband Auditions* is an understatement—I loved it! My favorite contemporary book of the year. With realistic, heart-drawn characters, issues that are all too relatable, and laugh-out-loud moments galore, I thoroughly recommend Strong's latest novel to readers who appreciate romance, comedy, and truth. Run and get it now!"

CAROLYN MILLER, author of the Regency Wallflowers
and Regency Brides series

"In Strong's signature way of weaving a story that's equally full of laughs and depth, *Husband Auditions* covers all the bases for a home-run rom-com and then delivers a grand-slam finish."

JAYCEE WEAVER, author of the Everyday Love series

"The moment I read the premise, I couldn't wait to get my hands on this book. *Husband Auditions* is a delightful abundance of comedy and chemistry interwoven with the rich themes and characters I've come to expect from Strong's writing."

HEATHER WOODHAVEN, author of *The Secret Life of Book Club*

"In *Husband Auditions*, Angela Ruth Strong delivers humor, romance, and a heartfelt message. Romance fans will laugh their way to a unique happily-ever-after."

TONI SHILOH, author of *An Unlikely Proposal*

"*Husband Auditions* is a fun and quirky romance. The perfect read to unwind from a challenging day."

KIMBERLY ROSE JOHNSON, award-winning author of Christian romance and romantic suspense

"*Husband Auditions* is a delightfully humorous bookish escape. Filled with outdated advice on how to snag a husband—and a quirky heroine willing to follow such suggestions as carrying around a hatbox—readers will snicker their way to an ending that may be even more satisfying than a simple happily-ever-after."

SARAH MONZON, author of the Sewing in SoCal series

"Perfect for fans of Becky Wade and Bethany Turner, this hilariously irreverent look at the lengths women have gone to for love is seventy years in the making. Readers will adore the oh-so-relatable Meri. And Kai? His lovable, sloth-with-a-heart-of-gold personality is a refreshing and delectable addition to the dreamy hero hall of fame."

JANINE ROSCHE, author of the Madison River Romance series

HUSBAND AUDITIONS

HUSBAND AUDITIONS

A Novel

ANGELA RUTH STRONG

KREGEL
PUBLICATIONS

Cataloging-in-Publication Data is available from the Library of Congress.

ISBN 978-0-8254-4710-5, print
ISBN 978-0-8254-7673-0, epub

Printed in the United States of America
21 22 23 24 25 26 27 28 29 30 / 5 4 3 2 1

To my sister Emily,
whose independence as a single woman
inspired me when I unexpectedly became
single again

CHAPTER ONE

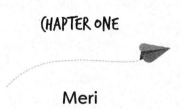

Meri

#16. Work as a waitress or nurse. Men love being taken care of.

I hated *My Best Friend's Wedding.* No, I'm not talking about the ceremony I just took part in, which was absolutely beautiful despite that the bridesmaid's dress I'm still wearing makes me look like an origami swan. I'm referring to the movie with Julia Roberts and Cameron Diaz.

Okay, honestly, it was a good movie until the end. Spoiler alert: The rich, beautiful blonde gets the guy, while the heroine is left alone.

Granted, Julia's character had been conniving and selfish at times, but since she learned a valuable lesson through the story, I can't help thinking that both she—and I—deserve a happy ending. As for Cameron being jilted at the altar—who cares? Again, rich, beautiful, blonde.

But I'm none of those, so what hope do I have? Not only am I still wearing this ugly grass-green dress, that's uncomfortably strapless and slipping dangerously low, but . . . I caught the bouquet! To make the situation even more embarrassing, my competition was a gang of eight-year-olds.

That's right. I'm the last of my nursing-school friends, or any of my friends for that matter, to be single.

Hmm . . . Maybe I'm glad Julia Roberts is still single at the end of the movie because now we have something in common. Me and Jules.

I wish I could claim to also be a tall redhead with a toothpaste-commercial smile. I'm actually an ordinary thirty-one-year-old woman who still looks twelve due to an exorbitant amount of freckles. And my boring brown hair is neither as curly as Julia's hair when it's curly nor as straight as Julia's hair when it's straight. My hair is wavy. Which sounds nice, but really means it can't be considered sleek nor bouncy. No, Julia's character and I are only bonded by the bare ring finger.

Said finger cramps as I grip my luggage tighter, juggle it with my other belongings, and struggle up the one step in front of my younger brother's townhome located in the West Hills of Portland, Oregon. The dum-dum can afford such a place because he's a workaholic, which has left him single as well as successful.

Scratch successful. Having your fiancée leave you because you pri-oritize your career over loved ones does not make a person successful. Let's call him prosperous. And maybe a little stingy too. Which is why he's rented out the spare bedrooms to a couple of his classmates from film school.

Of the three of them, he's the only one I *wouldn't* consider a starv-ing artist. Though they must all be starved for affection, judging by their singleness. Unfortunately, I'm about to join their Bermuda Tri-angle of relationships.

I'd usually go right in, but my hands are full. Stupid bouquet and such. I kick the door a few times in attempt to sound as if I'm knocking.

I don't want to live here for the summer, but I currently have nowhere else to go, and three months will give me some time to figure out what I do want to do. The only thing I know for sure is that I can't keep all my stuff in my old garage indefinitely, since Anne lives there with a husband now.

I stare at Charlie's trendy, cranberry-colored door. So misleadingly cheerful. And still closed.

Music drifts from inside.

I kick again and add a "Hello?" for good measure.

Nothing. My brother's Subaru Legacy is in the parking spot behind me, so I know he's here.

I do an upright row with a tote bag to press my elbow to the doorbell.

No footsteps tap to the beat. Fine. I'll perform a juggling act and open the door myself.

I slip the tote up to my elbow until I'm tilted sideways like the patient with back problems who came into my doctor's office last week, but at least I'm able to grip the doorknob. I twist and release. The door swings open to reveal the far windows with a view of the city skyline underneath the snowy white peak of Mt. Hood—like a Facebook frame on an Instagram filter.

This image is not picture perfect, however, because sitting on the kind of black leather couch you'd expect to find in a bachelor pad like my brother's is Kai Kamaka. Feet up on one of the two cube-like coffee tables, MacBook on his lap.

I'm surprised the guy is awake during the day. Five years after graduating, he still works at the same place where his school counselor got him an internship and, like a nocturnal college student, he prefers the night shift. He's a prime example of the shortage of mature men in the world and why I haven't been able to find one yet.

He grins at me and my charade of a pack animal. He has one of those grins that would have gotten him out of trouble for pulling the fire alarm as a kindergartner but can only be considered childish after the age of five.

"Hey, Meri," he says in a voice much too deep for elementary school. "Why are you wearing a dinner napkin?"

Now that I think about it, the folds in my bodice do resemble the aforementioned part of the table setting during today's reception dinner, but that's not the issue here. "It helps soak up all my sweat when I'm left standing in the burning heat by a lazy roommate who refuses to open the door." Okay, the heat actually feels warm and inviting. I always appreciate sunny days in Oregon. But again, not the issue.

Kai lifts his phone. "I'm not lazy. I checked my phone to see if anybody texted to say they were coming over. No texts."

The hipster definition of hard work. Though I'd consider Kai more of a skater than a hipster. Even though I've never seen him on a longboard, I'm sure he has one. He's lanky, wears baggy clothes, and his shiny, dark hair hangs almost in his eyes. If we lived in the state of his heritage, Hawaii, I'd call him a surfer. We do have some surfers here in Oregon, but due to water temperature, they must wear wet suits and be real diehards. Kai is not a diehard. So, we'll stick with skater.

"Dude," I speak his language. "You're not the only person who lives here."

"Oh, that's right. Welcome home." He turns his attention to his computer screen. "Why'd you even knock if you live here now?"

My dramatic motion toward my luggage is lost on him. Or maybe he's pretending he doesn't notice so he won't feel guilty for not helping me carry anything.

Charlie thunders up the stairs at the back of the living room. At least I know my brother will lift the load from my shoulders. In the twenty-seven years I've known him, I'm not sure I've ever seen him sit on a couch with his feet up. Even when he was a sick two-year-old, he was more likely to climb the fridge, looking for medicine to fix his problems. Of course, as his older sibling, I got in trouble for that stunt.

"Hey, sis." He grabs two of my suitcases without a hug. He'll remember to hug me later. Connection is always an afterthought with him. "Why are you still standing outside?"

If I had his energy, I would be moved in and painting my room by now. "My hands are full, and your roommate wouldn't get up to open the door."

Kai grins at that. No shame. "Next time you want me to open the door, yell, 'Pizza delivery!'"

Charlie rolls my suitcases toward the staircases, one of which goes up to the master bedroom, the other of which goes down to the daylight basement. "Kai. Get up and help, or I'll raise your rent."

Kai folds his laptop, pushes to his feet, and moseys my way. There's not much left for him to help with. Just my tote, purse, bouquet, and an evil card from the bride that I'm surprised I haven't put through a shredder yet. I adjust so I can carry everything without his help.

His eyes light on the bouquet. "How many single ladies did you knock over to catch that thing?"

If ever there was a time for a witty retort, this was it. Tragically, the place where I keep my witty retorts—my pride—is still wounded from the memory of standing in the middle of a ballroom surrounded by giggly elementary schoolers who had to have the idea of a "bouquet toss" explained to them by the DJ. My only hope is that these freckles served as camouflage. "None. I'm the only single lady left."

Kai clicks his tongue and reaches for my tote. "Well, now you're doomed."

My shoulders slump, which makes it way too easy for Kai to slide the bag from my elbow. I'd meant to refuse his help. "Doomed to be embarrassed at weddings," I mutter.

"No." Rather than turn and lead the way, Kai pauses, blocking my path.

Is he expecting a tip for his service as a bellhop? Is he going to hold my luggage for ransom? It's not as if I have much left to lose. My home, my best friend, my future? All gone. I'll open my purse and hold it out for him to take whatever he likes.

He doesn't look at my purse but narrows his eyes. "I meant you're doomed to have the next wedding."

Oh? Oh . . .

I stand up straighter. One's man doom is another man's destiny. But who could *my* man possibly be?

I'm a nurse. The only men I ever meet are either coughing on me or sporting contagious rashes. Unlike every other decision I've made in life, I didn't get into medicine for the men. I got into it because Charlie was always getting hurt as a kid and bringing him a Band-Aid made him smile. Which gave me the feeling I could change the world.

The little rascal thunders up the stairs again. "Meri, get in here. I didn't say anything before, but you're letting the cold air out, and now that you're subletting my room, you'll be paying part of those utility bills."

He'll remember to hug me eventually. I'm sure it's on his mental to-do list. Somewhere below "remind Meri to pay utility bills."

Kai saunters away. It's a saunter this time rather than a mosey because he's swinging my tote in a very sauntering way. "Where do you want this?" he asks, obviously lacking my brother's Thor-like affinity for stairs. He drops my bag at the end of the couch before I have a chance to answer.

I sigh and close the door, which momentarily distracts me from thoughts of both Kai and my future husband. Have you ever noticed how people in the movies hardly ever close doors? The actors simply walk into a room and leave the door wide open as if people in Hollywood never had to face the harsh reality of a utility bill. I'm sure Charlie won't let that happen in any of the films he directs. He's going to revolutionize the industry.

You know what would be cool? If he got nominated for an Oscar someday and took me as his date—since most other women in his life won't wait indefinitely for a hug the way I will—and that's where I meet the man of my dreams. I scrunch my lips, trying to remember if any of The Avengers are still single.

"You okay, Meri?" Charlie frowns. "Oh, I forgot to hug you, didn't I?" He strides over, and I find myself in his signature choke hold. Why did I want a hug from him again?

Kai kicks his bare feet back up on the cube I vow to never eat off and flips his laptop open without a glance my way to make sure I'm surviving WrestleMania. "Don't take her attitude personally, Charlie. She's just upset she caught the bouquet at the wedding."

I guess I'm being a little cranky, aren't I? It's not their fault I'm lonely and homeless.

Charlie grips my shoulders and looks down at the crushed peonies. At least they still smell fresh like summer. I'll dry them and store them in a vase for my flower girls to sprinkle down the aisle on my big day. Because maybe Kai's right. Maybe I'm doomed-slash-destined to have the next wedding.

"I thought women *wanted* to catch the bouquet." I know Charlie partly says this because he cares, so I'm okay with the knowledge that he's also asking as research for some future project.

I pull away and drop the flowers in question, along with my purse and the vile envelope, onto the shiny concrete breakfast bar that separates the living area from the kitchen at the front of the townhome. I hoist up the top of my dress as discretely as possible then head to get a drink. "My problem isn't with catching the bouquet as much as it is with *the circumstances* of catching the bouquet."

"I don't know what that means." Despite all Charlie's talent, he can't read between the lines.

I grab a glass from the stainless-steel shelves he has in place of cabinets and cautiously press it to the lever on a refrigerator. I'm cautious because I'm still getting used to my fancy acrylic wedding nails, and because the appliance is high tech enough that I half expect it to reach for the glass with a robot arm.

Water spouts into my glass anticlimactically, freeing me to resume our conversation.

Charlie wants to know my feelings in black and white? Then I'll give him black and white. I point to the envelope on the counter.

If I'd been less dehydrated from hauling all my belongings up the walkway, I would have taken the time to deposit the contents of the card into Charlie's fancy trash compactor. Though I'm probably better off letting him do that for me. Just in case the trash compactor has a robot arm.

"Look what Anne gave me as a parting gift." I lift the glass to my lips and lean my head back to guzzle the cooling liquid down my sandpaper throat. Doing so also helps me avoid looking directly at The List.

Paper rustles. Charlie separates the card from its contents. "Dear Meri, I'll never forget our time as roommates. I loved our pedicure parties, movie nights, and borrowing your grandpa's binoculars to spy on the firefighters—"

I set the glass down. Had it not been breakable, I would have slammed it down. "You can skip that part."

Kai snickers, though he could have been laughing at a SpongeBob cartoon with the way his gaze remains locked on the computer. That sounds like his kind of humor.

Charlie scans to the end of the card. "I always thought we should have a double wedding, since we were the last single girls standing, but now that it's down to you, I'm passing on The List. May it bring you the same kind of happiness I found with Damian."

Charlie blinks at me. "I'm still not getting it. You caught the bouquet. Your friend is wishing you well. What's the problem?"

"I'm last, Charlie. You know what it's like to be last, don't you?"

"No. And I never want to find out."

"Exactly!" How did the guy ever get engaged before me when he still needs people to explain the basics of emotion?

"Okay. That makes sense now." He looks from the card in one hand to the folded pages in his other. "What kind of list brings love? Is it from the Bible? The Proverbs thirty-one wife?"

Not even close. "It's from a 1950s issue of *Sophia Magazine*. Ideas on how to catch a husband."

Charlie sets the card down to unfold the thin, yellowed pages ripped from a magazine by Roxy's grandma once upon a time. Roxy was the first of our group from college to get married, though I doubt it had to do with any suggestions from The List.

Charlie smooths the creases. "Number one: *Volunteer with shelter dogs*." He looks up, hazel eyes lacking humor. "That's fine, but you can't bring any animals home. I have a strict no pet policy."

My suspicions of his being heartless are confirmed. "I'm not actually going to try these things."

"Why not? If it helps you find a mate . . ."

"First, you're not allowed to say *mate* unless you have an Australian accent." I wrinkle my nose at the word. "Second, as I said, I'm not going to do any of those things. This is supposed to be more of a good luck charm, passed around from friend to friend since we attended nursing school. I am both offended that I'm the last to get The List and by the fact that Anne thinks I need it."

Charlie lifts a shoulder. "There might be more to this than luck. Remember, G.G. grew up in the fifties, and she caught herself three husbands."

"Scandalous," Kai chimes in. Probably not talking about Sponge-Bob anymore. "Who is this GiGi woman?"

I wave him back to his computer. "G.G. is short for great-grandma, and she only remarried after the first two husbands died. Nothing scandalous about it."

Though I can't help wondering if she ever found her one great love. If she'd loved her first husband as much as my mom loved my dad, wouldn't she have stayed single the way Mom did? Or maybe it was too hard to be a single mother in those days. I shouldn't judge.

Charlie points to the pages from the magazine—proof that women in the fifties were anxious to wed. "The point is that she *did* remarry."

I shake my head. I'd shown Charlie these pages so he'd understand where I'm coming from. "Keep reading. Volunteering at a shelter is normal, but it gets weirder."

"Number two." He clears his throat. *"Fake a flat tire or pretend engine trouble."* He sets the papers on the counter. "Okay, that might have been safe back then, but I don't want you doing that now. If your car breaks down, call me. Or Kai, since I'm leaving tomorrow."

Kai? Really? "Do you even own a car, Kai?"

"Nope." He taps at his keyboard with finality. Apparently, skaters look down on practical modes of transportation.

"Okay then. Call Triple-A when your car breaks down. I'd help, but I'll be out of the country."

"I know." He's acting like an older brother even though he's four years younger. He thinks I need protecting. Just as Anne thinks I need help with relationships.

The front door swings open. The most beautiful woman I've ever seen walks in. Scandinavian-model beautiful. I was intimidated by her at first, as I'm sure most people are. Women anyway. Men probably look at her and instantly decide they want her to have their babies. Which is why Mom was originally against her being roommates with Charlie.

Then Mom met Gemma and her goofy playwright personality.

"Hey, roomie," I say.

Gemma is also the reason Mom is okay with me staying in Charlie's townhome with a male while he's gone. I tried to tell her that Kai shouldn't even count in the male/female roommate ratio because he's the opposite of my type, but she pulled out her trusty "appearance of evil" verse that somehow still gives me guilt trips as a grown woman.

"Hi, Meri." Gemma floats over. "You look pretty."

It's a good thing she's a writer, not a costume designer. "Thanks."

"Gemma." My brother turns her way. "Would you trust a stranger to help you if your car broke down, or would you call someone you know for help?"

She runs her fingers through her long golden locks and stares off into space with her ice-blue eyes for so long that she must have forgotten to answer. She's probably plotting the moment when her hero and heroine first meet, a meet-cute she calls it. But then she blesses us with her smile that's as gorgeous as it is innocent. "That's happened a few times. The men who have helped me have all been really nice."

I'll bet they were nice. "Gemma doesn't count. She doesn't need a list. Guys use lists to meet *her*."

"What list?" she asks.

I roll my eyes and motion to the pages. "Suggestions from the fifties of how to find a husband."

"You're looking for a husband?" she distractedly asks as she skims the article written over half a century ago. "Oh, if you volunteer at a pet shelter, you sadly can't bring any puppies home. I wanted one, but Charlie wouldn't let me."

She *is* The List. "I'm not really going to do these things."

"Why not?" She scrolls the page with her finger. "Look at number three: *Offer to take your dad's new car for an oil change. Have the cutest mechanic check your odometer, so he knows you're not the type of girl who gets around.* If you meet a guy who changes your oil, he'd know enough about cars to help when you get a flat tire too."

I'm ashamed to admit I almost consider it. Except my dad died way before I learned how to drive. And even if he were still alive and had a new car, I don't like the idea of being judged by my mileage. I always thought I would have traveled more by the time I reached my thirties.

"Wait." Gemma taps the page. "Number four says, *Move to a state with more men than women. We recommend Nevada.* You're not that desperate, are you?"

How did I suddenly get classified as desperate?

Charlie crosses his arms. "I was in Vegas last month for a film festival, and there seemed to be a lot of single women. I'm sure those stats have changed since this was written."

Why did he sound so serious? "I'm not moving to Vegas. And not only because it would send Mom to an early grave."

"Speaking of graves," Gemma lifts the page. "Number five suggests attending funerals to meet new widowers."

"It does not," Charlie objects without even reading it.

"Yes. It does." Maybe now both he and Gemma will realize this thing is only a joke.

Kai chuckles from his spot on the couch.

I glare. The only way Kai would ever get married is if a woman mistakenly tried #17. *Treat a bad guy like the hero you want him to be.*

"I know you won't do *that*." Gemma shrugs. "But you're already doing number sixteen."

"What?" I ask. "Move in with your brother's roommates when you have nowhere else to go?"

"You could go to Nevada." Kai.

I ignore him.

"No, sweetie." Gemma rubs my bare shoulder with her silky fingers. "Number sixteen says, *Work as a waitress or nurse. Men love being taken care of.* If you want to get married, I'm sure you'll find a man soon."

Her little pep talk is making me feel even more pathetic. Or maybe that's just because I'm standing in her angelic presence. Either way, I am hating this conversation.

CHAPTER TWO

Kai

#32. Act in a play with him. Preferably as Romeo and Juliet, but if he turns out to be brainless like the Scarecrow in The Wonderful Wizard of Oz, *play the part of a tree and throw apples at him.*

I am loving this conversation. I don't mean to eavesdrop, but the whole list of ways for women to trap a man is comedy gold. Especially since it has Charlie's little sister freaking out so badly. I mean, he's only twenty-seven, so how old can she be? Twenty-four, twenty-five? Hardly spinster material. Though I'm half tempted to buy a newspaper simply to hand her the obituaries section so she can start attending funerals.

I smother another chuckle and try to focus on my Google search. During my ride home on the light rail, I saw a camera crew filming in the Lloyd District. Based on what looked like actor Riley Avella in tights, it had to be that new superhero television show *Capers*. The tights were disconcerting, to say the least, but what bothered me even more was the angle the cameraman chose.

Hopefully the guy realized his mistake and asked for a retake. I would have. *If* I ever decide to give up my simple life of newsreel editing for Channel 7 at night. It's not glamorous, but it's easy. And it's a great excuse to sleep all day. Also, I recently got a promotion, so I don't have to work weekends anymore.

It's all right . . . until days like today when seeing something more creative being filmed gives me this itch inside, a desire to do more than follow a reporter around and clip the best part of interviews to paste together. I usually scratch the itch and quench the desire by going online and looking up positions to see who's hiring. Or I'll watch a few episodes of the show filming locally to see if it's anything I would want to be a part of. Then I can get rid of my discontentment.

I say things like:

Wow, that's honestly the stupidest show I've ever seen about unicorn rodeos.

Or . . .

Since they only film a few months out of the year, I don't really want to scrounge for another job like a bum the rest of the time.

Or . . .

I don't have as much experience as they require. I'd probably have to start as a camera assistant, and I'd rather be a bum.

This job listing, though. This one is going to make me dig deeper. I liked the show, the editing hours start in September and are the steadiest I've seen, and I have almost all the experience required.

I think I do, anyway. I keep getting distracted by Meri's list of dating tips. She's currently trying to kick off the high heels that are strapped to her feet. Either that or she's trying to kick Gemma. It's hard to tell when only watching from the corner of my eye.

"I know you're being kind, Gemma," says the bridesmaid dressed like Tinker Bell, "but my best bet is number twelve: *Make friends with beautiful women. They usually have a cast of unwanted suitors.* Do you have any leftovers?"

I don't even try to stop my snort. Gemma has no leftovers because she's too busy in her fantasy world of "plot and character" to ever notice the men falling all over themselves to open doors for her. I know this because I was once one of them. Got the broken toe to prove it. Though I think if I ever told her about that crush our freshman year of film school, she'd be shocked. She simply thinks the world is full of nice men who like to do nice things for women. All. The. Time.

But that's not why I snorted. I'm snorting at the suggestion of "leftovers." This is advice from the June Cleavers of the world? And they say men are pigs.

Gemma's long lashes flutter in confusion. "What do you mean by leftovers?"

I stretch my arms along the back of the couch to draw attention my way and help her stay sweet. "Gemma hardly has any leftovers because she's such a good cook."

Gemma beams at the compliment, while Charlie lifts one of his skeptical eyebrows.

Meri huffs. She was likely looking for a blind date out of the deal.

Gemma pats my head as she breezes past toward the stairway. "Don't judge him too harshly, Meri. He's got a good backstory."

I don't know about "good," but I say, "Thanks, Gem," anyway. I watch her grab the handrail to go upstairs, wondering if she'll realize her mistake. She doesn't and hops up the first step in her checkerboard Vans. "Where ya goin'?"

"I'm going to write . . ." She points the direction of her old room then lowers her hand. "Oh yeah." She pivots around to head toward the basement.

In the same way Charlie's mom made a big deal out of giving Gemma the master suite upstairs when she moved in so she wouldn't have to "share a bathroom" with a man, Charlie also made the two of us switch rooms while his sister is here. I think there's more that bothers him than the idea of simply sharing a bathroom, but I'm not going to complain. I get the master suite.

One might expect Gemma to be put out by her sentence to the dungeon, but with the way her eyes are glossing over, she's already in her fictional world.

I tuck my hands behind my head. "Don't rush back from Ecuador, Charlie. Not only do I get the master bedroom upstairs, but I get two lovely ladies to cook and clean for me."

Now that Meri has wrestled her shoes off, she's going for the earrings. "I'm not cleaning for you, Kai."

I'd seen the way she looked at the coffee table when I propped my legs up, so I just grin in triumph. "I'm gonna grow on you like the fungus on my feet." Ha. That will keep her cleaning late into the night. "You might actually like me by the time you leave," I assure my new maid before remembering she's on a mission to wed. I motioned toward the pile of papers on the counter. "Just don't try any of that stuff with me."

She narrows her eyes. I think she's trying to look menacing, but with all those freckles, she's as scary as a toddler in time-out. "Rats. There goes my whole plan."

Her sarcasm surprises me, and I laugh, then look back down at my computer. What was I working on again?

"As for your feet, you should really try using a blow dryer on them after you shower. Then put on talcum powder to keep them dry."

"I'll keep that in mind . . ." If I ever actually get athlete's foot.

Charlie leans on the counter in the kitchen, still engrossed in The List. "Even if you get your fungus taken care of, Kai, I don't think you have to worry about Meri trying any of these things on you." He looks up and studies me with the same intensity he'd been giving her. "I can't see her fainting in front of you as number ninety-five suggests, or wearing shoes one size too small as recommended in number thirty-seven."

I shoot Meri one more grin before focusing my own list: qualifications for a role as editor. "Too late for the shoes. You already kicked those off, revealing your giant feet."

"You really are a fun guy." She puts emphasis on "fun" and "guy" to make sure I know she was referencing the plural form of fungus supposedly on *my* feet. And she wonders why she's single.

"Don't worry, Meri. You might still have a chance with Kai." Charlie laughs because he knows this is a joke. "According to number thirty-four, you're supposed to wear a dress, so maybe following the advice for your outfit cancels out the shoe trouble."

"Yes. I only ever propose to women in dresses." I coat my words in sarcasm to keep out the chill of truth. As if our conversation is based on any kind of reality, other than the fact that women are manipulative. With a magazine from my grandmother's generation giving women advice on being dishonest, how was I ever supposed to trust another woman again?

This is one reason I don't worry about women besides my mom anymore. I don't need the headache. I prefer to avoid the difficulties in relationships by staying to myself.

I work for Charlie sometimes. With his documentaries, it's all similar to working for Channel 7 News. Nothing too creative. Plus, he's on the controlling side, so it can affect our relationship as roommates. I learned the hard way that I'd rather chill on his couch than hide out in my room to avoid talking shop. Not to mention the jet lag involved in all his travel.

But this. Filming a television show in town. I can't convince myself I don't want it. Blast the need for a demo reel.

I lean my head back against the couch and stare at the track lighting designed to look like spotlights. What material can I use? Interviews? Panoramas? Seriously, for a city that gets forty-four inches of rain per year, my footage is all incredibly dry. You'd think with the whole "Keep Portland Weird" slogan on buildings and bumper stickers that I'd at least have some video of the bagpipe-playing unicyclist.

Doing *her* part to "Keep Portland Weird," Meri speaks. "Charlie, stop looking at me as if I need help. No self-respecting woman would ever put on such a show to find a husband."

Put on such a show . . .

She keeps talking. "Did you read all the way to the end? Number ninety-four suggests learning how to use a lasso and roping the cowboy of my dreams."

I can see it now. Meri in cowgirl boots, swinging a rope over her head. I'd start with a close-up, making the viewer think she's on a ranch, then I'd pan out to reveal a city sidewalk where passersby shoot her startled and curious looks. Or being that it's Portland, maybe the citizens don't even notice. That could be funny too.

The Cowboy Way meets *The Bachelorette.* Who wouldn't wanna watch?

I have my phone out and in camera mode before I even realize what I'm doing. It's instinct. In hopes that my subjects don't notice they are being filmed, I keep my feet propped up. I zoom in. If only I had a boom mic to pick up every syllable of the conversation between brother and sister.

At least at this close range, I can really study my new roommate. She's not gorgeous like Gemma, for which my big toe is grateful, but she's cute. Sassy. Entertaining.

Her freckles are probably her most memorable feature. They will make her relatable, and viewers will find her sympathetic. Her upturned nose gives her kind of a cartoonish whimsy, which will tell an audience something unexpected is always right around the corner in her life. Her light-brown eyes flash with the kind of hunger that probably runs in the Newberg family and makes Charlie so good at everything he does.

Then there's her hair. She's got a lot of it, and you can tell she doesn't quite know what to do with it all. I've only seen it in ponytails when she's stopped by after work in her scrubs, but when attending her friend's wedding today, she probably wanted it to look all Victoria's Secret for the guy who caught the garter. Instead, her hairstyle resembles something out of *National Geographic*. Wild.

I smile.

Charlie chuckles at his own thoughts.

I wait for him to share.

"I'd love to see you on the street corner with a lasso. Too bad I'm not going to be in town for this."

Meri gives a jerky head shake, causing her layers of hair to sweep over bare shoulders. She throws her arms wide.

I pan out to keep her hands in the frame and also include Charlie.

"You're not going to be missing anything," she says, "because The List is going in the garbage." She picks it up between thumb and forefinger as if it's a dirty diaper and twirls toward the trash compactor.

I open my mouth to stop her. But why would she listen to me? How could I possibly talk her into making a fool of herself so I can get a job?

I needn't have worried. She clearly doesn't know to step on the lever at the bottom of the appliance. She pokes at it a few times with a finger, then slaps it with her palm.

The List is safe for a few more minutes at least.

Charlie doesn't step in to fix her problem as he normally would. "You should keep it. I know you're not really going to try to lasso a husband . . ."

I visualize cutting from this scene to Meri on the corner with a lasso.

". . . But that list has been passed down to you, and one day, once you're married and have children, you can pass it down to your daughter."

She stills in front of the trash compactor, and something in my chest twinges at the thought that she might be afraid she'll never be a mom. But then her fire returns.

She's tossing her hair and waving The List, and I'm slouching in relief. My favorite kind of slouch.

"Why would I pass this list down to my daughter? It's an embarrassment to my gender. It's a mockery of romance. It's a joke on society."

Melodramatic much?

"It's also a bridesmaid gift from your best friend." Charlie has a point.

Her arm lowers.

I zoom in on The List. If by chance she figures out the trash compactor and destroys it, I might be able to save some of the text digitally. Also, this is a great shot for promotion and teasers for our YouTube channel.

Though, how am I ever going to talk her into accepting a starring role in what she considers to be a joke on society? I wait. Which is pretty much my motto on life.

"You've had an emotional day." Charlie motions toward Meri's bridesmaid dress and its implications. "Someday you'll want to look back on this and laugh. Stick The List in your card and save it for that day."

Her bottom lip juts out in a pout that fits her freckles, but she trudges toward the envelope and dutifully stuffs The List inside. She's facing me from the other side of the counter, so I capture her at the perfect angle. "If I do ever give this to my daughter, it will be as an example of how changing your behavior to please someone else is a poor idea."

Poor ideas in real life often make the best entertainment. Just ask the Kardashi . . . *ahem*. Excuse me. This argument won't help my cause.

It's going to be tricky getting Meri to do a list of things she doesn't want to do, not to mention getting her to do them on film. But now that she's put The List back in the envelope, I've got some time to consider how to approach her.

Her lashes lift, and the enlarged image of Meri on my phone screen stares straight at me. My gut warms from the scorching glare I know I'll get when I look up at real-life Meri. With a strange kind of anticipation, like the itch I felt when watching the film crew work downtown earlier, I look up.

CHAPTER THREE

Meri

*#82. If he wants to never grow up, like Peter Pan,
don't make him face his consequences the way
Tinker Bell did. Be his mom, like Wendy.*

Are you filming me?"

Kai's phone is lifted into a position that looks like more work than would be required for him to simply text or scroll social media. From what I know of Kai, he never does more work than required. But why would he be filming me? If I look as sweaty and windblown as I feel, it's not a pretty sight. My freckles have probably doubled since I got up this morning. Not to mention, I'm about to burst into tears from talking about a daughter I'll never have if I don't get married.

He doesn't lower the phone. "Yes."

"Blackmail material?"

"YouTube material."

I snap my purse open and retrieve my own phone. Two can play this game. I tap on the camera icon to record and point it his way. "How much do you plan to charge me to keep from posting that recording online?"

He laughs. It's a deep laugh. Much more mature than his behavior. "Can you even see me on your screen? At the angle you're filming, I'm backlit from the window behind me."

I look down at my image of him. He might as well be one of those anonymous witnesses on the news where all that's shown is their silhouette. Not good evidence if I want to accuse him of blackmail. I step out from behind the counter and circle the love seat. He turns his phone to follow me, but at least I now have a clear image of him doing it.

Charlie joins him in the image, standing behind the couch, checking his watch. "Are we done here, Meri? Because I need to go pick up my shirts from the dry cleaners before they close so I can pack."

Charlie is leaving right now? I guess I'm not a guest anymore, so he doesn't have to entertain me, but shouldn't he at least be a little concerned his roommate is a blackmailer?

"Go ahead," I say to my brother since, being a single woman and all, I need to learn to stand up for myself.

Charlie grabs his keys, and I sink down onto stiff leather. If Kai ever gets up, I'm going to try out his spot to see if maybe he's worn the material down to be a little softer.

What I really want to do is climb into Charlie's bed and put an end to this day, but as he's not leaving until morning, I'll be spending a night on the couch. There's no getting away from Kai and his camera.

Charlie trots out. The door snaps shut.

I'm alone in a modern-day duel with one of the deadliest weapons of our society. Whoever pulls the trigger first can tarnish the social standing of their opponent. And I'd thought my day couldn't get any worse. "How is this my life?"

Kai's smile widens. He's enjoying our standoff way too much. "What's wrong with it?"

"Oh no. You're not going to get me to vent anymore for your viewing pleasure."

"Then don't vent. List all the great things about today. All the wonderful things about your life as a single woman."

If that's a joke, I don't get it.

"I'll start you off," Kai offers. He motions out the window at the golden sunshine of late evening. "It's a gorgeous night." He nods toward the wrinkled taffeta clinging to my sticky skin. "You got to dress fancy."

"Like a leprechaun."

"I was thinking Tinker Bell, but okay."

He only knows who Tinker Bell is because he's Peter Pan. He'll never grow up. I smile a little at the thought . . . and because he compared me to another Julia Roberts character.

He continues, motioning to the minimalistic decor around us. "You have a really nice place to stay."

My smile fades. "Because I couldn't stay in my regular house where I wanted to stay."

He continues in his uncharacteristically cheerful tone. "Your old roommate married the love of her life."

I press my lips together. It's hard to be happy for Anne and Damian when I feel left behind. But I'm not going to say that on film. The leprechaun thing was bad enough.

"And you are an inspiration for single women everywhere."

My lips burst apart with a *pshaw*. That's going to be attractive when this video goes viral. "I'm no inspiration."

Kai's eyebrows arch and hide behind his shaggy hair. "But you could be."

Really? Since single women everywhere want to be reminded how much it sucks to only dance the fast songs at your best friend's wedding? There was nobody to twirl me around. Nobody to hold me close. Nobody to catch me when my heel snagged on the edge of the dance floor as I was making a hasty retreat. Were my life a love story, that's when a hero would have swooped in.

I hope my facial expressions aren't revealing my memories. I shift on the overstuffed couch and curl my knees in to hide my discomfort. Then I nod at Kai's camera. "Is that what this is about? You want to make me a poster child for single women, which will encourage the girls you date to stop expecting you to grow up and propose?"

Kai tilts his head. His eyes roll to his left. That means he's thinking and that he's right brained. Which I'd already pretty much concluded. The right-brained part anyway. Finally, he shrugs. "I'm sure there could be benefits for me, but it would also benefit you. Let me film you doing the things on The List so you can show the world how silly it is for a woman to try to catch a husband."

"What?" My tone screams, *You're insane*. My goal here is to get him not to show anyone this footage, and he wants to make more videos?

"Yeah." He scratches his temple with his free hand. "It could be fun. And, hey, maybe you'd actually meet someone."

Okay, now he's trying to bribe me. But his offer goes against the whole principle of the idea. "By catching them with a lasso?" A giggle surprises me. The visual is ridiculous.

He chuckles. "Not all the ideas are that crazy. What else is there? Let me see your list."

I'd left it on the counter. I consider vaulting over the back of the love seat to grab The List and hide it from him, but with the way he's got his fungus feet up on the cube, such effort might be overkill. Also, I'm tired.

It's been a long day, and there's no reason to make it any longer.

"Forget it." I end my camera recording and tip sideways until I'm lying down, checking that both my skirt and bodice keep me decent. Not because I think Kai might find my body attractive, but because the world could be watching.

Once on my side, I can block out Kai. Also, he can't see that I'm contemplating his idea. Well, not really contemplating. More like letting my imagination draw pictures of the silliness like a SpongeBob cartoon. Only a character like SpongeBob SquarePants would try #100 on The List—*Get your personal ad in front of as many eligible bachelors as possible. Like on a billboard.*

My limbs grow heavy. Kai's lack of energy is contagious. But that's okay, since I'm already in bed for the night.

Kai moves the camera to get a better shot, though at the range he's holding the camera, it's probably a close-up of my nostril. "You're not even going to consider it?"

I grab a throw pillow designed to look like a movie clapboard and cover my face. "Why do you really want to film me, Kai? That would be work for you."

He's quiet for a moment.

I peek around the corner of the pillow in hopes that he's put his phone away. He hasn't.

"It wouldn't be work. It would be fun." He catches my eye and his jaw shifts in a way that makes him look guilty. "I also need footage for a demo reel, so I can get another job."

That makes more sense. He wants to use my plight for his benefit. I hug the pillow to my chest. "Why didn't you just say so?"

"Because I know you wouldn't do it for me." He taps his phone and sets it down. "But maybe you'd do it for yourself. You'll be like the superhero of single girls."

I sniff. Most single girls have other single girls to hang out with. If I'm a superhero, it's only because my world of single women has been destroyed, much like Superman's world of Krypton.

I'm an alien on a foreign planet. I must learn to survive in this new world, interacting with creatures like Kai and figuring out my purpose. Because it's obviously not what I'd thought it was going to be.

"It could be fun for both of us," he adds.

My body sinks deeper into the firm piece of furniture. "I miss fun." I'm not mumbling an agreement with his YouTube channel idea, just admitting that I don't have many better things to do now that all my friends are going on honeymoons and getting pregnant and stuff. For goodness' sake, I'm stuck sleeping on my brother's overstuffed couch.

I must have dozed off, feeling alone, but I wake up even more alone. The room is dark. Kai is gone. The only sound I hear is the mechanical clinking of the refrigerator making more ice.

I peel my thighs and shoulders from the leather so I can roll over, and realize there's a fuzzy blanket covering me. The silver glow from the city skyline in the distance reveal it to be the monogrammed throw I got Charlie for Christmas. Never in a million years did I think I'd be the one using it.

I grimace at the giant *N* on the blanket. *N* is my initial too. And, despite the bouquet I caught, Newberg might always be my last name.

Maybe it's time to stop wishing someone else would offer me their name and start making a name for myself. So what if I look like a fool in the process? It isn't like there's anybody left in my life to laugh at me. My best friend is flying to France tomorrow and my brother to Ecuador. When will it be my turn to travel the world?

Perhaps there are other women like me out there. I mean, this *is* wedding season. I can't be the only maid of honor left to clean up after the reception.

I'd like to think that rather than being an alien like Superman, I'm one of the X-Men. There are more of us mutants out there. We just haven't joined forces yet.

I wouldn't be the superhero Kai suggested, but I could do the You-Tube channel as a call to arms. My message could join us single girls together. Lonely hearts would watch me on their screens and not feel so alone anymore.

I close my eyes again.

I'm not really going to star in a YouTube channel. I'm just tired. Loopy. Tomorrow I'll sit by Mom at church and be inspired by the way memories of her one true love have kept her going as a strong, independent woman. Julia Roberts has nothing on my mom.

CHAPTER FOUR

Kai

#6. Sit in front of him at church. You're not trying to distract him from the good Lord. You just want to show him how bountiful God's blessings can be.

I sip my bitter dark roast coffee with satisfaction inside the modern entryway of West Hills Fellowship. Meri and I are waiting for Gemma's health-conscious order to be remade. I don't think my blonde roommate realizes that the youth group running the coffee bar isn't experienced with specialty drinks. We might be here awhile.

Meri avoids eye contact as if she's too good for me. Or maybe she's simply ruled me out as a possible suitor in her scan for eligible bachelors. If only she'd let me help. I read that list of hers last night after she started snoring, and there's enough stuff there that we could air our YouTube show daily for the entire three months she's staying in Charlie's apartment.

I smirk. "See any guys you wanna lasso?"

Meri's throat spasms as if she's choking on her drink. "Never." She wipes her mouth and scoots a few feet toward the edge of the room.

Is she instinctively following #44 on The List: *Hang out near the entrance to the men's room?* Or perhaps she's following #55. "Are you going to cry in front of me to let me know I have the power to cheer you up?"

"You can't cheer me up, so that would be a waste of tears."

"Oh, right. According to your list, any tears that aren't manipulative are wasteful. Better go cry in a corner so nobody can see."

"*You* go cry in a corner."

"Good one."

The edges of her mouth curve up despite her obvious attempts to be snarky. "You read The List?"

"I thought you left it on the counter for me." I innocently lift my cup to my lips.

She narrows her eyes. "Don't you have somewhere else to be?"

"Besides the corner?" I can't help it. Though I'm sure she isn't thrilled to have gotten up thirty minutes early to drive me to church only for me to hang out in front of Higher Grounds and make jokes at her expense.

"Do you want a ride next week?" she half threatens. I know it's only half because she's carrying half this conversation, and as she pointed out, either of us could have walked away by now.

It would have been nice if Charlie had agreed to let me use his car when he left for the airport this morning. At least if Meri refuses to drive me anymore, I still have Gemma.

Church is how I met my roommates. Gemma and I were the only ones at Portland State who responded when Charlie advertised a Bible study. So I'll cut his baby sister some slack. "Now that you mention it, I should probably go get my camera equipment set up."

"You do that."

I nod farewell to Little Miss Sunshine, and head into the spacious taupe sanctuary. It's the shape of half an octagon with four sections of seating angled toward the stage. I climb up the side stairs to my booth in the balcony. Somehow, when West Hills Fellowship decided they wanted to start filming sermons, I got roped into being the cameraman. At least it's an easy job, and it gets me out of having to work in childcare or pass the offering bucket.

I power up the computer monitor from where I'll run the slides of song lyrics interspersed with footage of the worship band. Sometimes I get the desire to spice things up by adding the shark from *Jaws* popping out of the water background of a song like "Oceans," but I know if I do, I'll lose my position and end up an usher. Thus, I do the same old thing every week without an ounce of footage that could be used on a demo reel.

After the slideshow is set and the countdown clock is running on the screens up front, I turn on the camera and adjust my focus. The stage is empty, so I pan around the room.

An older couple hobbles to their seats with the aid of walkers. A young mother tries to chase down a toddler running across chairs. A couple of guys my age move in on two women as if they think they're at a bar.

Ah, one of the women is Gemma. Makes sense.

And poor Meri. The sidekick. If only she would film her own show, she could be the star. I press *record*. And bring up the overhead lights for a better image. Just in case.

The guys smile at Meri in a friendly way, but they slap their thighs in laughter after Gemma speaks. Meri looks down at her bulletin, disconnecting. As the guys fight over Gemma's attention, Meri's gaze wanders the room.

Her eyes brighten. She waves her bulletin. Did she find a man who wants to talk only to her? I pan the direction she's looking and find Mrs. Newberg. She's always dignified in her blazers and scarfs, but her short blonde hair and genuine smile make her approachable.

She waves at Meri, which is normal. A man trails after Mrs. Newberg, which is not normal. The guy has hair that he's let turn silver, though his teeth cannot possibly be naturally that white. He's dressed in a long-sleeved black button down, which seems a little formal for Oregon summers. Of course, it hasn't yet warmed up today, and one never knows if it will here in the Northwest. That's not the point though. The point is that as I follow my subjects back toward Meri, I can tell by her stiffness that she isn't prepared to meet this stranger. Maybe his appearance will turn her off to men in collared shirts, and she'll start to see the appeal of baggy T-shirts like the ones I wear.

Mrs. Newberg motions between Meri and the stranger.

Meri holds out her hand and shakes his, but her smile is tight, and her eyes blink a lot.

Does Charlie know about this guy? I once asked if his mom ever dated, and he looked at me as if he'd never imagined such a possibility.

I could be making assumptions here. Maybe the stranger is a coworker. Or neighbor. Or friend's husband, and the friend is in the bathroom.

Meri follows them to a seat and sits on her mom's opposite side from the silver fox. She saves a spot for Gemma, but the dudes who were hitting on her earlier have talked Roommate Barbie into joining them.

Up on stage, the worship team takes their position, and I know I need to aim the lens their way, but I glance once more at Meri. If she hated having her best friend get married, she's going to completely loath her mom being in a relationship.

Hopefully the band will sing some songs about being in love with God today—get Meri's mind off how nobody else is pursuing her.

I focus on the stage and click the mouse to load the first Power-Point slide. Then I do my thing throughout the next hour and a half.

The sermon is a good one about selfish ambition. I pat myself on the back for not struggling in that area. There's something freeing about not even owning a car, ya know? And while I do want to work as a cameraman for a television show, I'm not stressing over it.

Now that the service is over, I should be filming Meri just in case she ever agrees to do the YouTube channel. I shut off the projector before trying to focus my camera on Meri in the crowd.

She's alone. Her mom must have taken off already. I keep focused on Meri as she crosses the sanctuary. Rather than exit, she climbs the stairs. Is she coming to see me? Wherever I am is the last place I expect her to go.

I turn the camcorder on the tripod to a forty-five-degree angle, so both the camera and I get a direct view of Meri walking along the balcony. Her eyes meet mine before she realizes she's on *Candid Camera*. Then her eyes narrow. When she gets close enough, she holds a hand in front of the lens. "What are you doing later today?"

I shrug. It's my day off, so hopefully nothing. "What are *you* doing?"

She lowers her hand from my camera to cross her arms. She glances at the sanctuary below. "I thought I was going to have lunch with my mom like usual, but she has a date."

I knew it. "Good for her."

Meri glares. "I didn't think my mom would ever date again. But now she has a boyfriend . . . while I'm all alone."

I cock my head, not sure where she's going with this. "Are you asking me out?"

She arches an eyebrow—very similar to the look I got from Charlie when I asked if his mom ever dated. She didn't have to act so bewildered. A simple *no* would suffice. "You're a little young for me," she says instead.

Does she mean young, or does she mean immature? Immature would make more sense, being that I still live like a college student. And because she's my roommate's little sister. "I'm thirty-one."

Her eyes clear. Her lips part. "Oh. I figured since you graduated with my younger brother—"

"I took a couple years off between high school and college. Then I worked my way through film school, so it took longer." Wait . . . "Did you call Charlie your *younger* brother?" I study her closer. She doesn't look as if she can be older than twenty-five, but if she'd thought I was too young for her, then what does that make her?

"I'm thirty-one also." Meri taps her nose. "It's the freckles. People think I'm twelve."

"Ahh . . ."

"But you're still too young for me."

I grin. She's desperate but not *that* desperate. "Well, I'm free this afternoon. What are we doing?"

She glances at her watch then frowns. "You don't need to check your calendar app or anything?"

What's a calendar app? "Nope. Never used one."

Her bewildered eyebrow puts on an encore. "How do you keep track of dentist appointments and such?"

"The dentist texts me reminders." Isn't that how everybody does it?

"Do you have any reminders for today?"

"Possibly, but I have a feeling that getting my teeth cleaned would not be nearly as fun as whatever it is you're planning."

She huffs.

I hold my breath, glancing at the video camera screen to make sure I'm getting good footage of what I think she's about to say next.

This is why I don't try to plan my life. Because I never could have planned this. Only God would know that Mrs. Newberg was going to bring a boyfriend to church on the very day I would need Meri to feel so lonely that she'd agree to go on a recorded husband hunt.

She doesn't respond. Camera shy? Nah. With the way she pulled out her camera on me the night before, she's going to be a natural. "Say it, Meri. Tell me what we're doing this afternoon."

She scrunches her eyes closed, and I'm not sure if she's about to laugh or cry. We'll go with laugh. If she's not laughing now, she will later. I'll make sure of it.

She peeks one eye open. "We're going shopping for a lasso."

CHAPTER FIVE

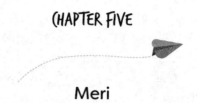

Meri

#33. Go to a rodeo. Rescue the Lone Ranger
from himself.

Kai bought the lariat—a fancy word for a lasso. He also bought me boots and a cowgirl hat from a consignment store. He tried to talk me into wearing chaps, but it's in the 80s today, and I'm already going to be embarrassed enough without getting extra sweaty in leather. He compromised on a costume of jean shorts, a white T-shirt, and a red bandana. He thinks the bandana is for the image, but it's really to pull up over my face in case I see anybody who might recognize me.

Plus, it kinda makes me wanna rob a train.

This is a much better sensation than how I felt at church when my mom told me she'd met a man. I'd thought my dad was the only man for her. If there's no such thing as soul mates, then how am I going to ever meet "the one"?

Definitely not by roping him like a calf, but, hey, it's better than being trampled by the herd.

Kai and I decided to film at Pioneer Courthouse Square. Known as Portland's living room, it's an entire open block downtown that's surrounded by tall buildings. Rows of bleacher-like steps lead from a coffee shop's outdoor patio to a lower level paved with bricks. There are often street fairs and open markets held here, but today it will be the location of my own private rodeo. We're serenaded with the splashing and trickling of a fountain that lines the entrance to the underground visitor's center.

This is the perfect spot because then I won't accidentally give any passersby a rope burn on their face. Also, I'm not the only freak. I'll fit right in with the guy wearing the lion onesie pajamas and the girl sporting a green mohawk.

Kai sets up his equipment and checks the lighting. At least having a video camera focused on me makes the whole thing seem less real. As if I'm putting on a show, not just being sad and lonely.

The Real Housewives of Orange County have nothing on me. Get ready for *The Real Single Lady in the Rose City.* "Hey, Kai. What are you planning to call the show?"

"Uh . . ." Kai scrolls through his phone apps. Maybe he's going to use it to film me from a different angle. "How about *Marry Me?* Except we'll spell it like your name. M-A-R-Y. It'll be a play on words."

My death glare is wasted on him since he's still focused on his phone. "First of all, my name is spelled M-E-R-I, short for Meredith after my great-grandmother. Secondly, no."

He grins at that. I think he likes it when I say no. It means he's succeeded in irking me. "I'm learning all kinds of things about you today. You're in your thirties and your name is Meredith. Do you want to come say that again for the camera?"

"No." My death glare hits its target this time.

He fights back with a killer smile. "Well, come say something for the camera before we begin. It doesn't have to be eloquent or even make sense because I'll be splicing all the best parts together in editing."

I swallow. Being on film is nerve-wracking enough when you're working with someone you trust, but with the way I've been treating Kai, I wouldn't put it past him to splice together my words in a way that makes me sound as silly as one of those *Bad Lip Reading* videos.

I take a deep breath and shake out my arms, ignoring the way the rope in my hand rubs a raw spot on my calf. Then I step toward the camera lens with the clomp of my thick heels. "What should I say?"

Kai presses a button and a red dot lights up. "Tell us your name, what you're doing, and why."

"All right." I bug my eyes at him in disbelief that he talked me into this then attempt a normal expression.

"Hi." I say to the camera. I explain the basics then loop the lasso over an elbow and reach into my back pocket for the notorious list. I whip it out with panache. "I brought this. Just in case any of you don't believe it really says to try lassoing a man."

I flutter the pages open and point to #94. "See? It also has crazier suggestions like using Christmas lights to decorate your roof with your phone number for curious pilots, but I'm not going to do that."

"What's wrong with pilots?"

I pause in my speech, considering whether to respond. I didn't know this was going to be a dialogue. "It's not about the pilots. It's about avoiding a charge of obstruction of aircraft lighting, though I've heard pilots don't make the best husbands either, with as much as they travel . . . and with women offering their phone numbers on roofs and such."

"The roof decorating must have been a fifties thing. It's easier to text nowadays."

I hold a finger to my lips to hush Kai and direct my next line to my future audience. "Don't mind him, he's just the cameraman."

Kai gives a good-natured chuckle. "Meri, perhaps the reason you're not married yet is because you're too picky. No pilots, no cameramen? How are you going to catch yourself a keeper if you throw all the fish back into the pond?"

I return The List to my pocket and plant my hands on my hips as a good cowgirl would. "The point of this show is not to teach women how to catch a husband, but to demonstrate how ridiculous it is to try."

"All right, then. Let's see you try."

I nod in approval then look down at my lasso. "I'm not sure how this thing works." It's a good thing I'm a nurse. At least if I injure someone, I'll be able to give them first aid.

Kai comes out from behind the camera with his phone. "I've been waiting for you to ask."

I look at his screen. He's loaded an instructional video. I watch it and follow the directions, making the adjustable loop about the length from the ground to my armpit. I hold the loop in one hand and the coils in the other. To swing it over my head, I have to keep my arm up and twist my wrist around.

I swing, knocking my cowboy hat off. I laugh in surprise.

Kai retreats behind the camera. Probably to get some awkward footage of me. But after enough tries, I finally take control of the rope like a student on the playground playing double Dutch.

"Yeehaw." I smile for the camera as the lasso swings round and round. I think I even managed a wink in there. "Now what?"

"Wink again." Kai's face is hidden from me, but I can hear the smile in his tone.

I like hidden Kai. His being behind the camera allows me to pretend I'm winking at a successful and mature man. I look around to see if there are any men like that close by. If so, they'd probably be in Starbucks.

Yes. A trim guy with stylishly messy hair, chinos, and a red polo shirt pushes through the exit. Unfortunately, he's not taking the stairs that lead down to where we're filming. "Rats."

Kai peeks up and follows my gaze. "You wanted to rope that guy who looks as if he works at Target?"

The guy strolls away. He actually does appear to work for the chain store, so no big loss, but I refuse to concede out loud. "I like Target."

"You do need some *target* practice."

"Very funny," I say sarcastically, though it's not a bad idea. I wouldn't want to ruin any stylishly messy hairdos. I keep twirling as I turn in a circle to find a target. A few people have paused to watch me, but none of them volunteer.

Kai points to a sandwich board set up in front of the visitor's center. "Throw it like a baseball."

I was never good at baseball. I preferred soccer, where I got to kick things. Too bad The List doesn't include attacking men like a ninja.

I count down mentally as the rope circles over my head. *Three . . . two . . . one . . .*

I squeal, close my eyes, and throw.

I hear something clatter, followed by surrounding laughter.

"You might have better aim if you keep your eyes open."

I peek out of one eye. Sure enough, I knocked over the sign.

Hopefully I'll get better at this, or our first YouTube show will be incredibly boring. Of course, a boring show would be a great example of how hunting for a spouse is a waste of time.

"Need some help there, Wonder Woman?" The male voice comes with a country twang.

I look up the steps to find a guy in jeans, a plaid shirt, and a straw cowboy hat. Surely he knows how to lasso. He's cute too, with sandy-brown sideburns and the kind of jaw romance novels are made of. Maybe I can simply let him lasso me.

I zero in on his left ring finger before my imagination takes me too far. It's bare.

I shoot him my sassiest grin. "Are you talking to me, cowboy?"

"Unless you know of any other women swinging lassos in the middle of the city." He flashes dimples.

I'm a goner, but I give a sweet little shrug and bite my lip for the camera. "Just me."

His boots clack down the last two steps.

Our audience grows.

He looks at the circle of people forming, then at Kai and his camera. "What's this for?"

I twist my lips while considering a response. Might as well tell the truth. "I'm trying to rope a date."

The cowboy hangs his thumbs in his belt loops and shifts his weight to one foot. He ducks his head low enough that all I can see is his smokin' hot smile underneath the brim of his hat. When he looks back up, I can tell by the crinkles around his hazel eyes that he's trying not to laugh. "You do this often?"

I motion toward the sandwich board now lying flat on the ground. "Obviously not. My cameraman friend needs material to show a television director, so he's asked me to star in a YouTube show called *Meri Me*." I did not just say that. Most ridiculous show title ever. Too late now. I let the rope hang from my left hand so I can shake his hand with my right. "My name is Meri."

The cowboy's hand embraces mine. It's warm and rough. It's the definition of hard work. In fact, it's better than dimples and sideburns. "Nice to meet you, Meri. I'm Luke."

He even has a man's name.

He doesn't let go of my hand but pulls me so that I twirl under his arm in a way that tells me he's no stranger to country swing dancing. We're not dancing though. He's lining me up to face off with the sandwich board. "Tell you what. I'll teach you to lasso your cameraman friend here, then you can go on a date with me."

My mouth falls open, but at least he's behind me so he doesn't see this look of pure glee I shoot Kai.

Kai stands behind the camera with arms crossed and the kind of expression I'd expect my dad would have had if he'd lived long enough to see me date. It's a mix of pride and wariness.

I don't have time to contemplate for long because Luke's body presses lightly against my back and his hands cover mine, taking control of the rope.

My heart does the "Boot Scootin' Boogie" inside my chest.

"Can someone pick up the sign for us?" Luke asks.

A kid in basketball shorts scrambles from the crowd to right our target.

I barely notice anybody else or even the camera.

"Thanks, buddy." Luke wiggles my arms a little to help me loosen up. "Here we go." He whips the rope over our heads and guides me into a smooth rhythm.

I let him lead, listening to his advice spoken quietly into my ear. I hear him, but I have no clue what he's talking about. I've never heard these terms before in my life.

Apparently, it doesn't matter because after we release our hold together, the circle part slips smoothly over the top of the sandwich board.

The crowd cheers.

"That was easy!" Perhaps as easy as getting a date—both would be very hard if Luke weren't here.

Luke turns me toward Kai, who is shaking his head in mock disapproval. I know it's mock because there's a small smile on his lips. Though that's always there, isn't it? As if he thinks the whole purpose of life is to entertain him.

"Don't worry," Luke calls to him. "This isn't my first rodeo."

"His name's Kai."

"Don't worry, Kai."

Kai lifts his thumb and pinky in the hang loose sign. "Shaka, brah."

My cowboy nods. "He's even giving us steer horns."

I giggle and don't correct Luke's misinterpretation of the Hawaiian hand gesture I learned on my graduation cruise.

Luke tugs the lasso off the sign and loops it up for the more advanced roping lesson. I grin out at the faces watching. I'm not sure if this is what Kai imagined, but if he gets as much interest online as he does live, then *Meri Me* might take him further than he's even realized he wants to go in life.

I don't even hate the title anymore, despite the humiliating connotation. It's the pun that makes it memorable. And fun.

Luke's arms surround me once again, and we circle the rope over our heads in tandem. I've always been a city girl, but the whiff of sweet hay that comes from my cowboy's musk gives me visions of horseback riding and barn dances. I've already got the boots for it.

Luke counts down, and we release with the exact right amount of power to toss the loop around Kai's shoulders. Because I can, I tug it tight. I keep tugging.

Kai stumbles around his tripod but catches his footing.

I reel him in like a fish.

His eyes snag on mine, that same smirk accepting his fate. He knows he's the one who dragged me into doing a reality show. He deserves to be lassoed, if not tarred and feathered.

"Howdy, partner." I smile up at him triumphantly. I hope the rest of the items on the outdated list turn out to be equally enjoyable.

CHAPTER SIX

Kai

*#46. Become famous. Hollywood is golden,
like a wedding ring.*

My alarm wakes me at five on Monday evening. Usually I'd hit the snooze button a few times, but today I instantly roll over to my laptop and power it on. I'd stayed up all night, working on putting together the first episode of *Meri Me*, as well as starting social media accounts for promotion.

I would have stayed up all night anyway to get myself back on schedule for graveyard shifts, but editing the video made it fun. I spliced together clips of Meri and her cowboy with the long shots I took after Luke left. Then I added interview segments, outtakes, and Saturday's footage of Meri saying there was no way she'd ever do this. The finished product makes me laugh, and I'm hoping others enjoy it enough for it to go viral. Or at least to be somewhat contagious.

I click my mouse and load the analytics page.

Less than a thousand views.

I rub my face. Why am I doing this again?

It's always the dumbest videos that go viral. If only Charlie was still here to bite my finger. But the truth is I don't need my videos to go viral. I just need footage for a demo reel.

I crawl out of bed, shower, and head downstairs to see what kind of crazy health food Gemma is making for dinner tonight. She claims to have allergies, but that seems to be the trendy thing to claim these days.

I find her sitting on a couch with some dude who looks like an advertisement for protein powder. This would not be unusual except I feel as if I've seen this dude before.

Usually after Gemma figures out a guy is only interested in dating her and not in listening to her discuss the craft of screenwriting or the intimate details of her characters' lives, the guy isn't invited back. Maybe this dude is a writer too, and they can geek out together.

I squint at him as I get closer. Because he doesn't look like a geek. He looks like a superhero.

Holy Hollywood, Batman. It's Riley Avella. On my couch. Just kidding—Charlie's couch. But he's seated next to my butt dent.

Since Gemma is on the other side of the couch from him, my butt dent (and gravity) could possibly bring these two together. Then Riley would owe me. He might even have to refer me to his director, Zach Price.

I want to introduce myself, but my hands have grown so clammy that if Riley felt them, he might worry about cameras slipping from my grip. What do I do?

Gemma glances up, totally chill. I don't think she realizes how much other women would pay to be across my butt dent from this movie star.

"Hey, Kai. I'm not going to get dinner made in time for you tonight. I was offered a role on *Capers*, and I'm running through my lines with Riley."

Riley looks me up and down with the kind of smolder that sells *People* magazine. He's probably wondering about my connection to Gemma and rightly speculating that she would never be in a relationship with me. "You are . . . ?"

"Just a roommate," I say quickly to get back on his good side. "I'm going to order a pizza. I know Gemma won't eat any, but would you like some?" See, I can be chill too.

Riley's stiff expression relaxes into his signature smile and focuses back on the reason he's here. "I'd rather take Gemma out for dinner."

Gemma barely glances up from her lines. She's obviously too busy rewriting the scene in her head to realize she's being asked on a date. "Oh no, that's okay. I prefer to cook my own food."

Crud, Gemma. You're going to ruin this connection for me.

The front door bursts open. Meri bounces in, wearing bright turquoise scrubs and running shoes. If Gemma doesn't ruin my chances with Riley, my new roommate might.

I should just be glad Meri is happy. It's hard to believe she's the same woman who struggled through the door two days ago. Amazing what making a date with a cowboy can do to one's mood.

"Hi, guys." Meri tosses her purse onto the counter, obviously not cognizant of the celebrity in our presence. "I saw the video, Kai. I watched it at least fifty times on my lunch break."

I mentally subtract her fifty views from the number listed on the website and sigh. At least one person is entertained.

"Hey, Gemma. Did you see the YouTube clip Kai made? A cowboy named Luke asked me out for Friday. I hope he takes me swing dancing." She pumps her arms and does this little step-kick I assume she thinks is dancing.

Gemma tilts her head. "I didn't see the clip yet, but I'm pretty sure the move you're doing is called the Charleston."

Meri keeps right on kicking forward and tapping back, an infectious grin lighting her face. "Is there a Charleston in country swing?"

"I'm afraid not."

I can't even imagine what Riley Avella is thinking at this moment. "Do you all live here?" he asks.

"Yep." Meri beams his way between kicks. "My brother owns the place, but he's overseas right now."

A crease forms between Riley's eyebrows. I can guarantee that we were not part of his plan for getting himself an invite. I don't want him to leave yet, so I hook Meri's elbow and tug her into the kitchen.

She sails past me, grabs a glass, and fills it with water. "It's a good thing I have all this energy because I'm not used to jogging on these hills. I should run uphill first, so that jogging home will be the easy part."

I momentarily divert my attention from Riley to Meri. "You're going jogging *now*?"

"Yeah, I always go right after work."

I scratch my head. Her workout doesn't fit into my schedule. Not that I'm schedule oriented, but with my graveyard shift, we only have a limited amount of time to make this happen. "We're supposed to film you trying something else from The List."

She chugs water and waves a hand dismissively. "I have to jog now, or I'll lose my energy the same way I did on the couch the other night. As soon as I sit down for the day, I'm done. We can film afterward."

I curl a lip. "But aren't you going to want to shower and, you know, look presentable?"

She shrugs and goes for a refill. "Well, yeah."

I open my hands as if displaying the obvious. "I work nights. If we're going to film, then we need to film now."

She sets her glass on the counter. "Okay, but we'll have to do it quickly. No more taking hours for you to shoot me from all directions."

I stop my eye roll at the ceiling so I don't come across as condescending. Shooting her from all directions is pretty much my whole purpose for this show.

"Hey." She taps me on the arm and points at Riley. She must have finally recognized him. "Is there something on The List I can do to get his attention? Then we could film right here, and I can leave for my run."

I'm not even sure where to start. Though I kinda wish I was filming already. In fact, I wish I'd started back at Meri's version of country dancing. You can't make this stuff up.

Unfortunately, for both of us, Riley Avella expects to get paid big bucks to be recorded.

"Yes." She claps her hands. "Remember that suggestion on The List about having a beautiful friend so I can get her leftovers?"

I seriously hope Riley cannot overhear this conversation. It would not get me a good referral. In fact, it *could* get me blacklisted.

I lower my tone. "He's not leftovers. He's Riley Avella."

Meri's eyes widen and she turns to stare at the movie star. "Am I supposed to recognize his name?"

I throw my hands up and shake my head. "Have you not seen him wearing tights downtown?"

She wrinkles her nose. "Oh, is he the guy who rides a unicycle while playing the bagpipes dressed like Superman?"

"The Unipiper? No." Pressure builds in my temples. "He's an actor on the show I want to work for."

"Ohh . . ." Her confused face softens into understanding, then scrunches back up. "You should have started with that. When you only state the guy wears tights downtown, it makes him sound like a weirdo."

"Says the girl who lassoed a man yesterday."

Her light-brown eyes sparkle golden. "No, I lassoed you."

I walked into that one.

Gemma jumps to her feet. "Are you still interested in seeing my screenplay?" she says to Riley. "I can go print it out right now."

Aha. The true reason she invited him over.

"Hey." Meri steps closer to me as if she has a secret to tell. "If Gemma is working for the television show now, you can just have her put in a good word for you with the director."

I wish. I pinch my lips together because I don't want to talk poorly about a woman I adore, but Gemma does have an MO that Meri hasn't yet discovered. I glance to make sure our gorgeous friend is headed downstairs before whispering, "She'll probably get fired."

Meri does a double take. "Why would you say that?"

I blow out my breath. "She's going to try to change all her lines, and she'll eventually offer to rewrite the script. The writers will respond by poisoning her or running her over with a train or dropping a building on her. That girl has died so many times she puts cats to shame."

Meri blinks. "I didn't even know she was an actress."

"She's not." I shake my head sadly. "Whenever she meets with a producer to pitch her scripts, they want to put her in front of the camera. That's why she gave up on Hollywood and came home to teach

English. Though, as you can see, she still pursues her passion during summer break."

"Hmm . . ." Meri purses her lips. "So, you need to make friends with this guy. What's his name again?"

I eye the guy who has now sunk completely into my butt dent. He doesn't seem the least bit interested in us, for which I'm not sure if I should be grateful or not. "Riley Avella."

"Riley." Meri marches across the room, arm extended.

Tingles shoot through my body—the kind you get when stomping on the brake to prevent a car crash. I'm a little late to avoid this disaster.

Riley looks up with eyes so blue I'm surprised Meri doesn't break into another Charleston right in front of him. If she was willing to dress up like a cowboy to meet Luke, then she's quite capable of tying herself to train tracks to get rescued by this superhero.

Riley stands. He shakes hands. He gives her a smile as if it's as routine as signing autographs.

"Kai told me you're a famous actor."

Where's Lex Luthor when I need him to cause an earthquake so I can disappear into a crevasse?

Riley crosses his arms. "I have my fans."

"Me too," Meri says.

What? Did I truly get up when my alarm went off, or did I actually hit snooze, go back to sleep, and am having a really strange dream?

"Really?" asks the only star in the room.

"Yes. Kai and I started a YouTube channel yesterday."

Riley looks at me as if I'm trying to hide kryptonite.

Any time, Lex.

Meri grabs the remote control. "Do you want to see our first episode?"

Riley sinks back into my favorite spot. "Sure. Why not?"

Meri clicks enough wrong buttons to disconnect pretty much every input.

I sigh in relief. "It's okay. He doesn't have to . . ."

Gemma reappears, stack of papers clutched to her chest. "Oh, I want to see it too, Meri. Here." She holds out the paper for Riley to take so she can click over to YouTube. She types in my name.

My belly warms. I wasn't ready for this. I mean, I had fun making the clip, but this is the pilot episode. We still have kinks to work out. We need to grow our audience to get more comments.

Meri's face appears on-screen, winking at the camera and swinging her lasso overhead.

Riley chuckles. My nausea reacts to the sound like a gulp of Pepto-Bismol.

Not everyone can get away with a wink, and most shouldn't try, but I have the feeling there's a lot of things Meri does that most people wouldn't. The Meri on YouTube whips out The List to prove my point.

"Oh my goodness." Riley rocks with laughter. "Is this for real?"

I cover my mouth and continue to watch him.

Cowboy Luke comes to the rescue, and Gemma clutches her hands to her heart. "He's such a gentleman. This is exactly how I would have written this scene."

Wow. I've never heard those words come out of Gemma's mouth before.

The crowd on-screen cheers. Meri tugs the rope and pulls me into the picture and grins up in victory. "Howdy, partner." Fade out.

Riley relaxes against the sofa back as if he's digesting a full meal. "You're holding husband auditions."

Gemma leans forward. "I love it. If you are going on a date with Luke, are you going to keep trying these tricks on other guys?"

They're into it. A famous actor and a wannabe writer are into my show. The thrill that tickles the hairs at the base of my skull is not an experience I get from editing the nightly news. Meri has to say yes. She has to say she wants to keep doing this.

She shrugs. "I'm excited to go out with Luke, but I'm not doing this to meet a guy. I'm doing it to help Kai put together a dummy reel—"

"Demo reel," I translate for Riley's benefit.

"—demo reel of his videography so he can get hired to work for shows like the one you two are working on."

That's not exactly how I remember our conversation going, but it sounds good. I hold my breath for the actor's response.

Gemma holds her arms wide. "Why didn't you tell me you wanted to work for the show, Kai? I could put in a good word for you."

"Uh . . . yeah . . . I didn't even know you got a role." I shoot Meri a warning sign with my eyes. I wish I hadn't said anything about Gemma's track record. "Congrats."

Gemma beams. "Thanks. I pitched Zach Price—the director—my screenplay earlier today and, what do you know? He was looking for a blonde to play Riley's love interest."

I do my best to look surprised. "What do you know?"

Riley nods. "Our screen test showed so much chemistry that they hired her immediately."

I paste a smile in place. "Great."

"Anyway." Riley rubs his palms up and down his legs. "We could put in a good word for you. But, honestly, if your YouTube channel takes off, and I'm sure it will, Zach will notice. He's always on the lookout for true talent."

True talent. I like the sound of that. It's a compliment, and also it makes it sound as if I'm so gifted that I don't have to work for it. Dream job.

Meri gives me a look, and I know what's coming. She'd make a horrible actress, but what a great personality for a reality show. "That's fantastic, Riley. You know what else would help?"

Riley grins. "What's that?" Obviously, he's a lot more comfortable around us now, and I partially credit the nice soft spot I created for him in the leather cushions. Let's hope he stays comfortable after Meri asks what I know she's going to ask.

She laces her fingers together and holds her hands by one cheek in a pose that I bet got her out of a lot of trouble as a little girl. It probably still works because she looks twelve. "How do you feel about being called 'leftovers'?"

CHAPTER SEVEN

Meri

#31. Be sure to laugh at his jokes, but allow a light, airy chuckle. Nothing boisterous.

Gemma twists my hair around a curling iron, and Kai watches through the lens of his camera.

Ever since Riley agreed to be in our second video, Kai has followed me around as a toddler would his mama—if a toddler had a toy camcorder, that is. He's even been taking the bus to meet me at my clinic after work, so we can film downtown before my daily jog.

I give him my most menacing look. "Scram."

"Okay, Oscar the Grouch."

See? He's a toddler. I wish I could stay mad at him, but I'm in too good a mood since I'm going on a date and all. I laugh, then regain control of my smile, settling on a neutral expression. "I need to take tonight off since I'm going on a date. I have a date. Did I mention I have a date?"

"Because of your date, you especially cannot take tonight off. We need to film you trying out stuff from the 'Get Him to Commit' section of The List."

I scrunch my nose.

Gemma smooths a finger over my skin. "Don't. You'll get wrinkles."

Back to my neutral expression. But does Kai really think I'm going to let him film my date? I have to appease him somehow.

"Hand me the folder," I say with a sigh.

Without taking the camera off me, Kai reaches toward a folder on what used to be his desk. Well, it's still his desk, but since he and Gemma switched rooms for the summer, the black wall unit is now covered in makeup and hair products. Gemma even propped a mirror in front of the corkboard. I haven't been up to Gemma's old room, since Kai sleeps there now, but I imagine his computer to be set up on a white French vanity with gold trim. Perhaps that's why he spends so much time on the couch.

He hands me the folder in which I've arranged pages of The List now protected by clear plastic sleeves. I have the originals, and I made him these copies. It's almost as if we're a professional business. Except, instead of an occupation, I do things like throw gutter balls at the bowling alley, pretend I'm too squeamish to bait my own hook at the local fishing pier, and shop for power tools so I can ask for advice. It's been an entertaining week, just not as fruitful as learning to lasso.

I angle the folder so I can look at it without turning my head in a way that will affect Gemma's job as my stylist. She's already given me smoky eyes that are so perfect I look like an avatar, and I don't want to mess up what she's doing with my hair.

I flip to the page on "Getting Him to Commit," sincerely hoping Luke never watches our YouTube channel and sees me doing this. "Here it is. When Luke comes to pick me up, you can film me *not* talking about having children with him, *not* discussing politics, and *not* letting him see my age on my driver's license."

Kai peeks out from behind the camera to show his disdain for my idea with a condescending scowl. "Let's ask the writer if your idea for a scene will make riveting entertainment. What say you, Gemma?"

"Hmm . . ." Gemma sets down the curling iron and starts twisting my hair up in different ways. "Where is Luke taking you?"

I join her in staring at my reflection. I've never looked so glamorous. It doesn't even look like me. If Luke asks me out again after tonight, he'll be disappointed when the real me shows up. "We're going to the Rose Festival."

"City Fair at Waterfront Park?" Kai asks so cheerfully I regret telling him.

"Yes." I eyeball his camera. "They'll have live bands so we can swing dance."

"And Charleston?" Gemma's words are teasing, but she says them in such a genuine way it sounds as if she'd be really proud of me if I performed my own moves on the dance floor.

"Why not?" It is my first date in months. Might as well enjoy it. "Taking dance lessons is on The List."

"You know what else you can do that's on The List?" Kai circles us to get a better camera angle.

"Play carnival games and eat pizza cones?" I hope.

"A Ferris wheel."

#97. There's nothing more romantic than a view. Ask a Ferris wheel operator to leave you at the top of the ride for longer than usual.

I roll my big, smoky eyes. "This isn't *The Notebook*."

"I know. It's *The List*. You must do what The List commands."

"You two fight like the characters on *The Notebook*." Gemma peers over my shoulder to get a better look at my folder. "What does The List command?"

I hold it up. "Kai wants me to ask the Ferris wheel operator to leave us at the top for a while."

"Oh, I wouldn't do that. It could be windy at the top, and you don't want to mess up your hair."

I nod smugly. "The writer has spoken."

Gemma points to another page. *#27. Practice blowing kisses in front of a mirror to perfect your pout.* "I like that one."

I guffaw. The only person I know who has ever blown kisses is my mom. That couldn't have been how she got my dad to commit.

"The writer has spoken," Kai mimics.

I make my pouty face.

"Yes, that's it." Gemma cheers me on. "But you don't want to scare Luke off. Try something more inviting."

I tilt my head and purse my lips.

"No, don't look at Kai. Look in the mirror. You want to see the expression for yourself."

Kai laughs.

I stick out my tongue.

The doorbell rings, saving me from having to play kissy face any longer. I jump up and smooth out the floral sundress I paired with my cowboy boots. I'm halfway out of the bedroom when I remember #26. *Look over your whole ensemble in a mirror before ever answering the door for a date.* I spin around.

Kai almost runs into me.

"What are you doing?" I demand like a parent.

"What are *you* doing?" he retorts like a teenager.

This could be good practice for raising those 2.5 kids Luke and I will someday have.

"Number twenty-six," I explain.

"You look good, Meri. Now go."

Wow, if Kai admits I look good, I must look *really* good. I give my full, knee-length skirt a little twist and squeal, "Wheee . . ." like Liesl in *The Sound of Music.*

Kai chases me up the stairs, and we stand at the door catching our breaths for a moment before I swing it open to reveal my date. He's holding sunflowers. It's as if we truly are dating in the fifties.

"Oh, Luke. You're so sweet."

"It's nothing more than what any gentleman would do." He hands me the flowers.

My toes curl. I'm not sure if I've ever gone out with a gentleman before. "Take notes," I toss over my shoulder.

Luke straightens. "Hello there, Kai. I didn't realize you'd be here too."

"I live here." With as smart as Kai's mouth is, he must be intentionally remaining vague.

"Pretend he's not here. That's what I do." I wave Kai out of the way so Luke can step inside. "Let me put these in water and grab my purse."

Luke takes off his cowboy hat before he enters, and the way his hair is kind of scrunched up in front endears him to me even more. I clomp into the kitchen, pretty sure there must be vases somewhere for all the flowers Gemma is sure to have received over the years. But since I don't want to leave Luke with Kai any longer than I have to, I go for a mason jar. The jar will actually match the downhome look of these yellow blooms. What a thoughtful gift.

"Are you coming with us tonight?" Luke's tone lacks its normal relaxed drawl.

"No, he's not," I call, willing the water pressure from the faucet to fill my jar faster.

"Meri wanted me to join you guys, but I told her that might make things awkward . . ." Kai's lie proves he enjoys making my life awkward.

I'll finish adding water later. The flowers can surely make it through the night like this, while I'm not sure Luke and Kai can. I jab the stems into the mouth of the jar, hook my purse across my chest bandolier style, and grab a denim jacket. I bet Luke has a denim jacket he'd put on me if I get chilly, but I'm used to taking care of myself. I march into the entryway.

I let out a huff at Kai's presence then smile sweetly at Luke. "While I'm sorry Kai has nothing better to do on a Friday night, I most certainly did not invite him to join us."

"Not with your words." Kai angles his camera my way and twists the lens as if he's focusing. He grins.

"Goodbye, Kai." I breeze past.

"Wait," he calls.

For some reason I stop.

With his free hand, he motions toward Luke. "You've got to tell him the three list items you're going to use to 'Get Him to Commit.'"

I bug my eyes. If Kai really wanted me to get anyone to commit, he would not be sabotaging me so. He just wants juicy entertainment.

Fine. I signed up for this. And I wouldn't have met Luke if I hadn't.

I give my date an apologetic smile. "Luke, just so you know, tonight I will not be talking about how many children I want to have with you, discussing politics, or letting you see my age on my driver's license."

He sets the hat back on his head and gives his slow, toe-curling smile. "That's too bad. Because I want four kids."

"Holy guacamole. I'm already in my thirties."

There went the plan to be secretive about my age.

"And cut." Kai lowers the camera and beams as if he won an Emmy.

I effectively usher Luke over the threshold and slam the door. As you might imagine, our date goes better from here.

There are carnival games, pizza cones, and swing dancing. Unfortunately, in that order, causing my side to ache from the demands of trying to digest during physical exertion. I step to the perimeter of the dance floor, wipe my sweaty forehead, and clutch my gut.

"You need a break?" Luke joins me, leading us toward the fence overlooking the river. City lights reflect off the inky water, helping to create an enchanting summer night.

I look at the array of bridges in the distance and the silhouette of boats lined up along docks. I imagine I can hear the lapping of the wake over all the night noises. What I really hear is the echoes of car tires humming on the highways, the live band behind us, and shrill calls from carnies. "It's so pretty."

"It is." He takes my hand.

My heart flutters for a moment before I realize he's pulling me toward the Ferris wheel. Memories of Kai's suggestion threaten to strangle my joy, but I won't let him ruin the moment.

"Let's get a better look at the lights from the top," Luke says, and we join the crowd of people that must remind him of cattle with the way they're lined up along the winding fence.

"Sure," I agree. I mean, it is a romantic idea. Speaking of romance . . . "According to my list, I'm not supposed to talk about the fun I've had with other guys, but it doesn't say I can't ask you about your former relationships. How is it that you're not married? Are you as averse to commitment as my roommate?"

"No." Luke drops my hand and turns to face me. He crosses his arms. "I was married for a while."

My throat constricts. I knew I was getting older, but I didn't realize I was at an age where the men I dated could be divorcés. How old was Luke when he got married? How long could it have lasted? Am I interested in pursuing a relationship with a man who has a poor track record? And if not, am I doing exactly what Kai said by being too picky? "Oh."

Luke presses his lips together and looks toward the water for a minute. "She couldn't handle me being gone so much for rodeos. So, she left."

I shake my head because I don't know what to say. My whole life, I've pictured marriage as the happily-ever-after fairy tales make it out to be. But apparently never getting married isn't the only way to fail at love. "I'm sorry."

"I learned a lot, and now it's time to move on." Luke's gaze returns to lock with mine. "I know this is our first date, but if we're going to keep seeing each other, I need to know how you feel about being in a relationship with someone who travels a lot."

I take a deep breath of air filled with the scent of sweet corn dogs and greasy elephant ears. Luke's offering another hypothetical I've never considered. I always assumed I'd get married to a doctor, and we'd travel together to do mission work in Uganda and visit our children when they signed up to be foreign exchange students in Japan and Germany. What do I say? "I'm sure a relationship with someone who travels isn't easy, but life isn't easy."

The corners of his lips curve up, making life a little easier. "What about you? No divorces?"

I shrug and move forward in line. "Not even any engagements."

He follows. "That's not a bad thing. It means you've avoided mistakes that many others—including myself—have made."

He makes me sound wise rather than unwanted. "That's kind of you to say."

"But you don't believe it." He studies me. "Why do you want to get married?"

Oh boy. We're unlocking the secrets of our hearts while in line for a carnival ride. I turn to move forward and to give myself a moment of privacy before responding.

I take a baby step.

All right. Here we go. "My dad died when I was four. I don't re-member him that well, so as a kid, I asked lots of questions."

Luke rubs my back encouragingly.

I've come this far, so I'll keep on going. "Mom would pull out her photo albums. You know the kind with the sticky pages and the clear plastic sheet over them?"

His smile softens. "Yes."

"The pictures came with the most spectacular stories." I look down, remembering the faded snapshots. "Dad . . . uh . . . Dad died in a motorcycle crash. But before that, my parents would take trips all over on his bike. Crater Lake. The redwoods. Yellowstone. My grandparents didn't want Mom to date him, but she didn't care. They eloped in Cannon Beach. Mom doesn't like to talk about it, but I get the feeling those were the best years of her life."

I don't add that Dad was younger than I am when he died. I don't say that I'm afraid I missed my best years. I just pinch my lips together and give a weepy smile. Hopefully Luke can't tell that the broken-hearted little girl has become a brokenhearted woman.

Luke lifts my chin, gently forcing me to look at him. "The best is yet to come."

I know he says that because he wants to believe it for himself. As I study his open and sincere eyes, I want to believe it too.

"Did your mom ever remarry?"

My mood is broken in the same way a scratch of a record ruins a song. "No." Luke doesn't need to know about Douglas. It's not as if the old man at church is marrying my mom. It was one service. One lunch. No big deal.

I try to relax by telling myself that if there was no Douglas, I would have gone to lunch with Mom rather than joining Kai at Pio-neer Courthouse Square. I never would have met Luke. So, it's okay. Maybe God allowed Mom to be curious about dating for a greater purpose.

I'd like to think God has created a man specifically for me, and

He will move mountains to bring us together. His hand is the hand of fate.

A seat on the Ferris wheel comes to a stop in front of us. The attendant unclasps the chain link blocking us from our ride. A woman and two little girls scurry out. Luke motions me forward, and I climb on first. He follows and the bar is locked down over our laps.

I sink into the vinyl cushion, happy to get off my feet. Cowboy boots really aren't that comfortable.

Luke slides closer to me and lifts his arm. "May I?"

"Please." I smile as he wraps a warm arm around my shoulders.

He's very handsome. He smells sweet and earthy. And his heat is nice as we rise into the night sky.

Maybe he'd made the mistake of marrying too young. Maybe Mom will make the mistake of marrying again. But I can't let those thoughts ruin my magic. I have a date on a glorious summer evening

I look around from the water to the skyline to the stars. I point toward the lights twinkling on the West Hills. "I wonder if we can see my house from here."

Luke points. "It's that one."

He can't possibly know. I laugh. "Where do you live? Think we can see *your* house?"

Luke clicks his tongue. "Probably not. I live in Pendleton."

I blink. A breeze or something gives me goosebumps. Pendleton is four hours away. It's famous for its rodeos and blankets, but that's it. The one time we drove through for a soccer tournament, I'd mistakenly assumed it had been the location for the movie *Footloose*. It's that dead.

Like our relationship.

I feel duped. "What are you doing in Portland?"

"I help my friends get ready for the St. Paul rodeo every year."

"Oh." Then he's going home? Why even ask if I was okay with dating a guy who traveled a lot when the only way I'd see him was if he traveled . . . or if I moved? But I'd rather move to Nevada. At least they have good entertainment.

He reads my hesitation and offers a rebuttal. "Lots of people meet online these days and make long distance work."

His wife couldn't even make long distance work. If his story is even true. I mean, maybe she left because he cheated. He could easily have a girl in every town. And he wants me to be Miss Portland.

"I don't ride a motorcycle the way your dad did, but I ride bucking broncos. That's cool too, right?"

"Luke . . ."

"I didn't realize you thought I lived here. One look at me and you can tell I'm out of place in the city."

Okay, that's true. He's being very sweet about this. And he did put up with my idiosyncrasies—aka Kai. But I have to be honest. "I don't see this going anywhere."

Luke looks around. "You're right. We've been up here for a while."

I sniff. Now that things have gotten all uncomfortable between us, this moment definitely stretches time. "I mean us. Our relationship can't go anywhere."

Luke meets my gaze. "I know." He removes his arm from my shoulders, and the chill in the air creeps down my spine.

I unfold my jacket from over my purse and slide my arms into the stiff material. The movement makes the seat rock, and my tummy flutters. We're a long way off the ground, and we seem to be stuck. Stuck?

"Oh no. Oh no, no, no." I smash my hands to the side of my face.

Luke's arm returns protectively. "What?"

I scan the ground for a lanky, Polynesian skater pointing a camera our direction. "One of the items on The List was to ask a Ferris wheel operator to stop the ride at the top. I think someone might have done that for us."

Luke pulls away, probably glad for an excuse to escape my crazy world. "You mean Kai?"

Despite all the color and sound surrounding the fair, my eyes are drawn to a glint of light off the glass on a camera lens. My lungs deflate. In response to Luke's question, I point toward Kai standing on the pathway along the water.

My roommate shakes his thumb and pinky at us. The last thing I want to do on a Ferris wheel is hang loose. Does he really think he's helping me, or is this about using me? Either way, he's crossed a line. I'm not famous, and he's not paparazzi.

"I think he has a crush on you." He sounds annoyed.

Though a crush is probably the closest Kai has ever been to a relationship. As for our relationship, I want to crush *him*.

CHAPTER EIGHT

Kai

#38. A man should never see you without makeup.

Had I known Meri would be this angry about the Ferris wheel stunt . . . I still would have done it.

Eventually she'll realize this isn't about what I did, but about the bad timing of when I did it. How was I to know Luke would use their moment at the top of the carnival ride to announce he lived halfway across the state? Any other guy would have just enjoyed sharing such a view.

I'm enjoying my current view. It's my favorite view—my legs propped up, computer on my lap. What makes it even better is the constant dinging sound when viewers comment on our YouTube video from last night. I usually get up at noon, on Saturdays anyway, but I couldn't have even slept in if I'd tried.

A breeze ruffles my hair when Meri storms past into the kitchen. She's finally getting up after a full night's sleep, and she calls me lazy?

"The least you could do is turn off the sound," she snips, then ironically starts banging pots and pans around.

"You're making more noise than I am."

She wields a frying pan like Rapunzel in *Tangled* and shoots me a look that is probably intended to make her silence seem terrifying. Unfortunately for her, there is nothing menacing about the way her bathrobe hangs open over llama-print pajamas and her ponytail of leftover curls spills down the side of her head.

I look back at my computer to keep from laughing. "Gemma left some chia seed pudding for you in the refrigerator."

The truth is that I left the chia seed pudding there. If it had been any good, I would have eaten it all. I usually enjoy Gemma's cooking, but sometimes her "superfoods" get the best of her.

Meri sets down her pan and opens the fridge with the slurp of its seal.

"The baseball game is at two o'clock," I remind her.

A friend from film school runs the media for the Portland Pickles. Yes, our home team is called the Portland Pickles. I told you we're weird. Anyway, when my buddy found out about *Meri Me*, he offered us tickets so Meri could complete #28 on The List by attending a baseball game. It's good promotion for them as well as for us. Win-win.

Meri doesn't respond, but the computer chimes fill our silence. I can't keep up with all these comments. I should set up ads because we could make some serious money off this.

I scroll through the feed. "Are you not at all curious about what viewers are saying?"

I look up in time to see Meri slide a spoon through her lips and frown at the deceptively inviting parfait glass. She sets it in the sink and makes a mug of coffee. "No."

"Okay." I hope she's lying and it's as hard for her not to hear me read them out loud as it is for me to read in my head.

Meri, you'll get past your fear to enjoy the view. Just hang on.

Poor Meri. She's fair-ever alone.

It's not the ride that went wrong. It's who you're riding with. Obviously, Kai wants to be there with you.

What in the world? Maybe I won't read these aloud.

Meri trudges from the kitchen, sinks onto the love seat, and criss-crosses her legs like a pretzel. She doesn't look at me but sips coffee and stares straight out the window at the white tip of Mt. Hood. "Fine. What are they saying?"

"Uh . . ." I scan for a safe comment. "Life is like a Ferris wheel. If you're down, that means you'll soon be going back up."

She hugs her mug close. "My life is a Meri-go-round. I'm stuck going round and round."

Here we go again. She's only been living here a week and she's gone from miserable bridesmaid to Charleston-dancing cowgirl to depressed in llama pajamas. "Maybe you shouldn't base your ups and downs on a dude."

Nothing moves except for the glare she sends me. "Should I be more like you, then? More uncaring of others?"

"Hey." I open my hands wide as if measuring off how much I care. "Just because I don't let other people's actions control my emotions, that doesn't make me uncaring."

"Right. It's part of hanging loose." She lets go of her mug with one hand long enough to mock my shaka sign.

I lift a shoulder to shake off the guilt trip. "You could try it sometime."

She gives me her full attention now. "That wouldn't be good for your YouTube channel. If all I did was sit around and chill the way you do, would you be getting any of the comments you're getting now?"

My computer dings as if to accentuate her point. She's right, but I'm not going to admit it. I just let her continue her rant.

"Yeah, I'm bummed, but that's because I want something out of life, and I haven't gotten it yet." She stands. "I may be stuck on a Ferris wheel, but you're not even in line for the ride."

Ouch. "There's nothing wrong with working behind the scenes. We can't all be superstars."

She tosses her floppy ponytail and marches back into the kitchen. "Have you put together your dummy reel yet? Have you sent it to the director of *Capers*? Or perhaps working behind the scenes is only an excuse to do nothing."

The familiar itch in my chest spreads. I shift side to side in my butt dent. "Riley Avella said that if our channel gets recommended on YouTube, then the director will notice. In which case, I won't need to apply."

She dumps the remains of her coffee. "Heaven forbid you might have to apply yourself."

I don't only roll my eyes but my whole head. "Just because you're unhappy doesn't mean you have to try to make everyone else unhappy too."

"You think you're happy?" She sticks a hand on her hip. "If you were happy with your life, you wouldn't have come up with the idea for this show in the first place. You wouldn't have freaked out when Riley Avella showed up in our living room. You wouldn't have followed me to the festival to film me without my permission."

I open my mouth to argue my happiness, but her last statement stops me. "So that's what this is about."

I thought we'd hashed out the show issues last night as Gemma drove us home. Though that had mostly been Gemma apologizing for going along with my idea. The writer in her just loves a good meet-cute, with which I see nothing wrong.

Meri sniffs. "Do you want me to keep doing the show or not?"

My stomach sinks. My nerve endings tingle. If I let her see how much I care, will she just use it to strengthen her argument about how I'm not happy? I swallow. "Yes."

She studies me. The anger in her eyes simmers into sadness.

Is this about me at all, or is it about her wanting to get married so badly that every false hope feels like a divorce? I know the feeling of false hope more than she realizes.

I lower my feet to the floor and set my laptop down. "Haven't you had fun doing the show?"

She nods.

I stand. "If your relationship with Luke had worked out, you would have been proving your own thesis wrong."

She looks away.

"You're showing women that it's silly to try to catch a husband with gimmicks."

She plucks the chia seed pudding from the sink. Has she gone that numb? Is life not worth enjoying anymore?

"Don't." I stride into the kitchen to ease the spoon away. "Go get ready, and I'll buy you a hot dog at the game."

She slides the elastic band from her hair and shakes the waves out with a coffee-scented sigh. "Give me half an hour." She pads downstairs.

Though I should be relieved that she's still doing the show, for some reason this itch continues to interrupt my peace.

CHAPTER NINE

Meri

#28. Root for his baseball team. As you know,
diamonds are a girl's best friend.

The greasy hot dog eases the rumbling of my stomach and temporarily coats my inner turmoil with satisfaction. I lick salty fingers and sip sugary soda from underneath the bleachers where Kai is setting up his tripod. "I should give up on men and become a hot dog vendor."

"You should."

A mascot that looks like Larry the Cucumber in a baseball uniform makes his way along the food vendors with the help of a cute little assistant. The back of his jersey reads *Dillon.* He poses for pictures, hugs children, and high-fives babies.

From Kai's location, he should have a clear shot of Dillon. "Hurry up so you can film me hugging the mascot."

"I'm already rolling."

I look over my shoulder to see if Kai is serious. His face is hidden, and in its place is a camera lens with the red light shining bright.

"You recorded me declaring I should give up on men and become a hot dog vendor?"

"I did."

"Why am I not more careful when I say things?"

"I have no idea. Now go hug Mr. Pickles, then find a guy to help you to your seat."

I scan the area for a cowboy hat. When all I see are a bunch of baseball caps like the one I'm wearing, I stick my bottom lip out in a pout. I wish Luke was here to help me find my seat. He could hold my hand again. And put his arm around me again. "We should have done this at a rodeo."

"Are you changing your mind about moving to Pendleton?" How does Kai read my mind like that?

I've been weighing the thought all morning. Because I did look really cute in my cowgirl boots. "The idea is only a little worse than becoming a hot dog vendor," I reason.

Moving to Pendleton wouldn't be that bad if Luke didn't travel. But were I to move there, and he was gone all the time, I don't know what I'd do with myself. Nursing wouldn't allow me to travel with him. If we had kids, I'd be stuck raising them by myself in the middle of nowhere. Then as teenagers, our kids would likely end up getting into trouble by playing chicken with tractors and such. No, I'd be better off eating away my sorrows with a never-ending supply of hot dogs.

"It's a *lot* worse than becoming a hot dog vendor. Now go pose with the giant pickle."

I suppose I shouldn't feel sorry for myself. I mean, I'm only posing with the pickle. I'm not the poor sucker dressed up in a sweaty costume on this gloriously sunny day.

I duck under the edge of the bleachers and wave at the mascot like a maniac.

Dillon strolls over, all Jolly Green Giant–like.

"Can I kiss your cheek?" I ask. Since I'm going to give up my dreams in exchange for becoming a hot dog vendor, this will be the extent of my love life. Bad for me, good for YouTube.

The giant pickle's head bobs up and down.

I make sure we're angled toward the hidden camera before gripping Dillon's shoulder, lifting onto the toes of one foot, popping the other foot back, and planting a big smooch on the rubbery green mask.

Dillon's assistant snaps a photo too. Probably for the team's website.

Only then do I have the thought that there is a real guy under that mask. I could be kissing anybody. I could be kissing my high school principal.

A wolf whistle splits the air, and a group of guys cheer at my display.

I lower myself and back away, face burning.

Dillon claps his giant green hands and reaches for me as if he wants another kiss.

"Oh, no, Dillon," chides his assistant. "Leave the pretty lady alone. She just wanted a picture with you, not a relationship."

Dillon holds his giant green hand over his heart, then hangs his head, and trudges away. I'd get a laugh out of it if I was here with some friends. But as nobody knows I'm secretly being filmed, I probably look pretty strange, running around kissing mascots by myself.

I stuff my hands in my back pockets and give a weak smile. "Thanks, Dillon."

"My turn," jokes one of the guys from the group. He's wearing a black ball cap, mirrored sunglasses, and has a little triangle of dark stubble between his bottom lip and chin.

The guys look to be in their twenties. Maybe even college students.

These aren't men I would normally be interested in, but neither were any of the other guys from last week. Of course, last week I didn't care because I had a date planned with Luke. Today is a little bit different. Today I have no one.

I look over my shoulder at Kai hidden under the bleachers and give a small shrug. Why not?

I pull my ticket out of my pocket. "Hey, guys. I'm lost. Can you help me?"

"Sure." The hipster in the group reaches for my ticket. He's wearing pants despite the heat, and his thick plastic glasses are not for blocking the sun's rays. I would have picked him to know the least about sporting events, but perhaps he's the most factual.

The guy with the soul patch holds out his hand. "I'm Justin. What's your name?"

His hand is beefy and rough. Maybe he does construction during the summer between college semesters. Or maybe he never attended college.

"I'm Meri."

He doesn't let go of my hand. "You look familiar. Have we met?"

I narrow my eyes for a closer look. "It's hard to tell with your hat and glasses on."

He lets go and removes what would be considered a disguise, were he famous. Without the getup, he looks completely different. Receding hairline and little beady eyes. I hadn't realized I felt intimidated before, but I must have been with the way my body is now wilting in relief. "I'm sorry. I don't recognize you."

The hipster points down the aisle between bleachers that leads to the field. "Your seat is that way, on the left. Just go up to row K, then look for seat twelve."

I nod, pretending this is all new information to me. "Thank you." I reach for the ticket.

"Who are you here with?" asks a third guy. This one is the most athletic looking. And completely bald. Or buzzed.

I study him while trying to come up with some brilliant answer. Why hadn't I expected this question? Things could get weird now. Even weirder than cheering for a team called The Pickles. "Oh, just a friend."

The athlete scans the area. "Did you lose your friend? Were you supposed to meet her here?"

"Um . . ." My friend is watching us through a camera lens right now. And he's probably laughing enough to have to edit out the sound later. "I stopped to get a hot dog and wasn't sure where to go next."

"Meri . . ." The over-friendly guy rubs his tiny beard. "What's your last name?"

Stranger danger. Though what am I afraid of? I'm not truly alone. Plus, when I tell these guys that I'm on a reality show, they'll learn my last name is Newberg. It's not a secret as if I'm in the witness protection program or anything. "Newberg."

Justin claps his hands. "Meri Newberg?"

I eye him closer. Maybe we did go to school together, and I simply don't recognize him because of the receding hairline.

"Oh my gosh, you guys. This is Meri Newberg."

I look at the other guys. Could we have all gone to school together? They look young, but maybe they just take really good care of themselves. Residents of Oregon don't get much sun damage to their skin. "Do I know you?"

"I'm your biggest fan."

Fan? My lips part. "I have fans?" I told Riley Avella I did, but that was so we could connect. My show's only been online a week. I didn't think anybody besides Kai spent enough time on their computer to religiously watch YouTube channels. And of all the people I would have expected to watch *Meri Me,* I would never have expected a man like this one.

"Yes." Justin steps forward, gushing like a preschooler with the pickle mascot. "My girlfriend has been trying to get me to propose for a couple of years now, so I'm showing her your show to help her realize how ridiculous she's being."

I grit my teeth. "Sweet." Not really. Pretty much the opposite of my goal. But I'm not going to make a fool of myself in front of my very first fan.

Justin looks over his shoulders at his buddies. "You guys remember Meri? I showed you her show."

The bald one pulls out his ticket. "Will you autograph this for me?"

The hipster lifts his phone to get a selfie.

Other people start to look and whisper among themselves. They're probably trying to figure out who I am.

I wave the ticket away. "I don't have a pen."

How are we ever supposed to film more shows like this if men only want to get their picture taken with me so they can show their buddies? And what if Kai's filming is only the beginning of my paparazzi problems? Am I ready for this?

The bald guy puts his ticket away but leans in to talk. "Last night's episode was brilliant. I know it's supposed to be reality television, but it's staged, isn't it? Is Kai your boyfriend?"

I give a confused shake of my head. "What?"

The hipster looks around. "Is Kai here right now? Are we being filmed?"

My heart trips like a base runner who forgot to tie his shoelaces. Dare I look over my shoulder at Kai? Will these guys find him, or will they give up and go away?

"There he is." Justin points past me.

No reason to pretend anymore. I turn my head and pull the brim of my hat down a tad lower as if sending one of those signals base coaches give.

Kai steps out from underneath the bleachers, camera balanced on his shoulder. He gives me a smirk as the three stooges whoop with glee.

"Which one of us did you want to go out with?" Justin demands. "I have a girlfriend, like I told you, so we can't date, but were you interested?"

"*We* can date," says the hipster. "We can start right now. I'll lead you to your seat."

The bald guy steps in front of his buddy. "He doesn't even know anything about baseball, Meri. Sit with me. I can explain the game, the history, and all the stats."

"Tempting."

"Also, I *don't* live in Pendleton," he adds.

Oh my. These men have seen my Ferris wheel ride.

I refuse to make eye contact with Kai so I can keep my tone light. "Sorry, guys. I was really hoping for a date with Dillon."

Justin's eyes practically disappear when he narrows them. "Who?"

Kai chuckles. "The mascot."

Since our cover is blown, and the guys seem to think we're celebrities, Kai's buddy gets us all into the VIP tent to watch the rest of the game. It's a gorgeous day, there's free food that doesn't involve chia seeds, the Pickles win, and I have so much fun that I forget about Luke for a while. But my energy fades into exhaustion once the fans disappear and we're left to pick up Kai's equipment.

Back underneath the bleachers, I coil a power cord from my elbow to palm and think over the crazy day. "Did you hear Justin ask if you're my boyfriend?"

Kai snaps a cover on the camera lens, then squats to lower it into a hard case. "Yeah."

He hadn't said anything before, so maybe it isn't a big deal. But just in case . . . "Do other viewers think that?"

"There seems to be some speculation online. You can read the comments for yourself if you want."

My belly warms. "This whole thing is backfiring," I say. "It's supposed to be about encouraging women who feel lonely, but instead men are using it as an excuse not to commit. It's also supposed to get me out into the dating world to meet more people, but now people assume I'm dating you."

Kai glances up. "Do you want to do a little video segment where you clarify those issues?"

"That's a good idea." I stuff the cord in Kai's backpack. This day wasn't at all what I expected. "Can you believe I was recognized already?"

"You're kind of a character." Kai grins. It's that same fatherly grin where he looks proud of me, so I don't take offense. He snaps the lens off his camera and focuses it on me from his squat. "Do you feel famous?"

"Kinda. But I don't know if I like it."

Kai shifts his head to make eye contact with me around the camera. "Why is that?"

I pull the hat off my sweaty head and shake out my heavy hair thoughtfully. "When I kissed the pickle mascot, his assistant told him that I only wanted a picture with him, not a relationship."

"Yeah?" His eyes sober as if he gets my connection.

I scrunch up my nose. "If I'm now famous like the mascot, people will only want my picture, not a relationship."

CHAPTER TEN

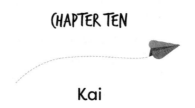

Kai

#43. Holiday at an adventurous location.

We sing "Oceans" at church again. As we sing about walking on the deep water, I picture Meri pretending to drown at the beach. She wouldn't drown, of course. It would just make for an adventurous holiday, as her list suggests. It's not the most sanctified of thoughts, but I suppose it's a step up from wishing I could freak the congregation out by adding a picture of the *Jaws* shark popping out of the water.

It's a beautiful day. We could make it a day trip to Seaside. And the good thing about Meri being filmed in the water is that nobody should recognize her and help her only to get their five minutes of fame.

Those guys from the ballgame yesterday were pathetic. I mean, it was cool they were so into our show, but they weren't even interested in Meri until they knew who she was. She deserves better than that.

I struggle to listen to the sermon—something about family, which doesn't apply to me—then I make my way down from my perch to rescue Meri from having to go to lunch with her mom and the boyfriend. I can tell by a pinched look on Meri's freckled face that she's not used to sharing her mother.

"Hey, Mrs. Newberg."

"Hello, Kai." Meri's mom gives me her full attention, as if she thinks I must want something. I guess she's not used to me just hanging out with her daughter. When I don't say anything, she turns sideways to include me in their small circle. "Kai, this is my friend Douglas. Douglas, Kai rents a room from Charles. They went to college together."

"Nice to meet you, Kai." Douglas holds out a tanned hand.

You usually don't see that kind of color on an Oregonian until the end of summer. Maybe he's not from around here, only visiting. Meri could take solace in that.

One glance at the burning embers in Meri's eyes, and I know she has as much solace as a smoke jumper during forest fire season.

"Would you two want to join us for lunch?" Mrs. Newberg glances across the sanctuary. "We could invite Gemma, as well. Where is that girl?"

Last I saw Gemma, she was sharing song lyrics she'd written with the new worship leader. I'm positive he's already invited her to lunch. "Actually, I was going to see if Meri wanted to go to Seaside today."

Meri's eyes widen my way. Surprise? Relief? A craving for clam chowder?

Mrs. Newberg's shoulders stiffen. "Just the two of you?"

"Yeah." I shoot Meri a questioning look. I know her mom isn't fond of the opposite sex sharing a bathroom, but our car ride to the coast will only involve rest stops if one of us drinks too much coffee. "I thought we could film an episode for our YouTube channel there today."

Meri closes her eyes and slowly shakes her head.

What?

"You have a YouTube channel?" Mrs. Newberg repeats as if this is news.

This should not be *my* news to share with her.

We both look at Meri.

Meri opens her eyes and smiles sweetly. "Yes. I'll have to show you later, Mom. If Kai and I are going to get to Seaside and back today, we need to be leaving. Sorry I can't have lunch with you." She waves me forward as if she can't get away from her mom fast enough, but she doesn't say anything else until we're in her car, headed down Sunset Highway.

The drive to Seaside is so gorgeous through the forested mountains and tunnels that it makes me want to buy my own car. Well, usually it does. At the moment, I'm too distracted by the tension radiating off Meri like sunshine off a magnifying glass.

She groans. "I didn't want my mom to know."

I eyeball her. "You were recognized by strangers yesterday. How did you think you'd keep this from your mom?"

She gives a stiff shrug. "Mom doesn't watch YouTube."

I scratch my head. I hadn't pictured Meri as the secretive type. She pretty much wears her emotions on her sleeve. The only way this makes any sense is if she's worried her mother won't approve. Mrs. Newberg *does* seem to be old-fashioned in ways, such as not watching YouTube. "You think she'll want you to stop?"

My breath hitches.

Meri wouldn't really quit filming, would she?

Her knuckles whiten around the steering wheel. She shakes her head and rolls her eyes a couple of times before finally answering. "She's taught me that there's only one man out there for me, and she's been praying for him since I was a baby. I don't think she'd see my husband hunt as either wise or godly."

I'd known Meri wanted a marriage like her mom's from eavesdropping at the Ferris wheel, but I didn't know that her mom had actually taught her such a fairy tale exists for everyone. "Does she want you to wait in a tower to be rescued by a knight?"

"Yes. No. I don't know." Her eyes slide my way. "Either way, she's not going to like the suggestions from viewers that my roommate is said knight."

I stare. She's worried her mom might think something is going on between us? My invite to the beach probably didn't help, but neither did Meri's overreaction. "This is where being more laid back would have come in handy. If your mom asks, 'Is anything going on between you and Kai?' you laugh it off. You don't squeeze your eyes closed, then run out the door."

She guffaws. "Oh, I did that, didn't I?"

"Pretty much." I lean against my seat and rewind our previous conversation to play from this new perspective. "Though I'd think your mom would know I'm not your type."

"I'm sure she does." Meri twists her lips. "Of course, I didn't think Douglas was Mom's type either. Though he does wear nice shirts."

I'm not going to speculate on the implication of such a statement. Meri didn't say that to suggest that I might be right for her or to get me to change how I dress. She said it because she believes Douglas is completely wrong for her mother. Which is too deep for me on my day off. "Well, if she's found a man she likes, maybe she can offer you some dating tips."

Meri presses her mouth together, hopefully trying to hold back a smile. "Should I get my hair cut like a twin on the original *Parent Trap*. Should I buy blazers in every color of the rainbow?"

"Yes." I want to offer to take Meri blazer shopping. Or to a salon. Or suggest that maybe Mrs. Newberg found Douglas in the obituaries section when his wife died, but that might be going too far.

"Stop it." Meri flips on a blinker, then guns it around a semi in a rare passing zone on this two-lane road.

I need to stop smirking if I want to survive our trip. And if I want Meri to bring me home rather than leave me in Seaside. It's just so hard when the whole show we're going to the beach to film pokes fun of the very thing that Meri is struggling with.

"I'm sorry." I rub my hands over my face. "I wouldn't be laughing if I thought you had a serious problem. I mean, you went on a date two days ago. Obviously, you can get a man." *Or a mascot*, I add silently. It's too funny to keep to myself. I have to say it aloud. "Or a mascot."

She laughs. She also hits me and orders me to "shut it." But at least she laughed.

I rub the slap spot on my arm and prepare to defend myself in case of another attack. "How many women can claim that?"

She purses her lips. "He *was* kind of a big dill."

I snort in surprise. She's better at the jokes than I am. How am I not getting this on film?

I pull out my phone and switch my camera to selfie mode so I can shoot some footage of us talking about the day's plan, but plans go awry when we reach the top of the Oregon Coast Range and the blue sky turns gray. Mist blurs the windshield.

Meri clicks her tongue. "Never fails. I think it's going to be nice at the beach because it's so beautiful in Portland, then I get out here and it's raining."

"And vice versa."

She slows for traffic, though on a Sunday there are more people going the opposite direction, back to the city after a weekend away. "If I pretend to be drowning in this weather, there'd be nobody on the beach to save me, and I'd probably really drown."

"Or die of hypothermia," I add. As a kid, I played in the ocean here, but after my first trip to Hawaii to meet Mom's relatives, I realized how much I hate being cold. I'm pretty sure surfers in Oregon have never been to Polynesia.

"No guy is worth hypothermia."

"I wouldn't think so." It's good to know there are some boundaries to what this chick is willing to do. Though with the way she broke it off with Luke because he lived out of town, I'm starting to think she's got some pretty high expectations. If she liked him so much, why wouldn't she date him for a while to see where things went?

"What else is on The List that I can accomplish here?"

I pull up the gallery on my phone. I know she made me a handy dandy folder, but I took pictures of it because carrying my phone around is more practical. "Hmm . . . We don't want to fake a flat tire in this weather."

She turns onto Broadway, which sounds a lot bigger than it is. It's a tiny street lined with rows of shops that ends at a roundabout above the beach. "Why is it that my life has to be in danger or severely inconvenienced for a man to notice me?"

I ponder the question as a man. "I'd say, first of all, this list is outdated. These are ideas from the fifties, when it was the norm for a woman to live with her parents until her husband provided a new home."

"Hence, the suggestion of having my father offer him an extra season ticket to the local theater. That one will be a hard one to fulfill, considering I don't have a dad."

"Maybe Douglas has an extra season ticket."

"I hate you." She scans the rows of businesses and points to the Shilo Inn at the end of the promenade.

An odd suggestion, considering she hates me. "I know The List includes adventurous travel, but I have the feeling your mom wouldn't approve."

She pulls into a rare empty parking space along the side of the road and turns to deadpan me. "My mom always approves of eating at Mo's."

I smile at her sidestep of the insinuation. "Oh, right. You're talking about the restaurant inside the hotel."

She blesses me with a tiny smile. Maybe she doesn't completely hate me. "Yes. I'm hungry, and you haven't come up with any better ideas yet."

"Number ten: *Pretend to trip or fall in front of him so he has to help you up.*" I show her my phone as proof I'm not inventing stuff to embarrass her. "Let me go in first and set up my camera. Then you stumble in."

Meri pulls her keys out of the ignition and grabs her purse. "I'm not waiting for you." She pops her door open, holds her purse over her head, and charges through the rain in her sandals.

When Meri is herself, she's pretty much the opposite of everything on The List. I have to race to keep up. It's exhausting. Could that be why she's still single? Because she doesn't need rescuing?

I grab an umbrella from her backseat to use as protection for the camera equipment I have to carry inside. I'm sure she was thinking of my equipment when she ran off without it. Meri has already claimed a wooden picnic table by the wall of windows, where she's watching the waves and braiding her damp hair. The long room is decorated with fishing nets and ship wheels and smells like buttery bread and grilling fish, but it's no match for the power and simplicity of nature's display outside.

I set up my camera to catch both of our profiles along with the view. This lighting even makes Meri appear relaxed. The beach is good for her.

A friendly waiter takes our orders, and I study him as he walks away. "Number thirty-one. You laughed at his jokes."

Meri sips her water. "Either he was funny, or I'm a shameless flirt."

I try to hide a smile. "You're a horrible flirt."

"Obviously. But at least I'm done with today's video."

"Or . . ."

We pay the day-use fee and get the indoor pool to ourselves for the moment. This is perfect for setting up my camera on a table and hiding it from view with stacks of white towels. It's also much warmer and quieter than the sea crashing outside the large wall of glass and obviously a much safer environment for having Meri pretend to drown.

"How's this?" Meri has changed into a black-and-white polka-dot swimsuit she picked up at a shop across the street. It's too modest to get her much attention in a normal situation, but with the way she drops into a dead man's float, it would be hard *not* to notice her.

I angle the camera toward her lifeless body with a chuckle. "I'm thinking it might be more believable if you fake a cramp."

She pops up, water dripping off her face. "That's a good idea. And not unlikely with how much food I just ate." She flops around to practice her performance, though with as lifeless as the hotel seems to be, her whole routine might go to waste.

At least I found some swimming trunks so I can use the hot tub. "Wanna soak in the Jacuzzi while we await your next victim?"

She wipes smears of black makeup under her eyes. "If I get into the Jacuzzi, it will put me to sleep."

"I'll drive home tonight." I tug off my T-shirt and head up the stairs to the landing with the perfect view of the beach. This is the life.

Meri climbs the ladder out of the pool slowly, eyes narrowed. "Do you even have your license?"

I narrow my eyes right back. "Yes." I don't tell her that I gave up my beat-up Honda to help out a teen mother at church. I like to keep people's expectations of me low.

She climbs the stairs and joins me in the warm water, sitting closer than I would have expected, but I'm sure it's so she can also look at the view. The ocean rages outside as water bubbles and splashes around us. The jets work their magic on my lower back and my eyelids grow so heavy that I'm almost disappointed when the hallway door squeaks open and a lone man enters.

Rather than look at the guy, I look at Meri looking at the guy. She sits up taller, the bottom part of her hair darker from the water. She glances over her shoulder at me, eyes sparkling. "No wedding ring."

Groaning, I push to my feet. I have to start the camera recording as well as disappear so that this stranger doesn't expect *me* to rescue Meri when she gets her cramp.

On my way across the room, I get a good look at the clean-cut dude. Meri certainly has her type—boring. Though for the life of me, I can't figure out why a man would be swimming in a pool at the beach hotel all by himself. I thought that only happened in James Bond movies. I'll just pretend the guy's a spy. That's less boring.

I nonchalantly click record, then grab a towel to use for drying off in the changing room. I hear water splash in the pool behind me as Meri jumps in.

I seriously can't wait to watch the footage tonight. With one last glance over my shoulder, I find Meri's legs sticking out of the water as if she's doing a handstand. I tug the bathroom door open and wish I had one of Q's inventions that could help me hear through walls. Of course, I'm not expecting the first sound I hear to be that of another female voice shrieking.

My heart lodges in my throat, and I charge out of the bathroom like Agent 007 only to find Meri being carried up the steps in a man's arms.

The other woman who has entered through the hallway door seems to be upset about this, yelling something about how she couldn't leave him alone for a minute or he'd pick up on other women.

Meri's eyes meet mine. They are as wide as life preservers. Apparently, her hero isn't single after all.

CHAPTER ELEVEN

Meri

#35. Be dangerous. Be well-read.

I play the Seaside YouTube video for Roxy, the only one of my college friends who works at the same doctor's office I do. Though, since she had a baby last year, I'm a little surprised she's still working full time. I hope that if I ever get married and have children, I'll be able to cut back on my hours to raise our family. But I've got to get married first.

In related news, I'm waiting for Kai to show up and I've already changed into cute jeans and a yellow blouse, so I look presentable for today's filming. As comfortable as my scrubs are, they are even less attractive than the swimsuit I bought yesterday.

The one-piece had been the only swimsuit in the store that wouldn't send my mother into cardiac arrest when she watches our YouTube show. I wouldn't want to give Douglas any reason to perform CPR.

Roxy points to my phone screen, where the guy who played my lifeguard at the Shilo Inn is carrying me out of the water as if he's Aquaman. "If he's married, why isn't he wearing a wedding ring?"

Had Lars been wearing a ring, it sure would have saved me a lot of embarrassment. I quirk my lips. "Lars and Shandra were newlyweds planning to get tattoo rings while on their honeymoon."

After Shandra freaked, the couple turned out to be pretty cool. We explained what Kai and I were doing, and they wanted to be on our show in a capacity other than Shandra's freak out. We ended up hanging with them for a while. Lars won the cannonball contest and

Shandra won Marco Polo, but Kai and I beat them in chicken. I guess his mom used to be a cheerleader, so he knew that for me to stay on his shoulders, I had to wrap my feet behind his back.

Roxy points to the video of me on Kai's shoulders. "Who's this guy again?"

"He's the guy who's been filming me. You've seen him when he stops by with his camera in the afternoons."

Roxy tilts her head to get a better look. "He looks cuter here."

I lean closer as well. I'd been too distracted with gauging the size of my thighs in the video to even notice Kai. "His hair is slicked back, and he's not wearing baggy clothes. I wish I had his tan." The front door whooshes open even though business is done for the day, but I'll let Roxy handle the ill-timed patient because I'm too intent on studying a shirtless Kai. "Wow. His shoulders are surprisingly well-defined."

"Whose shoulders are you talking about?" Kai's deep voice. And it's so close.

I startle, my heart skipping a beat. I don't want to look up from the little phone screen because I'm sure Kai will read the embarrassment on my face, but I do want to look up to read *his* face and see if he knows I'm talking about him.

"Kai." I take a peek before spinning away. "Let me get my purse." I stride back to our break room and force my breathing to slow.

Considering the question in Kai's eyes, his expression had been more curious than smug. He must not have known I was talking about him. That's a relief, as I especially wouldn't want him to get the wrong idea after our spending the day together yesterday. Granted, we'd stayed for the sunset, but that was only because we'd wanted to get the most out of our drive. Plus, Kai had to keep awake all night in preparation for sleeping today anyway.

While we didn't do our usual amount of arguing at the aquarium or arcade, the unexpected truce could only be a result of full bellies from our big meal and relaxing in a hot tub. Now that I can almost call the guy a friend, I don't want to do anything to disrupt our relationship. If he thought I was checking out his shoulders, things could get uncomfortable.

I hook my purse across my chest and force a smile when returning to the reception area.

"Hey." He thumps a round baby-blue box with a loop for a handle onto the reception desk. "I brought you something."

Roxy sits in a chair behind the counter and crosses her legs to watch our interaction as if we're doing a private show for her.

I shoot her a you're-a-weirdo look before focusing on the box. "What's in it?"

"Nothing."

I flip open the clasps to check for myself. Sure enough, it's empty. What had I expected? I wouldn't want *him* to make our relationship uncomfortable by getting me a gift. "Oh, you shouldn't have . . ."

"But then you couldn't attract a man by carrying around a hatbox. Number thirty-six on your list."

What? No . . .

I drop my head backward and groan. "We need to film something quickly. Men aren't going to care about a stupid hatbox anymore. It will take too long to find an interested stranger, and I won't get my jog in."

Kai adjusts his bag of camera equipment, and I find myself lifting my head to watch his movement and see if his shoulders look as well-defined in real life. It's hard to tell through his baggy T-shirt sleeves. Too bad skaters don't wear Under Armour.

He shrugs as if he's trying to shake off my inspection, and my face warms again, despite the fact that he can't possibly know what I'm thinking. "If no men are intrigued by the hatbox, we'll start asking *them* questions. It'll be interesting to compare our modern-day society to that of our grandparents'."

I consider his suggestion with a pout. "How long will this take? Will I be able to start my run by six?"

He glances at his watch. Wearing a watch is becoming more and more rare now that everyone has smart phones for checking the time.

Will watches eventually go the way of the hatbox? Then those who still wear them will be considered sophisticated, like Cary Grant. Or, in our day, Hugh Grant. Though his is probably a smart watch.

"Do you like running?" he asks.

That isn't the question here. "I hate running. But you saw me in a swimsuit yesterday. You know I need it."

One corner of his lips curves up, and I decide we're not friends anymore. Real friends know to lie to me about how I look in a swimsuit. "You're only running to look good in a bathing suit?" he challenges.

I grab the hatbox and head toward the door to get this new video checked off The List. "Doesn't everybody?"

"No." Kai stays planted. "Some people run for pleasure. Or to relieve stress. Or to win races. Come on, Nike Town's right around the corner. Don't you ever watch their commercials?"

I glance out the window. "I've seen them, but I run to look better in a swimsuit. No big deal. Let's go."

Kai holds up a hand, very theatrically. Gemma would approve. "Except it *is* a big deal. Because who are you trying to look better for?"

The half smirk at my mention of a swimsuit was bad enough to get him removed from my friends list. Now it looks as if we're not even allies anymore. Truce over. "Not you."

Roxy chuckles. I might have to take her off my friends list as well.

"I know not me, but . . ." Kai's eyebrows disappear behind his shaggy hair. ". . . perhaps other men?"

"So what?" I'm a woman. I want to be attractive in a swimsuit. That's normal.

"So . . ." Kai follows me toward the door slowly, as if waiting for me to get whatever point he's trying to make. "You're doing something you don't enjoy in order to attract a man."

"Ouch," says Roxy from behind her desk.

I ignore both her and the way Kai's point pricks my conscience. I don't want to admit the discomfort. Because while my behavior goes against everything I'm trying to prove through this YouTube show, Kai doesn't care about my goal. He only wants me to quit jogging so I can obtain his goal for him. I make my expression as blank as possible. "There are other benefits."

"There are also other forms of exercise. Such as swimming." He stops in front of me. "You got a workout in yesterday, and you didn't have to run."

Roxy hoots. Why is she still here?

I huff at her, then focus back on Kai. "I can't drive to Seaside every day to swim. With running, I have no excuse."

"True." Kai nods. "Though if you truly hate running, you should come to boot camp with Gemma and me in the mornings."

I blink. I figured Gemma worked out, but I thought Kai got all his exercise by walking to bus stops. "You go to boot camp?"

There's that half smile again. "It's where I get my surprisingly well-defined shoulders."

Roxy erupts with laughter.

I gasp and point at her. "You told him." My ears are ringing the way they should have been when these two were talking behind my back.

Roxy grabs her handbag and belly-laughs down the hall toward the rear exit. "Have fun with your hatbox."

"See if I show you any more videos," I call after her.

Though that really doesn't matter, does it? She could watch them herself online.

I press my lips together and face Kai. I guess it's a good thing he's joking about my compliment. No weirdness here. "Fine. You have nice shoulders."

His grin grows to full size. "I get that a lot. I pretty much have to wear loose shirts all the time to keep women from throwing themselves at me."

I contain a giggle and nod in mock empathy. "I can imagine. They're basically the male version of a hatbox in the fifties, huh?"

"Basically." His dark eyes crinkle at the corners with amusement in a way that keeps his confidence from becoming arrogance. They're nice eyes. Almost as attractive as his shoulders—you know, if I found Kai attractive.

"Well, let's go put my new hatbox on display and see how much attention I get."

Two hours later, I'm still waiting for some male attention. I've tried sipping coffee outside cafes, prancing past pubs, admiring art in galleries, and posing in parks with my new hatbox. Not even a double take. I'm starting to consider it personal.

It doesn't help that my feet are tired, and I haven't yet started my jog. Though maybe these steps should count. If only I'd worn my running shoes.

I stop and grab onto a pole for balance so I can kick a pebble out of my sandal. But it's not any pole I'm hanging onto. It's Portland's iconic street sign with signs pointing multiple different directions. At this moment, I am exactly 5,643 miles from Casablanca, 5,510 miles from the Great Wall of China, and 8,003 miles from kangaroos.

I let go to point up with my free hand. "I feel like this sign is symbolic of my life. I have no idea where I'm going." Though I'd be happy with going to any of those places, assuming kangaroos mean Australia.

Kai watches from behind his camera. Oh great, he got my last comment on film too. "If only there was clear direction on where to find a man who likes hatboxes."

"I've heard kangaroos like to *box*." I'm so helpful.

"Pardon me." A man no taller than I am peers through dark-framed glasses with intelligent eyes. He points to the signs above. "Do you know if one of those shows the way to Powell's Books?"

I squint to better read the small white words but can't find directions to the world's largest independent bookstore. Portland would never be so practical. These signs are better suited for those who typed Portland into their Google Maps, thinking it would take them to Maine. They're only 2,540 miles off course. "I don't think so, but I can give you directions." I nod at SW Broadway. It's the kind of street one might imagine when you hear the word Broadway. Unlike the Broadway in Seaside. "Go that way for about six or seven blocks, then turn left on Burnside. You can't miss it."

He gives me a pleasant smile. "Thank you, ma'am." As he passes, his gaze snags on my hands. He stops. Looks at me in wonder. "Are you carrying a hatbox?"

My eyes bulge, and I send the bug-eyed look Kai's way. He'd been lowering the camera, but at the mention of my hatbox, he raises it to his face and refocuses.

I look at the hatbox in a new light, then at the lost bookworm. He can't be more than ten years older than I am, so his interest in fifties luggage is unexpected. Refined. Cultured.

"Yes. Yes, I am carrying a hatbox." I can be cultured too.

The man strokes his well-trimmed whiskers. "I'd love to get one for my wife. Where did you find it?"

"Uh . . ." I hate to disappoint, but the last hat I wore was to a Portland Pickles game. Maybe I'm not cultured after all. I scrunch my nose at Kai. "Kai bought it for me."

We both look at Kai and his camera. The man next to me doesn't even seem fazed at the idea of being on film. He must be used to Portland's weirdness.

"I bought it at Goodwill," Kai says.

"I wonder how old it is." The man studies my hatbox. "The style must be making a comeback, though it originated in Victorian Britain. At the time, customers were using hatboxes for both travel as well as storage. Many milliners would include their brand of box with a hat purchase in order to advertise their business."

I'm fairly fascinated by the facts, but more fascinated with the man's fountain of knowledge, including, but not limited to, the word *milliner*. I purse my lips at Kai's camera to express my entertainment. "How do you know all this?"

"I write historical fiction." The man extends his hand to shake. "My name is Peter Leavell, and I'm in town for a writer's conference."

I shake hands with a real live author.

Gemma would be so jealous.

"Speaking of history . . ." I attempt to spin our YouTube channel in a way that will make me seem like an intellectual rather than another Portland weirdo. "I'm trying out a list of ways to attract men from a 1950s edition of *Sophia Magazine*. Carrying a hatbox is on The List."

Peter's gaze ping-pongs back and forth between Kai and me for a moment, likely ascertaining if I'm telling the truth or not. When we don't laugh as if it's a joke, he blinks and motions to the hatbox. "Carrying a hatbox is classic. I bet you've gotten all kinds of attention."

I scratch my head. "No. Not really."

"Well, don't give up." Peter is too kind. "A real gentleman always notices a lady."

Kai snorts.

I narrow my eyes.

Peter gives Kai a knowing smile, looks around as if getting his bearings, and orients in the direction I'd pointed him. "Maybe said gentleman has noticed but is waiting to make his move, because a gentleman always chooses what he wants *most* over what he wants *in the moment.*"

Sounds like the reason why all my diets fail. I want pizza cones in the moment more than I want a size-six waist in the future.

Though I kind of like the idea that there's a man who thinks I'm worth waiting for . . . or working for. I imagine Luke moving to Portland for me. Or Dr. Snyder from the office preparing to settle down with me after he pays off his school loans.

I walk beside Peter. He mentioned a wife, so it's not as if I'll ever be walking down the aisle with him, but I can get more advice on gentlemen as I lead him to the bookstore.

CHAPTER TWELVE

Kai

#24. Get a job in a male-dominated field.
You'll stand out, gain respect, and up your odds.

I sip my sugary soda, which is the only thing keeping me awake in the dark of an empty newsroom. Bleary-eyed, I click my mouse on the start and stop points for a video clip, splicing it into a segment that will be shown at six in the morning. It has to do with zoning for a new apartment complex, and it's so dull my brain can barely register the story. Though it probably doesn't help that I'm thinking back to Meri's run-in with the historical author and his quotes on gentlemen.

A gentleman drinks soda to stay awake at a job that bores him.

I doubt author Peter Leavell would ever utter such a quote, but I'm no gentleman. I'm a dude.

A dude drinks soda to stay awake at a job that bores him.

I sigh. That fits my life but not the life Meri was intrigued by. What had Pete said again?

A gentleman always chooses what he wants most over what he wants in the moment.

What does that even mean? I suppose to answer that question, I'd have to know what I want most.

I want to work on *Capers.*

But do I want it enough? Do I want it more than the comfort of having a news studio all to myself? Do I want it more than sleeping the day away? Do I want it more than the safety of avoiding rejection?

I look around at the blank monitors and computer equipment. There's ease here. This is known.

It might not seem like much, but obviously I get something from it. Enough that I've continued to ignore my longing for more.

I'm the kid who is happy playing in his sandbox because he's never been to the beach before. The kid might have seen pictures of the beach. He might have eaten fish sticks. He might even own a toy boat and enjoy imagining that there's something greater out there. But to travel to the beach for himself, he'd need to leave the sandbox behind. And what if the ocean was cold and stormy, or he got stung by a jellyfish? Then he'd have given up the little that he had in exchange for big disappointment.

Everybody has some kind of sandbox they settle for. Gemma settled for acting jobs and teaching high schoolers to enjoy *The Scarlet Letter* when she much prefers *The Scarlet Pimpernel* and wants to write her own adventure. Charlie settled for work instead of love. Meri even settled for moving into her brother's apartment, when it's obvious by how she'd looked at the sign for kangaroos that she wishes to travel the world.

So maybe I'm not alone in being a dude instead of a gentleman.

There's value in making the sacrifices to grow, but there's also value in being stuck. It takes less risk to stay stuck.

A light flicks on down the hallway, announcing the arrival of the producer for the morning news. Is it the end of my shift already? Work has gone by faster with all these deep thoughts distracting me.

Erin zips my way, a tiny Asian woman who seems to think she has to do everything at double speed to keep up with people who have longer legs. "Good morning, Kai. I'm glad I caught you before you left."

Uh-oh. Why do I always feel as if I'm being sent to the principal's office whenever someone wants to talk to me? I'm never in trouble, I just don't want to miss my recess. I cringe. "What's up?"

She pulls out a chair on wheels and adjusts the height so her feet will touch the floor when she sits. "I heard you're editing a show of your own now."

Is that all? I exhale and lean back, anchoring an ankle on my knee. "Have you seen *Meri Me* yet?"

She sits on the edge of the chair, a clipboard propped on her lap. "I've seen a few episodes. Well done. But what impresses me the most is how you've been promoting it through social media. That's how I discovered it."

I nod. Social media isn't my fave, probably for the same reason that working during the day isn't my fave—dealing with people. But it gets the job done. "The masses seem to like it."

Her smile twitches. "That's what I want to talk to you about. The masses."

I frown. I have absolutely no idea where this is going. "Oh yeah?"

Erin glances at her clipboard as if she has a whole speech prepared for me. "The masses aren't watching local news as much as they used to. We're a global society now, and people want to know what's happening on the other side of the world."

My heart flutters, creating even more of a tickle in my chest. This can't be good. "What does that mean for me?"

Erin meets my gaze, all business. "I have to let either you or Joel go at the end of the summer."

I drop my foot to the floor to sit up taller. How is this a contest? I've been here longer.

She holds up a hand. "I know what you're going to say, but Joel has a newborn to provide for."

Oh man. I'm worth less because I don't have a family? Never saw that coming.

My sandbox just got kicked over.

What now? I have to apply to work for *Capers*. But until I find out if I get that job or not, I definitely need to get some advertising on our YouTube channel. Maybe it could help rustle up business of doing my own videography for weddings. Though the summer wedding season is already in full swing, and brides will have hired their videographers by now.

I could film weddings for free on weekends to build up a portfolio. I'll just have to drink more soda to keep me awake.

"Before you get all worked up," Erin says.

Eh, a little too late.

"I have a better solution."

Better than filming weddings for free? Anything would be better than that.

"There's an opening in our promotions department."

I clear my throat to get rid of the panic creeping up. "Promotions?"

"Social media. Blogging. That kind of thing."

The very thing I hate. But as I pointed out before, it gets the job done.

"If you're interested, then we wouldn't have to let either you or Joel go."

I press my lips together. I didn't go to film school to post on Facebook. A Kardashi . . . *ahem* . . . could do that. Of course, editing newsreel has never been a dream either.

What about Joel? He loves editing newsreel. He loves his baby girl. How selfish would it be to compete against him for a job I don't even like just to keep from doing a job I like even less?

Erin pops to her feet. "You don't have to decide right now. The change won't happen until the end of the summer."

Is that any better?

It gives me time to pack for a figurative trip to the beach, at least. Should I not make it to the ocean, I could still have a little sand left to play in.

CHAPTER THIRTEEN

Meri

#41. Be the model of a glamorous housewife.
Do calisthenics to keep your figure.

I'd set my alarm for five in the morning to try out boot camp class, which I'm pretty sure is going to be worse than running, but my brother didn't even let me sleep in that long. Stupid Ecuadoran time zone.

I squint through the dark at the phone screen with Charlie's name lit up and consider not answering. If I don't, I'll probably worry he's been kidnapped and that I missed my opportunity to pay the ransom. Then I'll never be able to get back to sleep.

I swipe my thumb across the cool screen and close my eyes, curling into a ball with the phone by my ear. "It's four in the morning," I groan.

"I waited as long as I could, Meri. I'm going to be shooting all day, and this was my only chance to call." He's talking at a fast clip, and I picture him striding through a bustling third-world street. Way too awake.

At least he's not kidnapped. I could hang up and rest easy now. Except Charlie doesn't call just to chat. "You okay?"

"Yeah, yeah. I tried eating guinea pig last night before I knew it was guinea pig, and I feel a little nauseous, but that's not why I called."

Not only did he wake me up at four in the morning, but he's telling me he ate my elementary school class pet? I want to cry. I bottle the helpless feeling for use in the YouTube video where I'm supposed to let a guy see me cry so he can cheer me up.

"I talked to Mom last night. She told me about your YouTube channel."

She and I haven't even talked about it yet. I'd been wondering if she'd watched it. Now I know. Though it's not good that she's talking to Charlie about it before she talks to me. That's usually a sign she has "concerns" and wants to get feedback before addressing the issue personally.

I grunt in acknowledgment.

At least Charlie isn't kidnapped.

"I watched it too."

"Kai will be thrilled," I mumble. The producer/director/editor/cameraman is obsessed with our number of video views.

"It's pretty funny stuff." Charlie chuckles.

I sleepy smile.

"But I think what has Mom concerned . . ."

See, I told you she's concerned.

". . . are all the comments from viewers."

It takes my foggy brain a moment to process this. As I haven't been reading viewer comments, it doesn't fully compute. I sigh over the realization that I'm going to have to fully wake up for this conversation. "Why?"

Silence. Which might as well have been a cup of coffee with the way it pries my eyes open.

"You haven't read the comments?"

My brother is used to making movies for an audience, while I've kinda been doing this for myself. "No." I frown. If there was a problem, wouldn't Kai have known? He did mention a few comments about how viewers thought we were a couple. I drop my head deeper into my pillow. "We ran into some guy who recognized me and assumed Kai and I are dating. Is that what Mom's concerned about?"

"Mom. And me."

I give a dry laugh. "You know me better than that, Charlie. And I'd think you know Kai better too." If I were to hold actual husband auditions the way that tights-wearing Riley had suggested, Kai would never even show up to the casting call.

Charlie sighs. "That's the problem. I *do* know Kai. He's a good guy, but he's kinda lost in life. He doesn't know what he wants right now. If there's a woman in front of him who's looking for intimacy—"

"Stop." I squeeze my eyes shut tighter and rub at the growing tension in my temple. When The List suggests having your brother be his friend to spy on him, I don't think this is what it meant. I'm not sure which is worse—my brother talking about finding a "mate" or looking for "intimacy." Both sound institutional. As for Kai, I already know he's lacking ambition. Which is only one of the reasons I'm so not interested. And Charlie is wrong about Kai being interested in me. The guy definitely doesn't want a wife. I shake my head. "Kai's only doing this to make a dummy reel."

"Demo reel."

"And I'm doing it to show how silly it is to try to catch a man."

"Honestly?"

I stare at Charlie's bedroom ceiling fan, which is striped with streetlight from outside the blinds. The truth is that I'm lonely. But if I admit that to my brother, he might use the word "mate" again. "It's fun." And that's the truth too. Because filming with Kai is more fun than jogging by myself every night.

"I just don't want you to get hurt, sis."

"I know," I say. Even though I'm already hurt. But neither Charlie nor Mom could understand. Charlie is too busy for love, and Mom . . . "If you're going to worry about a relationship, you should worry about Mom's. Did she tell you about Douglas yet?"

I know, that was cheap to throw my mom under the bus. But it was self-defense. And it worked.

Apparently, Mom hadn't told Charlie about the only guy she's dated since Dad. Though, for the first time since I met Douglas, that's not what's eating at me.

I'm still trying to settle my stomach when Gemma holds the door open at the West Hills Body Shop. I don't like the idea that people are worried about Kai hurting me. He's a skater who rents a room from my brother. He works the night shift and doesn't own a car. I'm way out of his league. Do I really come across as so desperate that I'd settle for a slacker?

Speak of the slacker, he's wearing Under Armour today. And he's surrounded by women who are patting him on his surprisingly well-developed shoulders and oohing over him as if he's a rock star. Granted, one of those women looks to be as old as my G.G. and is wearing a puffy vest over her sweat suit, but there's also an exotic-looking woman in a sports bra. Just yoga pants and a sports bra. She must think this is the Nike campus or something. I look away to keep from staring.

"Hey." Kai nods at us from across the large fitness room with wooden floors and walls of mirrors.

He seems more stoic and contemplative than I've seen him at home. Could be from working all night or because of the half-naked female. My brother might be right about him being drawn to a woman right in front of him, though if he's got options like this, he's never going to make a move on me.

"Meet my mom, Nalani," he says.

I robotically extend my hand toward the G.G.-look-alike, as she's the only one in the group old enough to have a son in his thirties. Pretty cool that she comes to a boot camp class to be with her baby boy. Hopefully it doesn't kill her. The little one-pound pink weights that are keeping her from shaking my hand don't look too dangerous.

The fitness goddess steps in front of Kai's mom and grips my palm. How rude to interrupt. "You're Meri. I saw Kai's videos. They're hilarious."

I slant my gaze her direction, not sure how to respond. I guess I need to get used to being recognized in public, but I can't let the distraction keep me from meeting Kai's mom. "Thanks?" I try to pull my hand away, but her hold is as strong as her buff, tanned arms would suggest.

"I'm so glad he got you to come to class today. He's my favorite student." She finally releases my hand to squeeze Kai's bicep. "I hope you enjoy our workout more than jogging," she calls back to me as she moves away, tucks a microphone headset around her ears, and turns on some pounding music.

"Wow." Now I'm outright staring. "No wonder you come to class, Kai."

He stands up from where he bent over to retrieve dumbbells. "Why?"

He had to notice the instructor's attention. Kai just wants to hear me say it out loud. If his mother was still close enough to overhear, I wouldn't have said anything, because I know how moms can be, but she and her puffy vest have already claimed a spot by a mat in the corner.

I tilt my head toward Hula Girl. "The trainer obviously has the hots for you."

Kai's solemn expression cracks with a half smile. "She does love me, but that sounds weird."

Gemma's frown threatens a crease above her perfect nose. "The trainer is Kai's mom. She owns this gym. He gets me in for free in exchange for the meals I cook him."

What the what? I stare even harder at the tiny woman in charge of our class. Yeah, she looks to be the same ethnicity as Kai, with her bronze skin, full lips, and prominent cheekbones. But, at the very most, I would have aged her as an older sister.

Besides the age issue, I'm perplexed Kai's mother would be this hardworking. Not only is she a business owner, but her body is so sculpted that there's no way she ever watches television without being on a treadmill. Where did his laziness come from?

The final shock is her clothing. I guess I assumed all moms wore scarves with their blazers to prevent anyone from ever seeing a hint of cleavage. As for Kai's mother's chest . . .

"Who did you think I was introducing you to?" Kai stands close enough to be heard over the thumping of techno music.

Gemma already claimed a spot at the far end of the room where she does squats with a giant ball between her back and the wall. She makes wall squats look easy.

"Uh . . ." I glance sideways at the senior in the puffy vest.

"You thought Ethel was my mom?" Kai shakes his head, though a sparkle brightens his eyes. "I told you my mom was a cheerleader in college."

I blink. "They probably had cheerleaders back in Ethel's day too." He lifts his chin as if he wants to challenge me.

"Kai," his mom's voice booms over the loudspeaker. "Get Meri started at the jumping jack station."

Kai leads me to a corner. We are the last participants to claim a spot.

I feel the eyes of the rest of the class follow us. Many of them call greetings, as well. Kai is "Cute Kai" and I am "Proud Meri." I'm pretty sure no other boot camp has ever given out such nicknames. These guys are an eclectic mix of all body types and nationalities. I find their presence reassuring. If gym members like Ethel can handle this class, then it should be a breeze for me.

It should be, but it's not. By the time we spend a minute at each station and I'm back to my original spot, sweat rolls down my spine, and my arms hang from my surprisingly underdeveloped shoulders like overcooked spaghetti.

I plant a hand on the wall to help me balance so I can grab an ankle and stretch out my burning thighs. "Did you bring me back to this corner to practice my crying for The List?"

Kai smirks. He obviously enjoys my pain. "Are you going to cry happy tears because this is so much better than jogging?"

There is nobody in their right mind who would label burpees and mountain climbers as better than jogging. Ethel was pretty much false advertisement for boot camp, since all she did at those stations was march in place. "I'm going to cry tears of relief because we're finally done and can go home."

Kai tugs his T-shirt up, wipes his face, and reveals that six-pack abs run in his family. How did I not notice that when we were soaking in the hot tub?

"What do you mean we're done?" he asks. "We have two more rounds. This is just a break."

Two more rounds of torture? Would anybody notice if I laid down on my mat and simply rolled from station to station? "Okay, I really am going to cry in a corner now."

Mrs. Fitness bounces over and unhooks the headset so the microphone hangs around her neck rather than pick up her every word. "Kai, go get Meri a water bottle from my mini fridge."

"Here. Have this one." Kai hands me his unopened bottle before taking off to retrieve another for himself.

I unscrew the lid and suck down what I hope to be liquid energy. Or poison. Death seems the easier option at the moment. "This is harder than I expected," I admit. "Since I only ever see Kai sitting on the couch, I didn't realize he's in such good shape."

She watches her son mosey out the door. "He used to be in better shape. But after losing his track scholarship, he started coasting through life."

Kai had never mentioned a track scholarship, only that he had taken time off between high school and film school. Who'd have thunk? I guess Gemma did mention his backstory once. "How'd he lose it?"

Nalani grimaces. "He ruptured his Achilles junior year and never regained full mobility. His physical discomfort was the least painful part."

I hadn't realized colleges could take away a scholarship like that. It seems wrong. Like telling a person they weren't worth anything anymore. Though if the school kept giving him a scholarship when he couldn't compete, he might feel worthless anyway.

My guts twist, and not only from the bicycle crunches I did earlier. It's the same discomfort I feel every time my birthday rolls around and I get one year farther away from my dream of having a family. If I never marry and my dream dies, will I become as lifeless as Kai? "That's so sad." The story explained what Charlie said that morning. Kai was lost because he'd been hurt.

Nalani's eyes connect with mine—warm and wise. "There's more for him. He just needs his current life to become uncomfortable, like an old worn-out shoe, before he'll try on something new."

I smile in a way that I hope gives her encouragement. "Our You-Tube channel might do the trick. It could land him a cameraman position on a television show."

She smiles back. "I love that you're helping him. What's next on that list of yours?"

I purse my lips. "I was thinking about baking a pie to take to work. I'm supposed to bake for a guy, and I don't know who, so I figure the doctors would count."

Her eyes light up. As a health nut, she's probably about to give me a lecture on eating sweets. "Oh, I hope Kai will film you baking it too."

I picture myself in a messy kitchen with flour on my face. Hmm . . . If I'd lived in the fifties, my show would have probably looked a lot like *I Love Lucy.*

She snaps and points at me. "I'll get you my favorite apple pie recipe. It uses almond flour and coconut sugar."

I knew it. She wants me to eat healthier. No wonder she lets Kai bring Gemma to class for free in exchange for nutritious meals.

Before I can offer a feeble thanks, she's hooking the microphone back on and clapping her hands. "Break's over, people."

CHAPTER FOURTEEN

Kai

#80. Don't be catty. Unless you're purring like a kitten.

Meri is being her difficult self again. I'm pretty sure it's payback for inviting her to Mom's boot camp class. She's threatening to never attend boot camp again, but even worse, she doesn't want to film tonight.

She insisted on coming home after work, which is dumb because, since she's too sore to jog, we have a ton of time to film. Or we would, if she'd stop making excuses. With the threat of losing my job, I need her to do this now more than ever.

"Nooo . . ." she moans. "No to Mount Tabor Park, no to Cathedral Park, and no to Forest Park. I know they're beautiful, but there's too much walking involved. No man will want to stop and take the picture of a woman who hobbles around as if she's older than Ethel."

I choose not to mention the fact that Ethel doesn't hobble. On top of that, I let Meri sit in my butt dent on the couch. I'm really trying here. "Where do you want to go, then?"

She gives me an angelic smile. "The Rose Garden." Her voice even softens to the point I barely recognize it. I would appreciate this sweet side if only her suggestion isn't absolutely ridiculous.

I lower my camera equipment to the floor and drop onto the love seat across from her. "There will not be any single men at the Rose Garden. I promise you."

Out comes her pouty lip. "Where do you want to film then? A bar?"

"Or . . ." I hold up a finger. "The Moda Center where the Trail Blazers play. There's even a big sign out front that spells out Rip City, except you stand in the place of the letter *I*. It's perfect."

"I think it's perfect too. Especially since Ice Capades is performing tonight."

There goes that idea. No straight man is going to attend Ice Capades. "Never mind."

"I guess we'll have to skip filming."

"No way." We must keep going if we are going to build an audience that will get the attention I need. "You went to boot camp this morning specifically so we'd have extra time to film tonight."

"Boot camp is why I want to skip. I can't move."

I narrow my eyes. She can't be in that much pain. She's faking.

She lifts her arms from where they've been resting in her lap and slowly reaches her hands forward. The motion comes with some very unladylike grunts. So much for #88. *Always sit like royalty, with your legs crossed at the ankle. It worked for Grace Kelly, and it can work for you.* "I can barely do this," she says. "It hurts to straighten my arms."

Okay, that's real. I've experienced it. "T-Rex arms." While her heart is probably as healthy as can be from all her running, the girl isn't used to doing bicep curls.

She attempts a dinosaur growl, which turns into laughter. Then she clutches her stomach. "Oh, my abs."

Gemma was never this much of a baby after boot camp. Or maybe Gemma's just always so in her fictional world that she doesn't notice real-life pain.

"Here." I stand and climb behind Meri on the couch. I didn't want to have to do this, but if it's going to get her out the door . . .

"What are you doing?" Her voice is so high pitched that I know if she wasn't seriously sore, she would have leaped off the couch and thrown a coffee table cube at me.

"I'm stretching you out." I hook her elbows and pull them behind her with her hands hanging down.

"Ow-ow-ow . . ." Her moan turns into a sigh as I hold her arms wide. "Don't stop. That hurts so good."

If this was all I was going to do, I wouldn't have had to climb behind her. But I know with the number of push-ups Mom made us perform this morning that she needs her pecs stretched, as well. I lift her hands up behind her head as if she's under arrest then lean into her back with my chest, pulling her elbows wide.

"Ow-ow-ow . . ." She repeats the whimpering until her muscles release.

This is the position we are in when Gemma walks through the front door with Riley Avella. My first thought is that I'm surprised Gemma is still working with him. This might be a record acting gig for her. Then I see Riley's expression and realize how Meri and I must look.

Gemma, sweetheart that she is, doesn't even do a double take. "Are you sore, Meri?"

Meri moans in response.

I guess I'll have to be the one to explain what's going on to Riley. "Meri went to boot camp class with Gem and me this morning. I'm stretching her out, so she'll quit whining and go film another episode of our YouTube channel."

"Sure . . ." Riley drags the word out as if he doesn't believe me. "Gemma, want me to stretch with you?"

Meri's spine stiffens against my chest. "This just got awkward."

At least she didn't feel awkward before. Evidence that Riley is the only one who sees our position as anything other than personal-training related.

"Oh, that's okay," Gemma files through our mail as she leads him to sit on the love seat. "I've been attending boot camp for a couple of years now. I'm not sore."

Riley avoids eye contact, as if hoping we don't realize how our roommate keeps shooting down his advances.

I take the opportunity to release Meri's elbows and crawl out from behind her. I sit on the cushion next to her, expecting her to scoot over and give me more room, but either she's too sore or my butt dent is too comfortable. "So, Riley. For today's episode we're supposed to film Meri asking men to take her photograph. What is a good scenic area where single guys hang out?"

Riley shrugs. "Probably downtown. I always see people taking photos at Salmon Street Springs."

The fountain is along the river and is especially a hotspot in the summer, with kids splashing in the water and the walking path nearby. "How did I not think of that?"

"That's a good question." Riley grins. "Everything I've been watching of your show so far has been brilliant."

My belly warms. The star of *Capers* has been watching my YouTube show. And he thinks it's brilliant.

Riley's gaze shifts Meri's way and his expression goes from comedy to the tragedy mask. "Except for things not working out with your cowboy. Sorry he doesn't live here, Meri."

Meri grunts. Not exactly the bundle of energy she was last time Riley came over. But that's not what matters. Riley is here now, and he's talking about my show.

"Is anybody else at *Capers* watching it? Like, say, the director?"

Riley leans back, extending an arm along the love seat behind Gemma's shoulders. "I showed everyone the episode where Meri referred to me as Gemma's 'leftovers.'"

He did? He showed the cast and crew of a television show an episode of my little internet series?

"I still don't get what you mean by 'leftovers.'" Gemma holds up a magazine. "Hey look, they published my article in *Screenwriter's Digest*. Do you think that would impress the writers at *Capers*?"

Riley sends her a deer-in-the-headlights look.

"Did you tell the director about me?" I save Riley by asking him a different question that's not any better or less self-promoting but, in which case, the answer won't affect his chances at a love connection with my roommate. "Did you tell him I'm a cameraman interested in working for him?"

"Uh . . . yeah." Riley focuses on me. "He liked your work but really won't pursue you unless he starts hearing about your show from multiple sources." He leans into Gemma, pretending interest in her article as an excuse to drop his arm around her shoulders.

I may have been effectively dismissed, but my heart rate is thrumming as if I just won an Oscar. There's a chance the director of *Capers* may pursue me without me even having to apply. I could simply agree to take the promotion position at the news station and wait to be offered the better job. This option brings much relief despite the niggling reminder of our one conversation with author Peter Leavell.

A gentleman always chooses what he wants most over what he wants in the moment.

What if I could have both? What then, Pete?

A lucky dude only buys a lottery ticket to live happily ever after.

To strike it rich, all I have to do is keep filming until Meri does something wacky enough to go viral. Though that's a much harder task when I can't even get her out of my butt dent.

Eventually we end up at the round fountain that shoots straight from the cement. It only took bribing Meri with ice cream and the rental of a pedicab. She's still sitting in the back of the pedicab, licking her cone. It gives me time to set up my camera equipment in a way that I'm partially hidden behind the booth for dinner cruise ticket sales.

The Portland Spirit boards passengers from a platform below. Stragglers weave between parked bikes and squealing wet children to descend the stairs and escape the mayhem.

Meaty smells waft from food truck row and my stomach grumbles. Traffic roars along the road behind us, separating the waterfront from office buildings connected with glass skybridges. Meri hasn't moved.

I peer through my camera with one eye, focusing on her and hitting record. "Action."

Meri gives me a blank expression, then hands her phone to the guy who pedaled the bike taxi. "Will you take a picture of me?" she asks.

The gangly kid is wearing red Converse high tops that remind me of Ronald McDonald, and he's young enough that she wouldn't be any more interested in dating him than the clown who deals in Happy Meals. He looks at me hesitantly, then takes her phone and turns to snap a shot.

She poses with her oversized ice cream scoops right in front of her mouth, and it could actually be a cute image if the kid knew anything about photography. But even if he did, we're not here for him.

"Meri, you have to get out of the bike taxi," I call.

"That was never part of our deal."

The kid hands her phone back. "I'm sorry, miss. But I need to pick up other passengers."

"He has to pick up other passengers," I echo.

She wrinkles her nose at me, then slowly leans forward, steps one foot to the ground, and grabs onto the bike seat with her free hand to hoist herself up. She does a little laugh-cry along with the effort but is finally standing.

Our cabby driver jumps on his bike and peddles away as quickly as his clown feet will carry him.

Meri stays where she is, licking the drips from her cone.

"You're supposed to be catching men, not scaring them away," I admonish. Maybe I should let her go back to jogging rather than attending boot camp. At least then she has more energy during filming, even if our time is shorter.

"I'm not sure why I'm doing this item on The List. We already established that I'm not interested in either pilots or cameramen."

Nice of her to bring that up again while I'm breaking a sweat from squatting behind my tripod. "It's not about finding a cameraman. It's about finding a man who wants you to be his model." Take that, freckles.

She laughs at herself.

I relent and join in. Because being able to laugh at yourself is one of the best qualities in a person. And because she's way too real to be a model.

"Fine. I'll do my little turn on the catwalk." She steps one foot forward so she can pivot away, but mid pivot she's groaning in pain again.

It's so the opposite of sexy that we both laugh harder.

She plants a hand on her hip like a model striding down the runway, but with the way she limps along, there's no question that the hand placement is only for support. She throws me a grin over her shoulder. At least she's enjoying herself now, even if it's with self-deprecating humor. "I'm going for the cute guy in the collared shirt and fedora."

I'm pretty sure putting together "cute guy" and "fedora" makes an oxymoron, but it will keep the show entertaining. I pan our setting in search of the Indiana Jones wannabe.

Oh man. It's a *straw* hat. And to make it even cheesier, the guy has a chin cleft. It's as if he thinks he's a comic book superhero in hiding. Is he the kind of guy Meri is looking for? Just because he's wearing a collared shirt?

She staggers his way slowly. If this really were a comic book, she'd be a zombie. I can't keep from chuckling.

He sees her coming long before she reaches him. It's like watching a traffic accident in slow motion.

She holds out her camera. She points toward the fountain with her ice cream cone. He looks at the fountain and takes a long time to look back at her.

A woman sweeps in—a mother with little kids in swimsuits running circles around her legs. She reaches for the phone, then snaps photos of Meri from a variety of angles as if she thinks the photos will be going in her own scrapbook someday. The fedora-wearing jerk takes the opportunity to disappear.

Meri poses in multiple positions before retrieving her camera and being swarmed by the kids. She nods and smiles, then hobbles my way with the kids dancing along beside her.

"Do you know how badly that hurt?" she calls.

"What?" I peek up from behind the camera to see Meri's reaction in real life. "Having a guy refuse to take your photo?"

"No." She whimpers, then laughs. "Walking. Every step feels like a sledgehammer hitting against my thigh."

The kids see my camera.

"Are we on television?" asks one.

"Is Meri famous?" asks the other.

"No, no . . ." Meri tries to wave them away.

"Meri is on a YouTube show," I answer for her. If she would keep moving, her pain would lessen. But I'm not going to make her continue the husband hunt. It almost hurts to watch her move. Not to mention, I have another idea for this video. "I film her doing things like riding in a pedicab, eating ice cream, and running through the fountain."

She frowns and picks up her shuffle. "I didn't run through the fountain."

"You didn't?" I ask in mock disbelief.

"Kai . . ."

"Did you hear that, kids?" I turn my most animated look on the elementary school boy and girl who flank her sides. "If you run with her through the fountain, and it's okay with your mom, you can be in the video too."

The children's eyes widen in joy.

Meri's eyes widen in horror.

They grab her hands and tug. And it works. She laughs and gives in, splashing and playing with the kids even as she hobbles around in pain.

I zoom in to make sure I don't miss a drop of the action.

CHAPTER FIFTEEN

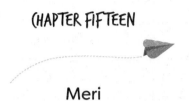

Meri

*#50. Bake his favorite dessert. Bad cooking will
drive your man to seedy saloons.*

I'm pretty sure hanging out with Kai is what life would have been like as a child if Charlie had been a normal brother. Though Kai's only a roommate and we are both in our thirties, I would consider our inter-action to be similar to sibling squabbles.

After Gemma had watched our video last night and saw Kai tricked some innocent children into dragging me through the fountain, she'd taken pity and baked his mom's pie recipe while I'd soaked in a hot bath. That's where I was when I'd overheard her giving him a lecture.

He hadn't argued, only laughed. I'd turned the water back on, so he couldn't hear me laugh along.

I wanted him to think I was mad. Then maybe I could get more free ice cream out of him.

Rats. I should have brought ice cream to go with the apple pie I'm serving right now in the office break room.

Kai shoots me a thumbs-up from outside the window, so I know he's ready. He came to the office early today to catch the action before the doctors leave. I hope they aren't too upset when they realize I've got a microphone tucked inside my scrubs. I'm not expecting to get a date out of this, but it's on The List, so here I am.

Dr. Snyder strolls in. He's the single one. Not bad looking, but he got into medicine due to headaches caused by blood clots as a kid.

Now he battles deep vein thrombosis, which makes him much more cautious about life than I've ever had to be.

"Would you like some pie, doc?"

Snyder retrieves a canister of whole almonds from the cupboard. "It looks great, but I'm trying out the paleo diet."

If I were as healthy as he is, my thighs and biceps would not still be throbbing at the slightest touch. I'm a little jealous of his discipline. "The pie is pretty close to paleo."

Snyder pauses. "It is?" He looks at me with a gleam of respect.

"Yes." If that intrigues him, he'll love this next part. "I got the recipe from a trainer in a new boot camp class I'm taking."

Snyder turns to face me, leans against the counter, and crosses his arms. "I mistakenly assumed you'd be more of the Zumba type."

Obviously, he's never seen me dance the Charleston. "I haven't tried Zumba, though this class is kicking my tail. I am so sore today."

He gives me more attention than he's ever given me before, but as if I'm a patient. "Have you stretched?" he asks.

I shoot Kai a sideways glance out the window, remembering the way he wrenched my arms behind me on the couch. Odd but helpful.

Kai waves my attention back to Snyder.

"Yes."

"Hot bath?"

"Yes." If I was a doctor, a hot bath would be my prescription for everything.

"Did you try eating pineapple or tart cherries?"

I purse my lips, trying to remember what I'd had for breakfast. Oh . . . I'd had the Pop-Tarts Kai smuggled me when Gemma decided to fix us all sweet potato-and-kale hash. Too bad I'd selected cinnamon instead of the cherry flavor. I could be pain free right now. "Nope."

I glance toward the window, wondering if Kai had known about the tart cherry cure.

He shakes his head and points toward Snyder as a reminder of who I'm supposed to be talking to.

I refocus but keep in mind the combination of a hot bath and cherry Pop-Tarts in case I ever decide to punish myself with boot camp again.

Snyder swings the cabinet open and retrieves a bag of dried fruit. "Here." He tilts it sideways as indication for me to hold out my hand.

I cup my palm, and he pours a handful of the little dried berries. Not how I'd planned to perform this item on The List, but has anything on The List gone to plan? At least, now my tender muscles might give me some relief.

I pop a tangy piece of fruit on my tongue. "Thanks."

Roxy sticks her head inside the door. "I have a patient asking for you, Meri."

I check on Kai outside the window to make sure he isn't the one who's come inside acting like a patient in order to give me some advice on how to land Dr. Snyder.

Nope. He's still positioned outside in the bushes at the angle where only I can see him. That's a relief at least.

"Okay." I stuff the rest of the dried fruit in my mouth, then motion Dr. Snyder toward my pie before washing my hands. "Go ahead and help yourself. I'll be back."

"Thanks, Meri." Snyder returns his snacks to the cupboard without another look at Gemma's pie. "I'm headed out, but I'm excited for your new ventures into healthy living."

That makes one of us. I give an overly bright smile, then hobble off to find Roxy, my calves throbbing. "Who asked for me?" I wrack my brain for patients that I'd seen listed on today's schedule.

Roxy stops outside an exam room and looks at her chart. "A Nicole Foster."

My eyes bulge. I've barely seen Nicole since she ended her engagement to my dumb brother. Last I've heard, she'd gotten engaged again. By now she should be married and have changed her name. Maybe the name change isn't legal yet. I take the chart and push open the door.

"Nikki," I greet.

She's as well put together as usual, with her dark A-line haircut, slacks, and heels. But the tip of her nose is red and her dark eyes water.

In my excitement, I forgot she'd be sick. I temper my tone. "How are you?"

"I think I'm getting pneumonia."

Most people with pneumonia would not be wearing high heels and have their hair styled, but I know that for Nicole to even be in a doctor's office, she pretty much has to be dying. It's probably killing her to have left work early for this appointment.

"Let's check your vitals." I can tell before I even stick the thermometer under her tongue that she has a fever. I'm starting to feel sweaty just from the heat emanating off her skin. Yep. 102.9.

I retrieve my blood pressure cuff from the wall and slide it up her left arm. I pause at her wrist and stare at her hand. There's no wedding band. Not even an engagement ring. Did she take it off because of swelling? Or has she been washing her hands so much due to illness that the giant diamond is getting in the way?

"I didn't get married." Her voice is raspy.

I look up at her, afraid to ask why.

"It has nothing to do with your brother. When he asks, tell him that." Okay. But why? Did *she* get left at the altar this time around?

I don't question because I don't want to inflate her blood pressure. Instead, I Velcro the cuff in place and slip the eartips of my stethoscope in my ears to count her pulse.

Her blood pressure is a little high, but that's to be expected when one is going through fiancés like Kleenex. At least she's been proposed to. Multiple times. Unlike me.

Paper crinkles as she lies back on the table. "He bought me a Porsche."

I gape, still holding onto the blood pressure cuff and sure to forget her numbers before I enter them into the computer. "Your fiancé bought you a Porsche?"

"Yes."

I'm not getting the connection. My eyebrows arch toward my scalp. "Isn't that when you put a 'Just Married' sign on the trunk and drive off into the sunset?"

She stares at the ceiling. "I liked Robert because he was so different from your brother. He never traveled out of town for work and forgot to call me, or stood me up to work late, or expected me to change plans at the last minute. I was his world."

My eyebrows stay up there. "It must be nice."

"It was. At first." She closes her eyes. "But then it became a burden."

My eyebrows might never move again. What would I give to have somebody care about me that much?

"It started to feel like his happiness was my responsibility. I felt smothered."

Like pneumonia would smother her lungs. Okay, I could get that. "I'm sorry. What did you do with the Porsche?" I just happen to know a guy without a car.

Not that I expect Nicole to give him the Porsche, but her old car might be up for sale.

She smiles sadly. "I gave it back. It was as conditional as his love."

I should feel bad for her, but this just makes me sadder for myself. If it's truly better to have loved and lost than to never loved at all, then she's better off than I am.

Back at the town house, I lament to Kai over paleo pie. We each slouch on stools at the counter. Dr. Snyder would be so disappointed in my eating half a pie, but the pastry is mostly fruit and nuts, so it's kinda like eating a Lärabar. Well, it's better for me than Pop-Tarts, at least.

I'm pretty sure from the way Kai has propped up his phone that he's filming us right now. I don't care. I have no pride left. There's not much I could do to embarrass myself more than I already have. I'll just be careful not to mention names.

Kai waves his fork in the air as if he's following along with the words to a story in a book. "She broke up with her new fiancé because he bought her a luxury sports car?"

I slide more cinnamon apples into my mouth. They're not as sweet as if Gemma had used real sugar, but maybe the tartness will have the same effect as tart cherries. Which, now that I think about it, is none at all. Dr. Snyder's natural remedy did nothing to help my aching muscles. It still hurts to move. "Yes."

He chews thoughtfully. "You don't think there's more to the story?"

I forgot that Kai knows Nicole too. He'd seen Charlie and Nikki together when they were crazy about each other. Back before Charlie's obsession and her ego got in the way.

I shrug. "She specifically said it has nothing to do with Charlie."

He narrows his eyes. "Why would she need to say that?"

"Because she knows he'll ask."

We eat in silence.

Kai swallows and his gaze snags mine. "Why did she want you to be her nurse?"

"She always does." Both times she's come in anyway. The only other time she'd scheduled an appointment was when her boss made her. By that point, she'd had a concussion for five days. She's lucky not to have any long-term effects from the lack of care. Or maybe all her canceled wedding engagements are a result of the brain damage. "I'm glad she makes an effort to keep in touch. We were almost family."

Kai holds up his fork again. "I think she wants Charlie to know she's still single."

"Maybe." I want Charlie to be happy, but I don't feel Nicole should get any more chances at love. She's already had two fiancés. What about the rest of us who have never been given an engagement ring? When's it our turn? "This really isn't fair."

"Eating apple pie without sugar? I agree."

"No. I'm talking about how I'm the one putting myself out there with the *Meri Me* show, and I'm the only one not in a relationship."

"I'm not in a relationship."

"You don't count."

"That's rude."

"You don't like commitment."

"True. What about your brother, then? He isn't in a relationship."

"Well, you think he could be." I tick off the relationships on my fingers. "My brother's ex possibly wants to get back together with him. Our roommate has got a certain famous actor panting after her without even knowing it. Even my mom is dating. Meanwhile . . ." I nod at my plate.

"You've got your own cutie pie."

The pun is so bad I can't help laughing. My belly burns. At least it'll give me an ab workout without boot camp.

CHAPTER SIXTEEN

Kai

#47. If he's riding a train, he's going places.
Sit next to him and find out where.

Saturdays I only sleep until around noon. It gives me a longer day to interact with humanity if I feel so inclined. I don't necessarily feel like it today, but as we're filming Meri riding back and forth to the airport on the light rail known as MAX, I'm sure to be interacting with some very interesting humanity.

For some reason, I'm not expecting the weirdness to start in my living room, but as I mosey down the stairs, I find Gemma duct taped to a chair in front of the television. Panic chills my spine until I see Meri eating Pop-Tarts on the couch, and everything makes a lot more sense.

I tuck my hands into my pockets and stroll down the remaining stairs. "Was Gemma trying to force you to eat kale again?"

Meri grins up at me from where she's facing Gemma with her knees tucked to her chin. "Yep. Don't mess with me."

I should be more alarmed than amused, but I can't help smirking at the situation.

Gemma rocks the chair back and forth as if she's trying to escape. "I told her to tape me up."

I continue into the kitchen. "I'm not sure how to respond to that." At least I'm more free to eat Pop-Tarts than I have been in a long time.

Gemma grunts as she wrestles with the tape holding her arms to the armrests. "Riley read my script and said he didn't think my escape scene is plausible. I'm going to prove him wrong."

I don't see Meri's box of toaster pastries, but there's some apple pie still in the fridge, so I grab that.

Meri waves me back into the living area. "Why aren't you filming this? It's better entertainment than my trying to lasso men."

"I don't know. That's pretty hard to beat." I tug a drawer open to find clean forks—one of the perks to living with two women.

Gemma throws her body backward with a groan. A clock clatters off the entertainment center behind her.

"Careful." I join Meri on the couch for breakfast and a show. "If you break any of Charlie's stuff, this might be hard to explain."

Gemma leans forward against the duct tape bound around her torso. "Read me the directions again, Meri."

Meri has her phone propped against her knees. She takes a bite of her breakfast and reads with the food in her cheek. "Pull your arms in as if you're trying to hit yourself in the chest."

This is going to be good. I set the pie on a coffee table cube and shift my weight so I can tug my own phone from a back pocket and hold it steady with both hands when pushing *record*.

Gemma fists her hands and bares her teeth. There's a lot of groaning and shaking involved, but the duct tape holds her in place. "Maybe I'm not strong enough." She looks at me. "My character in the script is male. You should try this for me, Kai."

I chuckle at the absurd mental image. "Not happening."

Meri scrolls down the website. "It says breaking free has nothing to do with strength but with speed and the angle used. Try one arm at a time."

"Okay." Gemma takes a deep breath. She shakes her head like a boxer getting ready for a fight, and I kinda want to play the theme song to *Rocky*.

"You can do it," Meri cheers.

Gemma narrows her eyes in concentration. "One, two, three . . ." She rips her right arm free and whoops with success.

That was actually kind of impressive. "Nice."

Meri claps. "Do the other one."

Gemma rips her left arm from the chair like Bruce Banner turning into the Hulk. Though she's still attached to the chair by the duct tape wrapped around her chest.

Meri looks back at her phone screen. "Now you have to jerk forward and stand up all in one motion."

Gemma braces her feet on the ground. She hunches forward with a mighty grunt, and her chair slams backward to the hardwood floor, barely missing Charlie's neatly arranged Blu-ray collection. "Yeah," she shouts, arms overhead, duct tape hanging from her sleeves. "My character can break free."

I motion to her. "And if you're ever kidnapped, this little lesson can come in handy."

She scrambles to right the chair. "I want to try it once more, now that I know what I'm doing. Meri, pretend to be an intruder again."

Meri has just gotten Gemma taped up and returned to settle next to me on the couch when there's a knock on the door.

"Police, open up."

Gemma's wide blue eyes grow wider.

Meri covers her mouth.

I've got that icy feeling crawling down my spine again. "Gemma, hurry. Break free."

Neither woman moves.

The police pound on the door again. Is their presence related to Gemma's experiment? Did a neighbor see her through a window? Or is there some other random emergency that sent the cops to our neighborhood? I won't know until I let them in.

I place my phone on the table, stand, and try pointing at Gemma to snap her out of statue mode as I pass, but she remains frozen. If this is how she reacts under pressure, I hope she never really gets kidnapped.

I scrunch my eyes closed and say a quick prayer as I grab the doorknob. *Lord, please let this officer of the law have a sense of humor.*

I open the door to find the man in uniform. If he'd been wearing a black leather vest and carrying a bow and arrow, he would have been a dead ringer for Hawkeye from *The Avengers*. He has the same bland coloring, messy hair, and serious expression. Unfortunately, I'm pretty sure that the reason Hawkeye is the only Avenger who didn't get his own movie is because he's the least funny. This does not bode well for our situation.

I wedge my body in the door opening and paste my face with an expression that I hope looks like the right amount of innocence and alarm. I should have let Meri open the door. Nobody would ever expect her of foul play with all those freckles. "What can I do for you, officer?"

He loops his thumbs on his belt, a little too close to his gun for my comfort. "Your neighbors called with some concerns about hearing loud noises. Is everything all right over here."

I shrug. "Perfectly normal morning for us." If only normal also meant boring in our case.

"Who else is here with you?"

"My roommates."

He narrows his eyes at me. "Mind if I look around?"

I am so getting handcuffed. "That's fine, but you should know—"

"Move out of the way, son."

I'm pretty sure this guy is not any older than I am, but his position of power has a way of making me feel like a little kid. I give a tight smile, swing the door open, and motion him in.

The man's look of caution melts into outrage. He draws his gun while simultaneously speaking into a radio for backup.

I don't hear a word he says, only a ringing in my ears as tingles explode through my limbs. I raise my hands in slow motion.

The girls shriek.

"No," Gemma yells. "He didn't tape me up. Meri did."

The gun barrel swings Meri's way. I want to leap on top of the guy, but that would probably make things worse. I bend my knees to spring, if needed.

Meri covers her face with her hands and half a pastry.

"I asked her to bind me to this chair," Gemma's voice resounds with a calm I don't feel. "I'm a writer, and I want to know what it felt like. She's reading me directions from the internet on how to break free."

The man's jaw twitches. He doesn't seem as entertained as we had been. "You can break free?" he asks slowly.

I motion for Gemma to do so, prompting a dirty look from Officer Angry Eyes. I lift my hands back over my head.

Gemma rips her arms from the chair then doubles over and stands to her feet like a queen rising from her throne. "I'm sorry I made so much noise earlier. I was just excited that the scene I wrote will work. Riley Avella told me—"

"Riley Avella—the actor?" He's still holding his gun up, but his finger is not on the trigger.

"Yes. I act with him on *Capers*, but that's only because I love story. I'm actually a screenwriter."

"Great." His gun lowers. "You're an actor." He says this as if it's a bad thing—as if he mistakenly gets phone calls to rescue actors all the time.

"No, I'm a screenwriter."

I give Gemma a shake of my head, hands still raised. This is not a moment in which to argue with the law.

The officer holsters his gun and glares at me.

Why me? All I did was eat pie.

"Don't let this happen again."

Uhh . . . "Okay."

"Even though this is a huge waste of my time, I'll need to take your statements for my report, since I drew my gun."

It's a waste of my time too, but I refrain from mentioning my side of the incident. He probably doesn't care that I have plans to film Meri riding around town on the MAX to sit by random men for our You-Tube channel. I let it go because I'm just glad not to have been shot.

Gemma, however, seems to be enjoying the drama she created. When Meri and I are finally allowed to leave, she hugs us goodbye and whispers, "Isn't he dashing?"

I have to admit I'm a little disturbed. Out of all the men who have shown interest in Gemma, including worship leaders and movie stars, the only one she's noticed is the guy who threatened my life with a gun.

I'm still pondering this as Meri and I take turns inserting our credit cards into the automated machine that will sell us tickets at the train station. "I don't get Gemma. Is it the uniform? Is it his authority? Does she have a history of emotional abuse?"

Meri retrieves her ticket. "I bet it's the challenge. He's the only man who hasn't fallen all over himself for her."

"*I* didn't fall all over her."

"I heard about your toe, Kai."

I focus on retrieving my ticket and mutter under my breath. "I didn't fall. I tripped."

A train squeals into the station and its doors open with a hiss, so there's a good chance she didn't hear. I don't want to talk about an old crush on my roommate. It's embarrassing.

"Anyway . . ." Meri leads the way, shooting me a grin over her shoulder. She'd heard. "I wonder if Gemma got a date with the cop."

"I'm sure she did."

We step inside the car and Meri examines the configuration of blue seats. The middle section has a bench along the wall facing in with loops overhead for passengers who want to stand. The front and back of the train car have rows facing forward like on a school bus.

I point at the sideways seats. Sitting there, I can record her from either the front or the back. I pull my earbuds from my pocket so I can act as if I'm listening to music. I didn't bring my good camera equipment, since there's not a place for me to hide. I'll film with my phone, and this way, I'll appear to be looking intently at my playlist.

Meri stays standing and grabs an overhead loop. That's a good location for her. Because it would be weird for her to get up from one seat to move to another right next to a man. Not that there are a lot of men on board.

Besides the guy who looks like a gangster and keeps glancing at me as if he's afraid I'll recognize him from an episode of *Live PD*, there's a small group that appears to be an occupational therapist with a couple of disabled patients.

Meri subtly points to the thug.

I pop in my earbuds, crank some tunes, and shake my head. She'd be better off snapping a pic of the dude to send to Gemma for her to report to Officer Hawkeye. Meanwhile, with the warmth of the sun shining through the windows, the hypnotic sway of the tracks, and my lack of sleep, I'm about ready to doze off.

The light rail nears the airport, and more people crowd the car. Meri smiles at every new person who gets on, which I'm sure makes her the friendliest rider there ever was. It also gives her a chance to study each opportunity.

Finally, I see her settle on a dude with glasses and a man bun. She catches my eye and tips her head his way, as if I haven't noticed.

I smoosh my lips together dubiously to say, *If you want.* I've never actually known anyone with a man bun to get married, so it's probably the collared shirt or the glasses that draw her his way. She must assume he's intelligent despite his hairstyle.

He's sitting on the aisle seat and has to stand for her to squeeze between him and an old man with white hair and wrinkly pink skin. She settles in, crosses her legs, locks her fingers together over one knee, and smiles up at him. Here we go.

I rub a hand over my mouth to hide a smile.

She says something.

Smarty pants shrugs.

The old man engages.

Repeat.

Until she's so deep in conversation with the old man, that we've reached the airport, and everyone is climbing off except for him. She finally realizes he wants out and stands to let him exit.

I pop an earbud out of my ear to eavesdrop.

"Where's your luggage?" the gentleman asks in a wobbly voice.

She holds her hands wide and looks around as if she's expecting to find the suitcase she never packed. "I don't have it here. I'll have to go home."

Good save. I stick the earbuds back in my ear.

She waves as he toddles away, and we have the whole car to ourselves.

"If only he were fifty years younger," she says. "His late wife was named Meredith too."

Perhaps Meri is single because she was born in the wrong generation.

The doors whoosh shut, and the train starts to move again.

She sinks beside me. "I'd wanted to talk to the other guy. I think he must be going through some personal issues because he wasn't very talkative, but I *did* like his glasses."

I nod. She should really stand, so we don't look as though we're here together when the doors open next. For the first time, I want to get filming over with so I can go to bed early. I don't think it's just my laziness this time. The stress of an uncertain career is getting to me.

"Hey, wasn't there a suggestion on The List about getting glasses? I should do that next. I think it will really work, because those glasses made that last guy look attractive."

I'm not going to talk about how attractive she thinks Mr. Man Bun was.

"Are you even listening?" She pops an earbud out of my ear, and with the pressure and noise change, it feels similar to rising above the surface of a swimming pool.

She sticks the earbud in her own ear, then reaches for my phone. "This music is so grungy. Can I pick a song?"

"By all means." I roll my eyes but pop my remaining earbud into the ear closer to her so we're not tethered together in an awkward position.

She takes my phone and checks out my playlist before opening YouTube. "I can't believe you don't have anything good. Like Katy Perry or Bruno Mars."

I should have known. "I make it a point never to listen to musicians who've played the Super Bowl."

"Oh, I know a song you'll like." She taps and we slog through a five-second YouTube commercial.

"Doesn't The List say something about finding out what books, movies, and music your guy likes, then making them your favorite too?"

"I can't help it if I have better taste than you."

Before I can think of a comeback, the familiar thrum of a ukulele fills my ear. *Count on Me* by Mr. Mars. Mom has taught hula lessons to this song.

Meri snaps along, singing the first verse.

I must admit it's kind of catchy. Should I let on that I know the lyrics? I surprise her by joining in on the chorus about being there for each other.

"You know it." She squeals, then sways into me, forcing me to sway in unison as if we're members of a gospel choir.

She only gets more animated from there, counting out the numbers on her fingers, and pointing back and forth between us to take turns as if we're singing a duet.

The train stops. A gaggle of teenage girls climb on.

Meri keeps singing. This is why she's a YouTube sensation. She has no inhibitions.

I might as well make the most of it. I lean in to harmonize on the oohs.

The girls laugh and point. Then they pull out phones to video us.

I feel like we're in a Disney musical, though that's not all bad. Everyone is always happy in one of those.

I smile down at Meri, and she smiles up at me.

We probably sound horrible to the girls, who don't have the background music to go with our voices, but we sound good to my ears. We're like the little five-year-old buddies in the music video playing on my phone screen. They climb trees and swing on tire swings. It's a good song for us.

Meri leans her head on my shoulder as the lyrics command, and we sing the last line together.

Our audience applauds and shrieks the way only teenage girls can.

The girl with long hair and a tank top leans forward. All the girls have long hair and tank tops, so I wouldn't be able to tell her apart in a lineup, but that's the only way I can see to describe her. "You're Kai and Meri, aren't you?" she asks. "From *Meri Me.*"

I'm surprised to be recognized. The shows have been all about Meri. Yeah, I get pulled into it by a lasso every now and then, but the girls probably only know me by my voice. Or from Meri's comments to me behind the camera.

Meri sits up, pulling her head from my shoulder. "We are. Hi."

"Are you filming today?" Asks another girl with long hair and a tank top. Or maybe it's the same girl.

"Yes." Meri motions to the empty train seats. "We're waiting for men to get on, so I can sit next to them and strike up a conversation."

The girls look at each other. The spokeswoman for them points my way. Or perhaps it's the third girl. I can't be sure. "You're sitting next to Kai. He's cute. Why not, you know, marry him?"

Oh boy. Here come the retorts about how Meri wants a real man.

Meri sticks a thumb at me. "This guy is never getting married."

I'm sure she'll add something about how I don't even own a car or take care of the fungus on my feet, but she doesn't. That's it.

That can't be the only reason she's not interested in me. Even if I were looking to wed, I know I wouldn't be good enough for her. She wants someone mature and driven. She's simply being nice.

"Too bad," says one of the high school clones with a shoulder slump.

The train comes to a stop at Lloyd Center mall, and the girls file off. Thankfully a few other people get on, so I'm not alone with my friend who just happens to be a woman.

My seat has grown uncomfortable, and I miss my butt dent. When I'm at home alone, I don't wonder what life would be like if I let myself want more.

CHAPTER SEVENTEEN

Meri

*#53. If you are going out to dinner, eat beforehand
so you can order something small. This will do two
things: show him you don't have a large appetite
and save him money.*

If my phone is going to ring before my alarm, it should never be on a
Monday. Monday's are hard enough.

I rub my stinging eyes and roll over in the dark to fumble for the
device that jarred me awake. With my brother in a different time zone,
I should really turn off the stupid ringer at night. At least now if he's
kidnapped, I'll give him the steps for breaking out of duct tape and
then go back to sleep.

I swipe the smooth screen and mumble, "Hello," before the phone
is even to my ear.

"Meri? Are you there?" The intense tone of his voice jolts me
awake all over again.

I grunt in reply. After my lunch with Mom yesterday, it's not sur-
prising that Charlie's calling to talk.

Mom has recently turned into a teenager. Even though Douglas
was out of town for work, she still giggled all through our meal as
if we were in a high school cafeteria. And she didn't ask one solitary
question about Kai.

The last time I'd seen her, I'd scrambled off to go to the coast with
him, and she must have watched the YouTube videos where everybody

else seems to think the two of us are in a relationship. She'd told Charlie last week that she'd had concerns, but she never once mentioned them to me.

How is she okay that Kai and I are living in the same house? I mean, I know nothing is going to happen between us, but *she* doesn't know that. Does she not care about my purity anymore? I should sit with Kai in the sound booth next week to see if she even notices.

"Did you talk to Mom about Douglas?" I guess.

"Douglas? You mean Mom's boyfriend?"

I shudder. "The guy who makes her use her scarves to dab at her face whenever she talks about him."

"Why does she dab her face?"

"Because she's flushed."

"Ew."

Ew is right. But there are worse things. "She's being weird. She's not even worried about the YouTube channel I'm doing with Kai anymore."

Charlie clears his throat. "That's what I wanted to talk to you about."

I sigh in relief, sinking deeper into my mattress. Mom must have talked to him more about her concerns, and he told her not to worry. She still cares.

"I just caught up on your videos and saw Nicole broke it off with her fiancé."

Now I'm the one trying to figure out who we are talking about. Nicole? Oh yeah. Charlie's ex. Kai included that part of our conversation in the apple pie video.

I scrunch my nose in a pained expression, though Charlie will never see it. "Then you also heard how she said canceling her wedding had nothing to do with you."

"But it does."

I flop onto my back. I don't want to be in the middle of this, but here I am. "Why do you think that?"

Charlie takes a deep breath. "The night before she was supposed to get married, I prayed that if God wanted me to marry her, she'd call off her wedding."

My eyes pop open. I grip the bedsheet in a fist. "You what?"

"Yeah, I don't know why. It just came out of my mouth. Then I totally forgot about it because I figured she'd gotten married anyway."

Charlie confirmed what I'd suspected all along. My brother is clueless when it comes to relationships. "So, you want to marry her now?"

"I don't know."

"That attitude is not going to win her over."

Charlie clicks his tongue. "I'd have to figure out the logistics of our relationship, but if God wants me to marry her, then I have a duty to do so."

I hold my hand wide because words fail me.

God's the only One who would see my motion, but I'm pretty sure we're both in agreement on the fact that my brother needs help.

"Since you're currently on another continent, Charlie, the logistics will probably have to wait. Which means it really wasn't necessary to wake me up at"—I pull my phone away to read the time—"four thirty in the morning."

"Sorry, sis." He sounds lost. Charlie is never lost. "I just haven't talked about this with anyone, and I thought maybe if I did, I could stop thinking about it."

I close my eyes to offer up a prayer for my future sister-in-law. Charlie may be no romantic, but he's a go-getter. Perhaps she was "the one" for him all along, and he just didn't realize it. If he comes up with a strategy to win Nicole back, she's going to lose her battle.

With "battle" on the brain, I decide to go to boot camp. I'm awake now. And a pitter-patter on the window tells me it's raining. If I went jogging, my new shoes would get all soggy.

More important than my new running shoes are my new glasses. I didn't take time to do the whole optometrist/insurance thing—I simply picked up a cute pair of reading glasses at the pharmacy yesterday when I was filming with Kai. The prescription took some getting used to, and I really did trip and fall, but not one guy was there to catch me. Well, except Kai. But he didn't seem too happy about it since I almost knocked his camera to the ground.

Anyway, at close range I can see better than before, which is an unexpected benefit. I've now got great vision for viewing myself looking super cute in my red plastic frames. Kai suggested I pair them with matching shoes as suggested in #45. *Wear red shoes. They make you walk faster, and if you have pretty legs, people will notice.* Not sure that my legs are pretty enough, so I'm sticking with my Nikes.

Hey, my shoes could be worse. They could be those white rubbery clogs Roxy wears that make her feet look as if they belong to a Smurf.

I got my workout in, and when lunch time rolls around, I feel I've burned enough calories to eat pizza. So here I am in the break room, wearing my new glasses and Nikes, when Dr. Snyder walks in. I know eating pizza is not going to impress him before I even see the unimpressed look on his face. Crystal clear vision isn't always an advantage.

"Hey, Meri." He grabs a fancy salad from the fridge and joins me at the table. "How's your boot camp class going?"

I swallow gooey cheese and yeasty crust. "I didn't hate it this morning as much as I expected to."

I'm not even lying. Though tomorrow when I'm hobbling around again, I might have a different response. This morning Ethel was next to me throughout our circuits, and she alleviated some of my push-up pain by telling stories of how she met her husband right before he was shipped out for war in Vietnam. They got married after only knowing each other a month. And they've been together over sixty years now. She hit the husband jackpot.

You don't hear stories like that very often these days. And you certainly don't hear them when you're jogging by yourself.

"That's good." Snyder nods, and I have to remind myself he's talking about boot camp and not Ethel's wedded bliss. "I watched your YouTube video last night."

I stuff another bite of pizza in my mouth so that it would be impolite for me to talk. Having strangers watch my videos is one thing, but coming from a coworker, it's different. Especially when he's in it.

"The whole premise made me laugh." At least he's not angry about being secretly filmed before we got his permission to air it. "I'm sorry I didn't try your pie."

I grin around the food in my cheek. "More for me."

He meets my gaze, dark eyes solemn. Did he not realize I was joking? Is he worried I've got an eating disorder? He touches my hand. His are soft but strong, and he has nice, trimmed cuticles. "I also want you to know that if I wasn't leaving Oregon at the end of the month, I'd ask you out on a date."

I start to swallow, and the pizza almost gets stuck in my throat. I choke it down in time to prevent Snyder from giving me the Heimlich. But which statement surprised me more? The fact that he's leaving or that he would've asked me out on a date?

If he's attracted to me at all, it's gotta be the glasses.

It's certainly not my mealtime etiquette.

I pull my hand away to cover my mouth and hide the way I'm licking tangy sauce off my teeth. Maybe I'll get to marry a doctor one day after all. "That would have been nice." Understatement. "I didn't know you were leaving."

He studies me as if he's never studied me before. And Kai's not even here to video it. I'm being almost asked out at work, but I have no proof.

He looks down. "I've taken a job with a ministry that travels the country, helping out with disaster relief."

He's going to take care of the sick after floods, earthquakes, and fires? With a Christian organization?

Even more than not getting to go out on a date with him, I'm bummed that I'm not the one leaving on such a mission. "That's incredible. You'll get to cure people all over the world."

He smiles up at me as if he's pleased I get it. "I wish I was traveling the world. With my vein issues, I can't sit in a plane long enough to fly overseas, so I'll only be helping out here in the States."

I clasp my greasy fingers together around my napkin and commence gushing. "You're still going to get to help people who need you for more than sniffles and sore throats. You'll be saving lives. I'm super jealous."

His dark eyes blink wider. "The ministry I joined is still looking for nurses. Though if you want to travel the world, you might want to check out their sister organization."

"Oh." I lower my napkin into my lap. I'd never considered such an option. I hadn't even considered ER work because the crazy hours would be hard on raising a family. Not that I have a family. But I was thinking ahead.

Of course, I can't tell that to Dr. Snyder. He probably already thinks I'm desperate.

He shrugs and stands. "I've got a brochure if you're ever interested."

"Thanks. I didn't mean . . . I'm just . . . That's not . . ."

He gives me a small smile. "I know. You're looking for a husband."

Well then. I don't have anything to say because he said it for me. But as he takes his salad to his office, I stare at my pizza crust.

Wanting to get married isn't a bad thing. But could it be holding me back from even better things? Like how I accepted this position working for a family practitioner over working in an ER because the hours would be more conducive to raising kids?

I would have enjoyed working in an emergency room. I do well with trauma because I can think quickly on my feet. And I'm one of the weirdos who enjoys that kind of pressure. I'd enjoy traveling to help people, as well. I'd feel I was really changing lives. Not just pushing antibiotics.

Roxy saves my thoughts from their nosedive by trotting in and lifting the lid to my pizza box. "Are you sharing?"

"Oh, so you'll eat my pizza, but you won't eat my healthy apple pie?"

"Yes. And you love me for it." She drops into the seat Dr. Snyder vacated.

"I do love you for it." In fact, now that I think about it, I'm kind of glad Dr. Snyder is leaving the state. He's a nice guy, but marrying him would be like marrying Gemma. I'd have to sneak Pop-Tarts. I smile in new appreciation at my old buddy from nursing school.

She attempts to smile back. I know it's not a real smile because my new glasses help me see the dull sheen of sadness in her eyes, despite the way they are almost hidden behind bouncy chin-length curls.

"You okay?" I ask.

"I will be after a piece of pizza. I'm getting hangry." She grabs a slice with shaved beef, green pepper, and onions, known as It's Always Sunny in Portland. I believe her even less than I believe the name of the pizza.

"Do you want to talk about it?" I hope she's okay. I mean, she was the first of my college friends to get married, and she has a one-year-old too. I would think she'd be the happiest.

Maybe she isn't happy. Maybe she hasn't been, and I just haven't noticed because I needed new glasses. And because she has everything I thought would make me happy.

She takes a tiny bite and chews slowly. Her eyelashes lift, and I see a shimmer of fear in her sage-green eyes. "Graham and I are separating."

The bread in my belly turns to stone. I'm afraid to ask what happened. I don't want to assume Graham cheated, but isn't that the only reason the Bible allows a divorce? "Was Graham unfaithful?"

Tears pool. "I wish."

My heart thumps in my ears. Where do I go from here? I'd heard the only thing more emotionally painful than infidelity was losing a child. I can't even imagine, and I especially can't imagine that Roxy could have kept such pain to herself. "Is Angel okay?"

Roxy grabs a pizza napkin to wipe her nose. "Yeah. She will be with me."

I exhale slowly. At least Angel is okay. Or as okay as children can be when their parents are separating. "Is this why you didn't cut back your hours?"

Roxy sets her pizza down. "I've wanted to tell you, I just didn't want to do it at the office, and I've been too exhausted to get together outside of work."

I place a hand on her forearm. "You don't have to talk about it now if you don't want to. I'm here for you whenever."

She glances at her watch, then toward the door. We have the room to ourselves for another fifteen minutes or so. "It's going to sound so trite, and I've been trying to deal with it, but I started counseling to help, and my counselor said nothing is going to get better unless I do something. She said staying with Graham is like keeping my hand on a hot burner and praying for God to take away my pain."

My chest tightens. Is she being abused? I can't imagine Graham would physically hurt her, but I know there's emotional abuse too. Or sexual. *Oh Lord, please not Angel.*

She bites her lips then meets my gaze. "He's lazy."

My body stills. My hand stays on her arm. But my mind is zinging around all over the place, trying to connect the dots.

"He doesn't do anything. Nothing. Except play video games."

I think of Kai's butt dent in the couch.

"He goes to work and comes home, just like I do. But I also cook, clean, make dinner, and take care of Angel. When I ask him to help, he doesn't take it seriously. Either he makes me laugh with a joke, or he gets angrier."

Graham does that? I remember he *did* like his video games, but he was always fun to hang around.

"I've tried not doing laundry for him or not serving him dinner, but he'll just wear dirty clothes and order takeout."

He sounds as if he's still living the life of a college student.

She sighs and stares out the window. "I could deal with all that, but . . ."

I squeeze her arm. I knew something bigger was coming.

"He hasn't gotten a vasectomy."

My eyebrows pinch together. This doesn't seem like the end of the world. Out of the two of us, at least she gets to have sex.

"We haven't had sex since Angel was born."

I rock back in shock. Angel turned one last month. I got her Dr. Seuss books for her birthday. That's a long time for a married couple to go without sex.

"Remember the blood clots I got during pregnancy?" She covers her face and her voice breaks. "I had to have that emergency C-section. I've been talking to Dr. Snyder about them since he's had issues with blood clots too, and he told me it wouldn't be safe to have any more kids."

I scoot my chair beside her and reach an arm around her shoulder. I didn't know she couldn't have more children.

She curls into me. "Graham's allergic to latex, so we can't use condoms, and because of my blood clotting, I'm not supposed to take the pill."

I smooth her coils of hair. All these little things are adding up into something big. Something too big for her to have to bear on her own. My heart breaks for her. For what I fear is coming.

"Graham says if I want to have sex so badly that I should get my tubes tied. But when would I do it? I'm working and raising a child and taking care of a house."

It boggles my mind. Why wouldn't *Graham* want to have sex with his wife? "Is he gay?"

She laughs dryly. "Again, I wish."

Wow. I rub my face. "And you know he's not having an affair?"

"He never leaves the house. He's too lazy to cheat on me." She reaches up to squeeze my hand. "It's very lonely being an unloved wife."

I'd always thought I had it bad. I never imagined there could be something worse than being single. Like getting married and being neglected. I squeeze her hand. "It sounds like he doesn't love anything."

One of her tears drips onto my collar bone, then soaks into my neckline. "Thank you for understanding. I tried to talk to some ladies at church, and they made me feel I simply needed to work harder to win his affection. I tried that. It only made him take more advantage of me."

This seems to be the Christian answer. *Turn the other cheek.* And I totally believe we need to be willing to surrender. But we also have to know where to draw the line. The way Jesus did when he flipped tables to protect the sacred.

Marriage is sacred. It was designed for more than a husband to treat his wife like a servant. "What are you going to do?"

"I asked him to move out, but he won't. So, Angel and I are moving." She sits up and grabs another napkin, visibly returning to work mode. She takes a couple of deep breaths and forces the quiver out of her tone. "I'm hoping he pays the mortgage, because it has my name on it. I'm hoping that without me there to take care of everything for him, he'll choose to step up. I hope he'll become the father Angel deserves."

I rub a hand down Roxy's spine, realizing for the first time how bony she's gotten under her baggy scrubs. "And the husband you deserve."

Her smile wobbles, but she meets my gaze. "If he doesn't, I'm going to have an opening for a roommate."

CHAPTER EIGHTEEN

Kai

#39. Never accept an invitation less than twenty-four hours in advance or he will think you're undesirable to other men.

Meri messaged that she doesn't want me to meet her at the office again. She didn't say why, but that's okay. I have a surprise for her.

Yesterday when she was at lunch with her mom, her best friend stopped by. Anne just returned from her honeymoon and wanted to tell Meri all about Europe. I agreed to a dinner with the four of us where she can do just that.

I figured it would make for good footage of Meri talking about marriage for *Meri Me*. Also, it will give her a chance to check off #13 and #18 from her list. *Ask your friends' husbands to set you up with eligible bachelors they know. Blind dates can be the best ways to open a man's eyes.*

"Technically," Gemma calls from the kitchen, where she's banging pots and pans around with extra force. "Meri can't check off number thirteen just by talking to Anne's husband. She must talk to a plural number of husbands. Hence the apostrophe after the word *friends.*"

"Is that what you're all angry about in there? Proper grammar?"

"I'm a writer. What do you think?"

I dig inside my camera backpack for a piece of gum because both Meri and Anne should be getting here soon, and I don't want to go all the way upstairs to brush my teeth. "I thought maybe you got let go from *Capers* for trying to rewrite your lines."

Gemma stills. "The lines are so predictable that I want to quit, but I haven't yet. Would you prefer pesto roasted vegetables and chicken or Indian shrimp curry for dinner?"

I'm hoping for a burrito the size of a Big Gulp. "Did I forget to tell you that Meri and I are going out with her old roommate, Anne?"

She shoves her pan back underneath the oven with a clang. "I didn't want to cook anyway."

I pop the minty stick of gum in my mouth and wad the wrapper into a ball. "Are you going to tell me why you don't want to cook, or do you want me to keep guessing?"

She slides the trash compactor open for me to make a shot with my gum wrapper. "I looked up the police officer who was here the other day so I could message him some questions about detective work for my screenplay, but he's not answering back."

I miss my shot, then lean back to study my beautiful roommate while I chew. I wouldn't put it past her to be this upset about her screenplay, but if there's more to her frustration, that would be very interesting.

How ironic that the first guy she shows interest in is the only guy who isn't interested in her.

"You could sign up for the citizen's police academy."

She straightens from picking up my wrapper, and her crystal-blue eyes gaze at me for a moment before she grabs her phone.

I hope I haven't created a monster. At least this way, the next time she tries a stunt like escaping duct tape, there won't be the chance that I end up on the wrong end of a gun.

The door swings open. Meri trudges in, looking as if she lost a patient. Probably just sore from joining us at boot camp again this morning, since family physicians are not known for losing patients.

"I have a surprise for you."

Her amber eyes don't light up. They barely even *glance* up. "I told you I don't want to film tonight."

"It's not that." Not really. "But you do need to go change." She's currently wearing scrubs with Winnie the Pooh on them. And her hair is falling out of a fuzzy-looking bun.

She stops at the love seat and plops down with a sound that could only be described as agony. "If you volunteered me for the historical society the way number fourteen suggests, I'm going to break your laptop in two."

"I would never do that." Though I do smile inside at the suggestion. And slide my laptop into my camera bag. "I wouldn't do it until after number twenty-two anyway."

She drops against the couch cushion, head back, arms wide. "Is number twenty-two attending my high school reunion? Because I did that a few years ago. My high school boyfriend is now a sniper in the military."

Wow. I can see why she might not be interested in marrying the dude anymore, though he left some very manly shoes to fill. "Don't tell Gemma. She might start stalking him for writing research."

Gemma looks up from her phone in the kitchen. "I don't have a sniper in this story."

She said that way too seriously. I widen my eyes in concern before returning to my previous conversation that will hopefully get Nurse Eeyore to change into something more attractive. "Number twenty-two is getting a job at a hardware store. I hope you don't mind that I turned in applications for you."

She grunts. "If I thought you were capable of turning in an application, I might believe you."

My chest tightens. She's right to call me out, but as I know she's joking, I'll play along. Keep it light. Just like the videos we're making so that I don't have to actually put myself out there with an application. "You know how to hit me where it hurts."

She smiles smugly.

The doorbell rings.

She frowns. "That better be pizza and not part of your surprise."

I second guess my plans. She wouldn't really be upset about seeing her best friend again, would she?

Since neither Meri nor I move to answer, Gemma strides out from behind the breakfast bar. "Even though you invited Meri's old room-mate over for her, I'll get the door."

Meri sits up, eyeing me in disbelief. "You should have told me."

I motion to the outfit I'd been trying to get her to change out of. "You should have listened."

Her eyes close long enough for me to know the smile that overtakes her face in the next instant is not genuine. She runs a hand over her head before standing and turning. "Anne."

The bride and groom look extremely happy for having jet lag. Anne resembles Scarlett Johansson when she had short hair, and the guy is a little goofy looking with hair like Kramer's but more outdoorsy. They both have smiles so wide I'm pretty sure they were one of those couples who posed for honeymoon photos while making heart shapes with their hands.

"I didn't know you were coming over, or I would have changed."

Anne claps, then hugs my roommate in a way I never will. "I wanted to surprise you. And you look good."

"As good as an overstuffed bear who eats too much honey."

"As good as the most gorgeous single nurse I know."

I have a suspicion the Halloween costume industry would disagree with Anne's take on Meri's outfit. But now that I think about it, the nurse's costumes sold in October more closely resemble what one might have worn in the fifties than today. Perhaps that's why Meri's list suggests becoming a nurse. Nowadays, what nurses wear to work looks more like pajamas. And not the kind you wear on a honeymoon.

Meri excuses herself to change, and Anne follows for "girl talk." Damian and I nod at each other, and thankfully Gemma steps in. She has all kinds of questions about Paris, since that's where her next screenplay will be set. She's describing the time-traveling plot in full detail when Meri arises from the dungeon.

Were this moment being filmed, the director would have had her make a grand entrance down the stairs, but then they would have missed out on the suspense of her being revealed from head to toe. Her hair has been let loose, and it plays peekaboo with bare shoulders.

She's wearing a black dress that wraps around her neck, and I'm not sure how long it is until I see her knees below the hem of a flouncy skirt. She finally steps onto the top step, revealing platform sandals made to appear more casual by their soles being covered in what looks like tiny esparto ropes. Beachy but classy.

I've seen her in a dress before. So my belly shouldn't be warming like this.

I meet her gaze, and it's clear by the deadness there that she's not having this same warm-belly feeling. But whether she's excited to hang out with me or not, she should be excited to hang out with Anne. Why the deadness?

"Ready?" Damian heads toward the front door without waiting for our response. Probably trying to escape Gemma's inquisition.

I grab my camera bag.

Meri's eyes follow me. "You're planning to film tonight?"

Is she surprised? I motion toward her friend's new husband. "This is an opportunity for you to do number thirteen. I think just talking to the one husband will be fine, though Gemma pointed out that *husbands* is plural, so if you want to talk to Roxy's husband another time, we can film that too."

Anne and Damian wait for us at the door.

Damian grins like a Muppet. "You want to ask me something?"

"Number thirteen?" Anne says. "That sounds unlucky."

Yeah, they'd been out of the country, but I figured all Meri's friends knew about the YouTube channel by now.

Meri stands taller and sniffs then precedes me out the door. "We'll tell you in the car."

Though she says that, I'm the one to explain as Damian drives us over the I-5 bridge to one of my favorite restaurants, Who Song and Larry's. I pull up a couple of video clips from *Meri Me*, and they laugh hysterically. Meri doesn't join in. She pretends to, but I'm not fooled. There's something going on.

Damian finally finds a parking space in the crowded lot next to the well-known Mexican restaurant. We're greeted by the scent of sizzling beef brought to us by a gentle breeze off the Columbia River. It's the perfect evening. Or it would be, if Meri didn't look as if she couldn't wait to get it over with.

"I reserved an outside table." Anne is too excited to notice her friend's hesitation.

"Why don't you guys go find our seats." I tug on Meri's wrist to hold her in place. "We'll be there in a minute."

"Okay." Anne takes Damian's hand and smiles up at him.

Meri peeks at me but remains quiet as her friends walk away. Is she upset that I arranged this dinner without her knowledge? I guess it would be hard to hang out with happy newlyweds when she's the last of her friends without a spouse. Usually she's good about laughing at such situations. Maybe she's getting tired of filming. Though it's going so well.

Since I need it to keep going, I'm going to have to stay on her good side. "Hey, I'm sorry if—"

"Roxy and her husband are separating."

Oh no. "Nurse Roxy? Your friend-with-the-baby Roxy? The one who's grandmother started this whole list thing?" A heaviness seeps into my heart, despite not even really knowing the woman. I only know what it's like to want something you can never have.

Meri nods slowly, eyes dull with despair. This isn't simply her friend's loss.

"You found out today?"

Her chest rises as she takes a breath. "Yes. I don't want to tell Anne. I don't want to think this could possibly happen to her marriage."

Meri's not saying what happened, but it doesn't matter. If the guy wasn't going to keep his commitments, he shouldn't have made them in the first place. It's that simple. "I'm really sorry."

She shakes her head as if she's trying to shake off the grief. "I feel bad for Roxy, but I also feel bad for me. In all my thoughts of finding 'the one' to spend the rest of my life with, I just assumed it would last . . . the rest of my life."

"Yeah." I study her eyes without their golden fire. They seem to be looking at me for answers. But I don't have any. And I've quit looking for them. "Fairy tales make it seem that only the bad guys lose, when really we all win and lose every day."

She purses her lips. "Do you think we can all be bad guys some-times?"

Her question rings with innocence. I don't know how she could ever be the bad guy. "That's a question for an expert on stories. You should ask Gemma."

She sighs and stares out at the water. In a moment, she'll paste on her smile and we'll go sit on a crowded patio with loud music and stuff ourselves with salty chips and salsa so spicy it makes our noses run. She'll be fine, as she always is, but she's not here because she wants to be. She didn't even want to film tonight.

I nudge her with my shoulder. "You didn't let me finish my apology earlier. I'm sorry for making plans without your knowledge. I won't bring my camera."

She looks at me again, her gaze tracking back and forth between my eyes as if she's actually reading them. One corner of her lips quirks up. "I can't let our viewers miss the craziness that happens here."

By craziness, she means customer birthdays that the whole restau-rant celebrates together, sombreros included, dancing on tables op-tional. Just part of the Portland experience.

"You sure?"

She shrugs nonchalantly. "I almost got asked out today because of our show."

With the way she'd danced in anticipation of her date with Lariat Luke, I'd think she'd be a little more excited by this. "What do you mean by 'almost'?"

She pivots on the heel of her fancy shoe and forces me to follow in order to hear.

I loop my camera bag over a shoulder and trot to catch up.

"The doctor you filmed at work said he'd ask me out if he wasn't leaving for a yearlong disaster relief job."

I think back to the doctor. I could see how he'd be everything she wanted. Hard working. Intelligent. Successful. Perfect, except for the fact he didn't eat pie with her. "Really?"

"Really. Though he did invite me to join the disaster relief company."

Something snags in my chest. I stop to knock it loose and have to lengthen my strides to catch up. "Are you thinking about going?"

She stops at the restaurant's entrance, sorrow haunting her expression. "I'm thinking about moving in with Roxy."

CHAPTER NINETEEN

Meri

#40. Never outshine your man in any athletic activity. Men have sensitive egos and usurping their sportsmanlike prowess will lead to the demise of your relationship.

While #13 on The List had an unlucky start, it turned out rather pleasant. I knew from experience that my relationship with Anne would change when she got married, and I'd worried that I'd be the third wheel around her and her new husband, but with Kai there, things rolled right along. It also helped that Damian offered to set me up with a couple of his single friends. I was able to meet them throughout the next few weeks and try items from the "Attract Him" section of The List. This sounds simpler than the section on trying to catch a man's attention, but . . .

#48. *Don't forget to wear gloves on your first date!* The article probably didn't mean latex gloves, but as a nurse in the summer, that's all I had available. It was trendy for a while with Covid, but my date didn't seem very impressed with my healthcare background.

#60. *Compliment his car. How he takes care of it will symbolize how he will take care of you.* I didn't mean to make a big deal out of how clean the back seat was at the beginning of a second blind date. It wasn't until Kai doubled over laughing that I realized how forward my compliment might have come across. Then I was self-conscious for the rest of the night, more concerned about my mom's reaction than my date's.

#8. Check out his grocery cart. If you like what he buys, you might like him as a person. I unfortunately went the Friday night of Fourth of July weekend, when men were mostly buying hamburgers, chips, watermelon, and beer. This made it really hard to judge, not to mention that the stores were crowded, and everyone was in a big hurry. I gave up after a nice man invited me to join his family of five at the Cherryfest NW, where I am happy to report that though I walked the 5K and lost the hula hoop contest to Kai, I beat him in the limbo challenge and water balloon toss. I wasn't even sore, perhaps thanks to all the tart cherries I ate.

#58. Let your date do the ordering. Never directly ask the waiter for anything. I tried to smother my laughter at this one until water came out my nose. Poor guy. Chances are he'll never go on another blind date again. Though I had fun chuckling over it again with Kai when he showed me the video.

All that to say, if #13 wasn't unlucky, then I'm not expecting #7 to be lucky. In fact, I dread learning to golf. The best thing about our plan for today's show is that Gemma let me wear some cute golf clothes, though I bet they aren't this tight on her.

Kai sits in my passenger seat, filming me from underneath his golf visor. This might be as exciting as our day gets, since I'm driving to some fancy country club where I doubt anybody ever wears latex gloves or refuses to order their own food for laughs.

I give a big sigh in direct rebellion of suggestion *#65. Breathe as little as possible around him and make them shallow breaths. No man wants to see the full girth of a woman's rib cage.* "Why can't we play disk golf?"

Kai shakes his head in disapproval, then points to where I need to turn down a lane shaded with giant evergreens waving in the breeze and lined by a stone wall that almost gives it a fortress feel. "If you're going to marry a doctor, you need to learn to golf."

"Why?" I slow and turn into the picturesque setting. "Can't I just drive the golf cart and look pretty?"

Kai's eyebrows arch.

"*I'm* pretty."

"I never said you weren't."

"You lifted your eyebrows."

"Maybe I was going to do this." He wiggles them.

"You definitely weren't going to do that." I can't help but chuckle as I pull into the pristine parking lot. "And please never do that again."

He smirks. "The reason I lifted my eyebrows was because I don't see you simply sitting in a golf cart while your husband plays the game."

Huh. He's probably right.

A long two-story white building with balcony dining shines in contrast to the recently tarred asphalt. I find an open spot and squeeze my eight-year-old turquoise Mazda between a Lexus and a Lincoln SUV.

Were I really to marry a doctor, would I want a luxury car, or would I keep driving colorful compacts? Furthermore, would a doctor want to marry someone who prefers cute and bright?

I guess Dr. Snyder wasn't deterred by my car. Though what really matters about his being a doctor is that it's proof he's not lazy like Roxy's husband, Graham. I'm not after someone rich. I'm after someone who cares about life. And hopefully me.

I grab my purse and hop out of the car. A gust of wind whips at a ruffle on the back of Gemma's black golf skirt. I hold it down, allowing hair to curtain my face. I hope it's not this windy the whole time.

I anchor the skirt in place for a moment longer, then am forced to let go of it so I can use the hairband on my wrist to secure my mane into a ponytail. At least the skirt comes with undershorts to protect my decency. As I pull a few more strands back, I find Kai watching in amusement. My cute outfit doesn't seem like a perk anymore.

I rush to twist the band, looping it around my hair a second then a third time, but I must have tugged too hard because the band snaps apart and shoots away. Long hair whips into my face again.

My shoulders sink. I give up on my hair and re-anchor the skirt against my thighs. "There's no way I'm going to meet an interested man on the golf course when I look like Cousin Itt."

My hair parts. Kai holds it to the sides of my face and smiles from inches away. His eyes almost disappear when he smiles.

I like searching for them.

"You're not getting off that easy," he says.

I'm not sure what he means, but with the way he's grinning, I'm intrigued.

He tugs the visor off his head with one hand, then bundles my tresses with his other so he can loop the thing around my crown like a headband. "There." He adjusts the bill in an almost flirty way.

This is okay though, right? Flirting isn't real love. It's only playing at love. Like they do in tennis—another game I will probably have to learn in order to marry a doctor.

He steps away and retrieves his golf clubs and camera from where he's set them down. "My visor will keep your hair back, but unfortunately, it might also prevent you from letting the sun kiss your skin as recommended by number twenty-nine on your list."

"What do you know about sunburns, Mr. Hawaiian Tropics?" Oh no. I'm flirting too. Maybe he won't notice . . .

"I know that in the fifties they must not have been as worried about skin cancer as we are today. We're going to cross that one off your list."

Whew. That was a close one. There's nothing flirty about skin cancer. Plus, I can run with his crossing-things-off-the-list idea. "While we're at it, let's cross golf off too."

He shoots me a not-gonna-happen smile before turning to open an ornately carved door.

I huff and enter in front of him onto the shiny wood floor. My skirt and hair fall into place. At least I'm escaping this wind for a moment.

Kai heads to a desk that has all kinds of golf equipment for sale and engages the clean-shaven, polo-wearing employee. Though I do like collared shirts, this guy seems kinda boring.

I pick up a brochure covered in photos of perfectly manicured grass and flip it open. Inside are more pictures of a golf course, but with giant holes. It takes me a minute to realize they are advertising something called "foot golf." It appears to be a cross between golf and soccer, where instead of golf clubs, players use their feet.

I loved soccer in high school. This is more my speed. I hold up the brochure for the man behind the counter. "Do doctors play foot golf?" If they have foot golf courses at places like this, then it must be classier than disk golf.

The man shoots me a curious glance. "I suppose." He turns toward a back room. "I'll go get your clubs, miss."

Kai turns to face me, resting a hip against the counter. "You want to play foot golf now?"

"Yes." I motion to his T-shirt with a screen print of the classic VW Bus, bummed this isn't one of those fancy golf clubs that requires a collared shirt because a polo could really improve his look. "I assume foot golf to be more your speed, as well."

He crosses his arms. "Because I'm not elite enough to like golf?"

"Because . . ." That's not what I meant. Well, not entirely. "You don't own a car in which to haul your golf clubs around." I tap my chin. "Though, I would think if you have money to golf at places like this, you could afford a car."

He studies me in a way that has me questioning everything I think I know about him. Was he planning to get his PhD in college when he lost his scholarship? Did he used to be a pro golfer? Is he secretly a millionaire?

"My dad has a membership."

Maybe his family *is* wealthy. His dad has a membership to a golf club and his mom owns her own business. What happened to Kai? Just because he has an Achilles heel . . .

"My dad's a mason. He built the rock wall at the entrance to this place. I was only two years old when he did the work as trade for his membership, so I grew up golfing."

"Oh wow." I want to ask more questions. Like how Kai ended up working the night shift at a news station when his parents are the ambitious type. I don't ask, because he's already feeling judged by me. And it's really none of my business. I'm here for the doctors. "Have you played foot golf then?"

He narrows his eyes begrudgingly. "Yes."

The country club employee returns empty-handed. "I hate to tell you this, but our last set of ladies rental clubs is currently being regripped. If you don't mind waiting half an hour, I could give you the two o'clock tee time."

I do mind. This is my get-out-of-jail-free card. "Or . . ." I look to Kai expectantly.

"I'm wearing golf sandals, not soccer shoes."

Rats. I wrinkle my nose and continue our ongoing joke about his feet. "Is that to air out your foot fungus? You could also try tea tree oil."

His look is unamused, which is rare. "We'll go get iced tea while we wait," he tells the employee.

Iced tea? He's all kinds of high society now. Though I probably ruin his image when a waitress leads us out onto the balcony and a gust of wind blows his visor off my head. I chase it through a maze of middle-aged couples sitting at little round tables, only running into a few of them when strands of hair block my vision.

I barely grab the visor before it blows over the edge. I'm strapping it to my head extra tightly as I return to find Kai already settled in and sipping through a straw. He looks as comfortable here as he does on Charlie's couch, and I wonder if he's a product of our entitled society. Even if his family isn't wealthy, he could have been spoiled by parents who thought they were giving him the world. After my last failed joke, I choose not to make this comment aloud. Though he seems to be laughing at me.

"You okay there?" he asks, full lips twitching at the corners.

At least he isn't filming, so the only people who will witness my little chase are the restaurant patrons. I hold the edges of my golf skirt and give them all a curtsy before taking my seat.

They golf clap. Such a PC crowd.

Despite Kai's visor, hair continues to whip me in the face. The ends even dip themselves in my water glass when I try to take a drink. "I hate my hair."

Kai sets his glass on the table. "I'm enthralled by your hair."

"Pshaw." I wave a hand and look away in dramatic fashion until I catch the eyes of other patrons, remember where I am, and realize

I'm making another scene. I fold my hands in my lap. "That's why I don't cut it."

His head tilts. "You don't cut your hair because I'm enthralled with it?"

"Enthralled is a little extreme, and I'm not talking about you in particular but men in general. Men prefer long hair."

"Really?" He leans forward, elbows resting on our table in a way I'd been taught was bad manners. He might get us kicked out of here. I hope he does. "Your friend Anne found a husband, and *she* has short hair."

I smile dreamily. If I were enthralled with anyone's hair, it would be Anne's. Though . . . "She had long hair when they met."

The corners of Kai's lips aren't fighting against his amused smile anymore. They outright mock me. "What I hear you saying is that you want to cut your hair, but you're afraid that if you do, you'll never find a husband. Should we add 'grow hair long' to your outdated list?"

I try to give him my best glare, but a lock of hair gets in the way. I sweep it back and catch the rest of it in my palm as if my hand is a hairband. "I'm not afraid."

"Then let's go get your hair cut right now. I'd give up golf for that."

My heartbeat wobbles similar to the way Kai's lips had done when he was trying to fight his smile. My pulse wants to turn up with excitement at the idea, but what if I cut my hair and then the man of my dreams doesn't find me attractive?

I told Kai I'm not afraid, and I'm not. I'm being realistic.

As realistic as a list from the fifties on how to catch a husband.

If I'm honest with myself, I had a list of my own ways to catch a husband before Roxy's grandmother ever gave us the article from *Sophia Magazine*. I ran to lose weight even though I hated running. I took the less exciting job in order to be there for a family I don't have. And I grew my hair long because I'd heard men loved long hair even though I'd rather chop it off.

I take a deep breath to empower myself in making the bold decision. It's either that or sit here with these stupid long tresses in my face as I wait to play a game more likely to put me to sleep than set me up on a date.

I shouldn't have to change for the right man. I should only have to become more me. "I'll do it."

Kai has his camera out as Beatrice braids my hair so she can donate it to Locks of Love after she chops it off. My hairstylist isn't usually available on this short of notice, but when she learned her salon would be on our YouTube channel, she made time.

My chest still throbs with anxiety at what I'm doing, but even if I look hideous when this is all over, I know that some child going through cancer treatments will receive a beautiful wig from my sacrifice. I remember Julia Roberts's character nursing a cancer patient in the movie *Dying Young*. *I'm doing this for you, Jules.*

Kai, on the other hand, believes our fans will love seeing me get my hair chopped. He vows my decision will inspire single women. I'm pretty sure he's more enthralled with his viewers than he ever was with my hair.

The scissors snip and Beatrice holds up a braid no longer attached to my head.

"Number forty-two," Kai reminds me. *"Keep your hair perfectly coiffed, even if he's completely bald. Bald men are more eager to please."*

I ignore him.

Beatrice doesn't. "Bald men have more testosterone."

I barely hear their argument. I'm too busy staring at the chin-length strands of hair sliding easily around my face. The waves I'd hated for so long are free to bounce and curl. They are almost beachy. Which fits my freckles.

Beatrice trims and styles.

I stare, entranced. I love the new look.

She hands me a mirror and spins the chair around so that I can see the back of it. I shift the mirror to different angles and pose for myself. When I look back down, Kai's camera is practically in my face.

"What do you think?" he asks.

I try to come up with something sophisticated for any golfers out there that will only ever know who I am from watching our show. But, let's be honest, I was never going to appeal to them anyway. Thus, the new me says exactly what she's thinking. "I'm so cute."

Kai's teeth flash in a grin underneath his camera.

He may have preferred my longer hair, but I don't want to hear it. "Look how cute I am."

"I'm looking."

I hand the mirror to Beatrice and fluff the ends of my hair with my palms. Beatrice spins my chair so I'm admiring myself again. "I look edgy. I need a biker jacket and black choker."

"That might not attract the kind of men you're looking for."

I picture the cast of *The Fast and the Furious*. Kai may be right.

"How about my glasses, then?" I dig my new frames from my purse, slide them up my nose, and strike a pose. "I'm practically a sexy librarian."

Kai chuckles, and I remember my audience. People like my mom. I spin around and point at him. "You can't put that on our show."

"Really?" He's got this deep chuckle.

I can almost feel the rumbling in my belly.

"After all the crazy stuff you've done on camera, you're drawing the line at 'sexy librarian'?"

"Yes."

Beatrice watches, hand on hip. With purple streaks in her hair and more than one nose ring, I'm guessing she and I draw lines in different places. "I think you should leave your quote in, but even if you don't, people will see for themselves. Huh, Kai?"

"Uh . . ." Kai backs away, refusing to call me sexy. "I think we need to get her in front of more people. You ready to rent that billboard now, Meri?"

Ooh, a billboard. I'd never taken #100 seriously before. "Charlie's ex works for an advertising company and could probably get me a good deal . . ." Wow. How vain am I? Just because I feel like a sexy librarian is no excuse to plaster my face above the city for all to see. "But I'm not going to spend that kind of money when I have Kai right here to tell me how good I look." I purse my lips to make it appear that I have high cheekbones.

He shrugs. "I'm a guy, so I preferred your longer hair as you knew I would. Of course, how you feel about yourself right now is more important than what anyone else thinks."

I do feel good. And it feels good to have a friend like Kai encourage me to do what's best for myself. "Admit it or not, I know you think I'm cute."

CHAPTER TWENTY

Kai

#66. Send a note to his pastor explaining why you're a good candidate for marriage.

I'm admitting nothing. That is dangerous ground. If I admit how attractive I find Meri's newfound confidence, then I might have to admit to myself that this growing itch inside my chest is really a desire to kiss her.

Then I might imagine sliding my fingers into the silky, pomegranate-scented strands of her sassy new haircut. I might imagine stepping close enough to cover her lips with mine and finding out how she responds to my touch.

Oh man. This is stupid.

It's not that Meri looks like a sexy librarian, because I honestly prefer her long, wild hair. It's the way she looks at life. Including the way she looks at me. As if, despite my flaws, there's nobody she'd rather hang out with. Though I'm sure she doesn't even know she's doing it.

No matter how much fun we have together, I'm not the kind of guy she sees in her future. Which is probably why she's herself around me. She's not trying to impress me the way she tries to impress other men.

But even if she didn't think of me as a loser, the truth is that I'm not able to offer what she's looking for. Yeah, she might let me kiss her if I tried, but whether it's a good kiss or not, it wouldn't satisfy her desires. She wants marriage and a family. And as she likes to point out, I don't even want the responsibility of a car.

What I have is time. A lot of time in which to edit another episode of *Meri Me* where, in every scene in which she looks at the camera, the itch in my chest grows stronger.

Over and over again, I watch her spin the salon chair to point my way, and I debate whether to leave in the "sexy librarian" bit or not.

No. I can't. She asked me to take it out.

I finally finish editing and post on YouTube only to realize from viewer comments that there is something else I should have taken out.

Kai, why didn't you tell Meri how good she looks?

I think Kai wants to tell her in private, off camera.

Kai, why are you holding back on the way you feel? Is it to get more viewers? Publicity stunt?

As much as I need more viewers, I also need someone else to step into the show as potential for Meri's happily-ever-after. If she sees that viewers think I'm her Prince Charming, things could get very awkward.

I like hanging out with her. I don't want to lose that. But unless I can get this itch back under control, I need to avoid her.

I stay in my room until both she and Gemma are ready for church. I do the gentlemanly thing of letting Gemma ride shotgun, then when we arrive, I head up to the balcony to run audiovisual and create some space.

But like an addict, I focus the camera on Meri below. She smiles at everyone filing into the sanctuary, flounces her hair, and adjusts her glasses. Then she heads toward the stairs.

I roll my eyes toward heaven. "Really, God?"

Before God responds with a peace that passes all understanding, Meri has climbed the steps and is smiling, flouncing her hair, and adjusting her glasses. At me.

"What's up?"

She grimaces over the edge of the balcony. "I don't want to sit with my mom and Douglas today. Can I join you?"

She's so casual that she couldn't possibly have seen the YouTube comments. I'll play along. I'm chill like that. "Yeah. Sure." I point toward a chair she can drag over.

Nobody has joined me up here before. It's distracting. Twice during worship I'm delayed in switching the slides for song lyrics. I hope the congregation knows these words by now and is praising with their eyes closed.

I know Meri is. Her hands are lifted. She's singing slightly off-key but with all her heart. Like she does everything.

Forget the peace that passes understanding. God should really strike me with a lightning bolt for the way I can't take my eyes off her when I'm supposed to be focusing on Him.

Will Pastor Mick have us hold hands during prayer? Will he tell us to hug someone during the benediction? Because it's just Meri and me up here. I'd have to hold her hand. I'd have to hug her.

The music finally ends, and I dread trying to ignore her through the whole sermon. I don't even hear what Pastor Mick says when he steps up to the pulpit.

I tip my head down so she can't tell I'm watching her take notes out of the corner of my eye. Her hands are small and dainty, though it looks as if her fingernails have started to grow out underneath her fake nails and need to be replaced. Is this because she doesn't have the money for the upkeep or because she's been too busy with me? If it was a money issue, marrying a doctor would take care of that. Though, knowing the way Meri always plans ahead, it's not a money issue.

How would a doctor feel about marrying a woman who doesn't make having a perfect image her first priority?

Meri writes the word MARRIAGE at the top of her notes. Is she reading my thoughts or is holy matrimony always at the forefront of her mind?

The pastor's words break into my conscious. "Let's look at what Jesus had to say about marriage in *The Message* translation of Matthew nineteen."

Oh man. Meri isn't writing down her thoughts or even mine. She's writing down the thoughts of Jesus. I prepare to tune out, since they don't apply to me.

"'Not everyone is mature enough to live a married life. It requires a certain aptitude and grace.'"

I sit up a little taller. This is what Jesus said? Should I feel validated or offended? Does it have to be that I'm immature? Maybe I simply don't have the desire to be a husband.

"'Some, from birth seemingly, never give marriage a thought.'"

Okay, that's better. I sink deeper into my seat, happy to avoid conviction for another Sunday. I may have thought about marriage once upon a time, but now I fit into this category.

It's not that I don't want to be a godly person. I just don't believe a person has to have a family to be godly. So often it seems as if the church bows to the idol of marriage. Everyone is always asking me when I'm going to settle down. I just shrug because, hey, I'm settled.

Pastor Mick continues. "'Others never get asked—or accepted.'"

My spine stiffens. I glance over at where Meri is taking notes.

Her hand has stilled.

"'And some decide not to get married for kingdom reasons.'"

I'm okay with this one. The apostle Paul never got married for this reason. Mother Teresa never got married for this reason. But I'm pretty sure Meri is not in this category.

Pastor Mick looks up from his Bible. In fact, he seems to be looking up into the balcony. "'But if you're capable of growing into the largeness of marriage, do it.'"

I rub clammy hands along my jeans. He's not talking to me. These words aren't meant for me. I'm in the "never gave marriage a thought" category. Or I am now.

"This last line is where we are going to spend our time today." Pastor Mick rubs his hands together. "Because I'm honestly tired of officiating weddings that don't last."

That's harsh.

"Jesus gave lots of reasons *not* to get married. He only gave one reason to wed. And I want to unpack this statement."

As uncomfortable as I am sitting next to my resentfully single roommate, I want to stand up and cheer. Finally. A message about *not* getting married. Maybe it will help make Meri not so desperate.

"We already examined the word *if*. Marriage is not for everybody. The next word I want to examine is the word *you*. You can be both singular or plural. That means you have to examine both yourself and the person you want to marry. I believe this is why the Bible says a husband and a wife need to be equally yoked. No matter how committed you are to marriage, you can't make it work on your own. The truth is that your life might be better off without the person you love."

Uh . . . ouch?

"The next word is *capable*. To me this means willing and able. You and your significant other have to be both willing and able to keep your commitments."

Makes sense. Though I hate thinking how this applies to Meri's coworker. From what she'd told me, Roxy's husband is able to step up for his wife—he's just not willing.

"What do you both have to be willing and able to do? *Grow*."

I hate the word grow. I relate it to growing pains. I relate it to the Christians who see someone hurting and tell them God will use it to grow them. I prefer to think pain is like a warning sign from God about what to avoid.

"The next word is *largeness*. Another word for largeness is *giant*. What happened when Bible characters came in contact with giants? They usually ran. There are going to be scary times in your marriage. You're going to want to run."

I used to be a good runner. Maybe I still am.

"In order to overcome, you have to do what David did when he faced Goliath. You have to be a man or woman after God's own heart."

Huh. And I thought I was going to be able to avoid conviction today.

"The final requirement for getting married is to understand what that means. *Marriage*. It's an example of how Christ loves the church. He died for us. And you have to be willing to die for your spouse."

If that's a requirement, there really aren't many people out there who should ever get married. Most people seem to get married for selfish reasons. I'm pretty sure Meri isn't desperate for a wedding just so she'll have someone to die for.

Pastor Mick closes his Bible. "That's it. That's the checklist Jesus gave us. 'If you are capable of growing into the largeness of marriage, do it.'"

Much better than the Nike slogan that once made me think I'd be their next spokesman. It's more like a warning sign on wedding rings. I consider myself warned. Great sermon, Preach.

Meri stands and wraps an arm around my shoulders, leaning in since I'm still in my seat. Mick must have called for hugs during his benediction, and I missed it. I missed the moment I needed in order to prepare myself for Meri's fruity scent and the tickle of her new do against my cheek. I don't even get my arm up to wrap around her before she's pulling away.

I don't want to marry her, but I also don't want her to pull away. I stand and stick my hands in my pockets for safekeeping.

I hesitantly meet her eye contact to see if she can tell I'm itching to reconnect. Hers are watery. She's not thinking of me. She's thinking of how the man she wants to marry may not even exist.

I want to cup her face in a hand and run my thumb over her cheekbone to comfort her. But that would only complicate things. I need her dream man to exist. I need her to find him, so that I'm not tempted to be his placeholder.

"Want to go to lunch with me, Mom, and her . . . boyfriend?" she asks.

I do. To support her. But instead I'm going to help her find a man who will *always* be there to support her. "I can't today."

I'm going to be a gentleman and choose what I want most over what I want in the moment. I'm going to call Charlie's ex to find out how much it costs to rent a billboard. Then I'm going to start a GoFundMe account to pay for the biggest personal ad that ever existed.

CHAPTER TWENTY-ONE

Meri

#62. Listen to your mother. Adam and Eve's issues may have stemmed from the lack of a mother's wisdom.

I can't get marriage off my mind, but I don't want to talk about it with my mom. Not when she has a better chance of getting married than I do. So, when she asks me what I thought of today's sermon, I eloquently say, "Uh . . ."

Thankfully, I'm interrupted by the hostess at La Provence, a froufrou French restaurant where even their hamburgers come with a wine-and-cheese sauce. You can tell you're in for a treat simply by the delectable but unidentifiable scents that greet you as soon as you open the arched black door with gold trim. The hostess leads us past the bakery display window with rows of macaroons so colorful that I feel like Dorothy in Oz for the first time.

We make our way up to a wrought iron balcony flanked by windows with heavy draperies. I love this place. And I love that I get a girls' day with Mom because Douglas went golfing with his brothers.

Note: I did ask him if he plays foot golf, and he didn't know what I was talking about, so clearly, he is too boring to ever be my stepdad.

We settle into our wicker seats, and I busy myself with the menu. "Are you doing breakfast or lunch?" I ask. It's so hard to decide at places like this.

"Let's do breakfast." Mom apparently isn't as conflicted. "I'll get the crepes, and you get the hash. Then we can share."

There goes my excuse to hide behind my menu. If only her sharing idea didn't sound so good. "Sure." I set the long skinny list down to find her watching me with folded hands.

"You never answered my question about the sermon."

My chest constricts. Memories of our pastor's words about being single shakes me like an overdose of caffeine.

There are married people. Then there are the "others."

Others never get asked.

I unwrap the linen napkin from around my silverware and spread it over my lap. "It scares me."

Mom studies me, her dark eyes serious yet understanding. "What are you scared of?"

I'm scared of crying in a froufrou French restaurant, for starters. I blink and look down so I can take a step away from emotion and unclog my throat long enough to speak. "You once told me there's a man out there just for me, but Jesus said marriage isn't for everyone. Maybe you were wrong."

Mom reaches across the tiny table and hooks my elbow to pull my hand up and clasp my fingers with her cold, smooth ones. "Have you talked to Him about it?"

A dry, derisive laugh surprises me. As do her words, obviously. "You know I've been praying for a husband since middle school summer camp, but now those prayers feel more like a fairy tale. As if I were a Disney character wishing on a star, or paying a sea witch for a magic spell, or rubbing a genie's lamp."

"God's not a genie in a lamp." Mom smiles softly. "Talking to Him is more about trust. Let Him remind you how much you are already loved. He'll calm your fears with the truth that He has good things planned for your future. The more time you spend with Him, the more your desires will come in line with His desires."

I fiddle with my napkin with my free hand, hesitant to voice how I want God's desires to come in line with mine, not the other way around.

"I've been a bad example of this, I'm afraid," Mom says.

I look up. Is Mom going to dump her boyfriend?

"Rather than trust God with you, I've placed myself in His position of authority in your life. I wanted you to look to me for answers about marriage."

I squeeze Mom's hand in case she's going to try to pull away. "Is this about Douglas?"

"No, honey." She looks down. "This is about your dad."

My dad? The perfect husband? Her hero? "Stories of Dad have always been my inspiration."

She rubs her lips together. "I know. I wanted you to think of marriage as a beautiful thing. I wanted to encourage you to save yourself for your soul mate. And I wanted you to think I had done the same."

My lips part. I don't speak. Simply breathe. I don't know what Mom is trying to say, and I'm not sure I want to.

"I didn't marry your dad for the right reasons."

My world spins. Or maybe that's just my stomach. Breakfast doesn't sound so good anymore.

Black is white. Right is wrong. And marrying my dad was a mistake. "But you told us all kinds of good memories."

Mom nods. "For every good memory is a bad memory. It was a roller coaster."

I can't picture it. Grainy photos of my dad come to mind.

Taking me fishing as a toddler.

Pushing me on the swings.

Building my tricycle.

That's how I want to remember him. "He's dead now. Why bring up the bad memories?"

Mom's chin crinkles. Her eyes shine. "Because I want you to know the truth about marriage. I want you to know that the reasons I haven't dated isn't because my first relationship was so good, but because I didn't want to put myself in another bad situation."

I cover my mouth. How bad could it have been? How bad could my dad have been? "Did he . . . beat you?"

She shakes her head. A tear leaks out. It draws a glossy line down her cheek. She grabs a fancy napkin to wipe her nose. "No. But he was an alcoholic. When he was drunk, he'd say some very cruel things. And he . . . cheated on me."

My dad?

"My parents had good reason for not wanting me to marry him."

Am I shaking, or is that my whole world?

"I was warned. But I was also pregnant and scared of being alone."

I understand being scared, but I never imagined my mom that way. Like when taking my last test at the eye doctor, I see two different images that are not congruent. The image of a rebellious, pregnant teenager. Then the image of my pious, concerned mother. Can they possibly line up?

"He was drunk when he died in the motorcycle crash. And so was the girl on the seat behind him."

My hands drop to my chest, where waves of pain crash into my heart. Like a hurricane. They threaten to roll me in the surf and submerge me until I don't know which way is up. I need Mom to be my life preserver more than ever. "Why are you telling me this?" I was happier believing in the fairy tale.

"Today's sermon spoke to me." Mom scoots her chair around so she can be closer. She's blocking the walkway, but there's a second set of stairs on the other side of the balcony the waitresses can use.

If they knew what we were talking about, I'm sure they'd want to avoid us anyway.

"I realized that while I'd been capable of growing into the largeness of marriage, your dad was not. And maybe, now that I know what to look for, I might be able to have another chance at love."

Douglas. I want to hate him, but as little as I know of him, I can see he's not a drunk who would emotionally abuse or cheat on my mother. He's a better man than my father.

Mom is like Roxy. While I thought she'd had a wonderful marriage, it had been a show. Underneath, she'd been hurting. Afraid. And only love can overcome fear.

Do I want my friend to find love again? Even if it's not with the same man who vowed to love her forever? Yes.

Do I want my mom to find love again?

I sniff. "I'm sorry I haven't given Douglas a fair chance, Mom. I'll go out to eat with both of you next week."

She wraps an arm around my neck and pulls me into a Tea Rose-scented hug. "That would mean a lot. But that's not why I'm telling you this."

I dab at my face with a napkin and exhale slowly. I can handle the dad thing because I still have a mom here for me. That hasn't changed. There's great security in her presence. But I don't know if I can handle anything more.

She smooths my hair the way only a mom can. "I'm telling you because I'm going to step back from trying to control *your* relationships."

I never pictured her as controlling. She always just had red flags to wave. There was a disapproving purse of her lips when Bryant decided to become a sniper in the military. There was the shake of her head when Dalton dropped out of college to work for the post office. There were the raised eyebrows as if surprised I might want to wait for AJ to finish medical school in California. And all that time I thought she was giving advice from her experience with true love.

"What do you mean?"

"I wanted to help you avoid going through the pain I went through, but nobody can avoid pain in life. My job as your mom is to point you to your heavenly Father who can heal your pain. His love is the only kind that never fails."

Her words settle over me like a weighted blanket, almost calming the fears she's stirred up.

She pats my leg. "Marrying your dad wasn't wise, but I don't regret it because if I hadn't done it, I wouldn't have you."

Oh wow. She'd been hurt, but she'd do it all again for me. This is what it's like to be loved.

I hug her tight. "I love you, Mom."

I may be an "other" when it comes to marriage, but I'm not alone. And I wouldn't trade this in for anything.

"I love you too, honey." She rests her head on my shoulder. "And that's why I'm going to let you make your own decisions with Kai."

"Mom thinks there's something between me and Kai." I continue my rant to Roxy every time we pass each other carrying boxes into her new house. It's actually an older house, like one you might expect your grandparents to live in, though it's been partly remodeled. Which means that while the fireplace is brick with a brass insert, the kitchen looks like an Ikea display.

The box in my hands says *Bathroom* in black marker. I carry it to the only tiny bathroom in the place and head back out to the U-Haul.

Roxy meets me at the doorway and hands me a lamp so she can pick up Angel before she toddles down the three steps. "Are you surprised she thinks that?"

"Yes." I set the lamp on a white shabby-chic end table. "In fact, I'm surprised you asked if I'm surprised." I join her on the front steps to better hear her response.

She sits down on the cement and bounces Angel on her knees. "You know she's not the only one who thinks there's something between you two."

I join her, enjoying the shade from the overhang. "Yeah, but there's not. Dating him would be like when you started a relationship with Graham after he dropped out of college rather than retake biology."

Roxy shoots me the side-eye. "My parents warned me about dating Graham. But does anybody ever listen to a warning when they're falling in love? They think those feeling will carry them through."

I lace my fingers and hook my knees. "Sorry. I'm being a very selfish friend right now. I wish I knew what to say to make you feel better."

Roxy shakes her head. "You're here, and that's what matters."

I give a weak smile. "According to my list of ways to find a husband, moving furniture is supposed to be one way to get a guy to your house. We must be doing something wrong."

"We already knew that, though." She lifts a shoulder. "At least my dad came over to move all the heavy stuff this morning."

I nod and study Angel's ivory skin, round eyes, and full wet lips. Is this how my mom felt about me when I was born? When she was left to raise me on her own? "Would you do it all again for Angel?"

"Of course I would," Roxy says in baby talk, then blows raspberries on Angel's chubby cheek. "Though I wish I'd done it differently. I wished I'd gotten help sooner. I wish we would have both grown healthy before bringing my Angel into our mess."

"You think you'll ever get back together? Renew your vows?"

"I want to. But I can't want it enough for both of us. I have to be okay with whatever choice he makes." She looks up, and I see the clarity of peace in the depths of her sage eyes. "It took me a long time to learn that's how a healthy marriage works. Rather than stay in a place of dysfunction, I move out of the darkness and invite him into the light."

I like that image. The sense of freedom that comes with it. I wonder what would have happened if my mom had learned to set those same boundaries in her marriage. Would my dad have joined her? Or would he have continued down his self-destructive path? I hope Graham chooses the light. For both Roxy and Angel.

"Graham begged me not to leave this morning. He promised he would change. But I've heard it all before." She sighs. "My counselor said that every time I reconcile with him before seeing true change, I'm not loving him unto life. I'm loving him unto death."

Whoa. "That seems extreme. Like putting the responsibility on your shoulders for his change."

She smooshes her lips in thought. "It's actually the opposite. If he says he'll change for me, then I'm taking up the responsibility for his change by staying there. He has to change for himself. True change has to happen in spite of me."

Angel reaches a hand toward my glasses, so I hold a finger out for her to grab instead. I wiggle her little fist and consider all these deep thoughts. "I guess that makes sense. It's like the hiring process at work when we had that group interview to pick a receptionist. We were told to discern who would be a good fit based on what they'd done in the past, not on what they say they will do."

"Yeah." Roxy sighs. "My counselor told me that out of all the abusive issues she deals with, the lazy heart is what upsets wives the most. Because there's nothing you can do to make the guy care enough to get up off the couch."

A plane roars overhead, making her last words hard to hear. I look up at it, then at the house across the street with its chain-link fence and yappy dogs. This neighborhood is a big step down from where Roxy had been living. If I were a dad, I wouldn't want my child living here.

Yet, Graham sits in his nice, new home while I help his wife and daughter move out. I want to shake him. His family deserves so much better.

"You won't be here forever."

"What?" Sarcasm drips from her tone. "You don't like it here? Because there's an extra room for you if you decide to move in."

I tug my finger out of Angel's grip. She laughs and reaches for it again. It might be kind of fun helping raise this little girl. "I've still got more time at my brother's. Hopefully by then Graham will have decided to turn his life around."

"I appreciate your optimism." She huffs. "Which brings me back to you and Kai. Is his laziness the only thing keeping you apart?"

I shrug. No sense in getting all offended over her question. There's nobody here I have to defend myself to. Just a hurting friend with a husband whose flaws remind me of my roommate's. Roxy certainly isn't trying to push us together.

I let myself imagine what it would be like to date Kai. Could there be something more than friendship between us? I've thought of him as a brother. Though he's more fun than Charlie. And I did like the way he put his visor on my head yesterday. "Even if he were the kind of husband I'm looking for, there's still the issue of him not wanting a wife."

Roxy smiles sadly. "Better to know that now than after you've been married for six years."

CHAPTER TWENTY-TWO

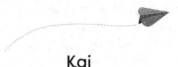

Kai

*#15. Plan an outdoor trip. That way if you get
angry at him and accidentally tell him to "take a
hike," you won't have to apologize.*

Believe it or not, the GoFundMe account has almost reached the thousands needed to cover a billboard. Crazy what people will pay for. Now all I need to do is design it. Which means more staring at Meri's freckles and fiery eyes on my computer screen.

Not only will a billboard draw male attention Meri's way, it's sure to bring new viewers to our YouTube channel. It's a win-win. We'll both get what we want from all the hard work we've put into our show over the past couple of months.

Until then—until Meri's inbox is full of invites, and I get noticed by the director of *Capers*—I shouldn't get too close to her. I need the comments about us as a couple to cool off, not to mention this ridiculous attraction warming inside.

But that doesn't mean I'm okay with her excuse that she needs to blow off some steam by jogging tonight. She attended boot camp again this morning, so I know she got her workout in.

I run through her dwindling list. When we check everything off, I won't have an excuse to hang out with her every day. By then I'll either have the cameraman position of my dreams, or I'll be stuck posting news clips to Facebook.

Only being hired for my dream job will get rid of this antsyness.

That's the whole reason I'm spending so much time with my room-mate. It's all for my "dummy reel," as Meri calls it.

I smile.

Okay, if I want to make a good demo reel, I need more stunning footage than just Meri sitting in a salon. We've been to the beach and the waterfront. Time to take her hiking at Multnomah Falls. #15 on her list will both help her blow off steam and give me a beautiful background.

I grab my camera equipment and head out the door. If we're going to make it to the top of the falls and back in time for my graveyard shift, then I need to meet her at her office as soon as she gets off work.

I take the bus and stroll into her office right at the stroke of five.

Roxy looks up from a file cabinet behind the front desk. "Hey, Kai. I've been watching your show." She doesn't say anything else, but the uncertainty in her gaze tells me she suspects I'm attracted to the star. Has she mentioned this to Meri?

"Yeah?" I lower my camera equipment to the ground and drop into a simple blue seat in the waiting area.

"I like that you're encouraging her to be herself." Roxy files a folder and slides the cabinet closed. "So often, people think they have to find someone else to love them in order to be happy. But that's not love. That's codependency."

"Yeah," I say again. I don't know anything about codependency, but it doesn't sound like something I have to worry about. Unless we're talking about a relationship with food. In which case, "I'm in a codependent relationship with pizza."

Roxy gives a small shake of her head. "If that's all you want for your life, may you live happily ever after."

"It's all I want in the moment." I spread my arms along the backs of the chairs next to me, cross an ankle over a knee, and frown. Some people can't take a joke, but I guess she *is* dealing with pretty serious relationship stuff right now.

Meri appears from the back of the office, her flip-flops making a slapping sound. She's changed into a striped T-shirt and short overalls, and she's fluffing her hair the way she's been doing ever since she got it cut.

She sees me and her hands drop to her sides. Her shoulder bag even plops to the floor. "No, Kai. I told you I need to decompress this afternoon."

It's a good thing I don't rely on her love for my happiness, let alone expect a warm greeting.

I look her up and down pointedly. "You don't look ready to go for a jog."

"I'm too sore. So, I'm going to take myself on a date."

"And where are you taking yourself?" I try not to get too jealous. Just because she'd rather be alone than with me.

She scoops her bag off the floor. "I was going to window shop at the mall and treat myself to an iced mocha. Maybe even get a mani-pedi."

I assume by the way she flashes her hand that she's talking about getting new fake nails, but I have a better idea. "If you need to refuel, you really should get into nature."

She pauses, her eyes flitting about as she mulls over my offer.

She hasn't turned me down yet. That's good.

"What do you mean by nature?"

"I mean the second tallest year-round waterfall in the United States."

"Ohh . . ." She looks at her fingernails.

I know if she looks too long, I'll lose her. I push to my feet, hoist my backpack over my shoulder, and cross the room in two large steps to grab her hand and pull her toward the door. "They sell iced mochas at Multnomah Falls too."

Meri lets me drag her a few feet before pulling back. "I don't really want male attention today." She says this as if my attention doesn't count as male.

"I promise to ignore you the whole way up."

Her seriousness cracks. A giggle escapes. "Besides when you're videoing me?"

"I'm only going to video the beauty of nature. If you get in the way, that's your own fault."

Roxy laughs and Meri looks over her shoulder, chuckling as well. This is my chance. "Laughter is the best medicine. Come on." I tug her forward.

"Fine." She stumbles after me out the door. "Though you should have warned me we were doing this, so I could have brought my hiking boots."

I wave to the other nurse. "The whole path is paved. You'll be fine."

Except I know she's not fine.

Why was she trying to get out of filming today? I wait until we are safely in her car on the way toward the Columbia Gorge Scenic Highway to ask. That way she won't back out of our trip, because she's too entranced by the healing beauty of mossy rocky walls, overgrown ferns, and numerous waterfalls tucked along the side of gorge.

"What's going on, Mer? We didn't film yesterday, and you're trying to get out of it today? Is there something you need to tell me?" I try to keep it light. I pray her answer is just as light. This is when I hope for PMS to be the worst of life's problems.

She grimaces at the road.

I let her grimace.

"I'm dealing with the reality that not all marriages end in happily-ever-after."

Okay . . . Most of America already knows that. Statistically speaking, half of Americans already know that. As she was raised by a single mom, I would have thought she'd be one of them. I guess she just never expected one of her friends to split from a spouse. "I'm really sorry about Roxy."

She bites her lip, focusing on the curvy road. "It's not just Roxy."

"Oh . . ." There must be others. From what I've seen, divorce happens in waves. Like an epidemic.

"My parents too."

I slant my gaze her way and frown. Did I hear correctly? "I thought your dad died a long time ago. You said at the Rose Festival . . ."

She glares at me.

I point at the curvy road in front of us.

She glares straight ahead.

"You said their marriage was the best years of your mom's life. You said you wanted to get married so you could have that."

"I didn't say that to *you*."

I tilt my head in a semi-apology. "I accidentally overheard when bribing the Ferris wheel operator to get you stuck."

"Why am I still speaking to you after that?"

"Because I listen. And I make you laugh."

She huffs. "I really am desperate."

"I'm not going to argue, but back to your parents . . ." I soften my tone. "Did you recently find out?"

She slows for a sharp turn, then to squeeze across a skinny bridge that is probably the reason they had to replace this road with I-84. She sighs. "After the sermon yesterday, Mom wanted to talk about marriage. About how my dad was with another woman when they died due to his driving under the influence."

That's a doozy. I'm lucky to be in the fifty percent whose parents stayed married. I'm pretty sure moving to the mainland from Maui has been challenging for my mom, but that's not the same as finding out your late father was not the guy you thought he was. "No wonder you want some alone time."

"A little too late now."

It doesn't have to be. "I'll give you some alone time when we get to the top of the falls."

The hardness in her jaw releases. "No video footage?"

"Not unless some guy sees you crying and stops to propose."

Her lips turn up at that one. "If you film me, I'll make *you* cry."

I really didn't mean to film Meri. Once we hiked up the steep mile of zigzags, the trail split. I headed down to the overlook of the falls. Meri hiked back along the river into the forest, where you can use fallen logs or rocks to cross. Either direction is really as close as you can get to heaven on earth. Well, I should say heaven on the mainland. Maui offers this kind of beauty along with tropical flowers, bamboo, and black sand beaches.

Anyway, Meri wandered off into the woods, while I filmed the 620-foot waterfall, bridge, and lodge below, along with a view of the Columbia River. Various tourists from around the world joined me, so I ended up taking pictures of them too.

I'm filming my jaunt back up to meet Meri when I see a lone red flip-flop float by. I adjust my camera for a close-up.

"My flip-flop." Meri's voice.

I lift my camera to catch her splashing through the shallow part of the river, holding only one shoe. I should have known.

Men emerge from all sides of the woods. Young, old, fat, skinny, Asian, and Hispanic. They leap to rocks and hang off the edge of the bank, trying to swipe the shoe with sticks. But as the water nears the ledge, the stream picks up speed.

Before anyone can stop it, Meri's bright red flip-flop disappears under the protective fencing that prevents larger things from floating over the edge of the waterfall. It emerges on the other side, swirls once, then rushes to its doom.

All these men watch with astonishment. Then they turn to face Meri.

I pan the camera to catch her response.

She's struck frozen with horror. Always overreaction with her. It could have been worse. At least it wasn't one of her new Nikes.

The men converge. All telling their tales of attempts at shoe rescue. Then they ask Meri how they can help.

If any woman ever wanted to get male attention, this was the way to do it. Unfortunately, Meri didn't want that today. And she'd made it very clear she didn't want me videoing her up here either.

Her gaze lifts my direction. It heats.

Seriously? She let her flip-flop float over the edge of a waterfall, and she's going to blame me?

"I'll be fine, guys." She shoos the men away. "Thanks for trying to help."

They take off, chatting among themselves as well as sharing their endeavors of heroism with awaiting family and friends.

Meri wades my direction.

"That was brilliant, Meri. We need to add 'let your shoe float over a waterfall' to your list. Though you really should have asked one of those men to give you a piggyback ride back down the trail."

"Oh yeah?" She looks up, her smile overly bright. "You think I need someone to give me a piggyback ride?"

My stomach does a flip-flop of its own. I'd made the mistake of touching Meri's hair at the golf course. I cannot have her hanging onto me for a mile hike.

I shrug the shoulder holding my camera bag. "I've got to carry this. Sorry."

She points a finger at the camera in my hand. "You mean your camera equipment that you used to film my shoe floating away?"

She's got me on that one. And she's coming closer, which, though I know I should avoid her, I kinda like. I hold the camera in front of my face as a barrier. It will keep me from kissing her, and it will also make her angry enough not to kiss me back. "How was I to know it was *your* shoe? I think too highly of you to assume you'd let your shoe simply float away like that. How'd it happen, anyway?"

She stops directly in front of my camera. Her fiery eyes glare straight through the lens. "I slipped on a rock, and my shoe floated off. I seem to remember you being the one to say I'd be fine walking up here without hiking boots."

"Most people would be. I forgot you're an exception to every rule."

"Well, as a reminder, you get to carry me back down." She snags the camera from my grasp, and tugs to lift the strap over my head.

I don't fight her. I'm too busy fighting myself. I'd been planning to keep my distance from her for this very reason. I could not have failed worse.

"Here." I reach to loop the strap over her head. Her hair tickles. My chest itches. "I wouldn't want you to lose this over the waterfall too." I dare to look down to see if she feels the same itch.

But she's lifting the camera between us, pointed my way.

Does she really want to film me, or is she just giving me a taste of my own medicine to keep me from tasting something else?

The flash of smile beneath the camera hints that she's enjoying this way too much. She doesn't even realize what she's missing out on.

"Everybody, this is Kai." Oh man. She's talking to the audience that she thinks will watch this video. As if they need more evidence of my crush.

Yes, I have a crush.

I roll my eyes. Both at myself and at the show Meri is putting on.

"He made me come hiking in flip-flops today, and now that one of my shoes has floated over the waterfall, he has to carry me a mile down to the bottom of this thing." She peeks over the top of the camera. "I hope you get sore. I hope you get T-Rex arms."

She's asking for it. "You think you're that heavy?" I step forward and drop down to wrap my arms around her legs and hoist her over my shoulder along with my camera bag.

She squeals and wiggles, and I really wish we were alone.

Instead, all the tourists who have been talking about Meri's shoe watch me head for the trail with a shoeless woman filming them. They wave and cheer.

An ache in my back tells me I can't make it very far like this. I stop at the first bench and lower her until she's standing above me.

I don't move away. Just shake my head at her. "You planned this, didn't you?"

She laughs with so much glee that it's all worth it. She spins me around and takes off my backpack to wear herself. She wraps her arms around my neck, leans against my torso, and lifts her legs to my sides.

I hook my elbows underneath her knees and start down the hill for the longest half hour of my life. Also, the shortest.

Her warm breath tickles my neck. Her fingers run from my shoulders to my chest, depending on which way she twists to film or point or wave. She doesn't even argue that we're not a couple when other couples see us and the girls beg their guys for a lift.

"You're so lucky," they tell her.

She just guffaws.

I pause to catch my breath at a switchback. I look over my shoulder to find her using the camera app on her phone in selfie mode. "You seem to be enjoying yourself."

"Oh, I am." She leans her soft cheek against mine and smiles for the camera.

I crack a grin, so I don't look like an ogre on her Instagram page later. I also take a deep breath of her pomegranate shampoo. Were a girl to ever ask me to buy her perfume like The List suggests, I'd have to find something with pomegranate. But Meri would never do that. I'm not even sure if she'll turn to look at me again.

She does.

"I told you laughter is the best medicine," I say.

Though I'm thinking about doing something that would take the laughter out of her eyes. It's also something that could potentially wound more than it might heal. I can't take that risk unless I get some kind of signal she wants me to.

Like an ear nuzzle. Or if she were to clutch my T-shirt collar in her fist and pull.

"You're right." She takes a deep breath, her ribcage pressing against my back. "The laughter. The nature. The exercise. This is perfect."

So close to perfect. So close. "Anything else you might want?"

Her eyes dilate. I seriously watch the dark pupils overtake her bronze irises. That's a natural reaction to attraction, right? Instinct. Basic desire. It has to be a sign.

"Yes," she says.

That itch in my chest has gone viral. She's about to tell me exactly what she wants. Then I can kiss her without risk. I'll simply be giving her what she's asked for. If she gets hurt by expecting me to give her any more than that, it will be all on her. She knows what she's getting into.

"I want . . ." Her eyes drop to my lips for a fraction of a second. ". . . An iced mocha."

CHAPTER TWENTY-THREE

Meri

#84. The wrong wife can break the right man.
Let him be right, so he knows he won't go
wrong with you.

I'm not sure whether to laugh or cry. At least I didn't kiss Kai.

Sure, it would have felt good in the moment, but then we would have had to go back to being just friends. Or roommates. Or whatever we are. And it would be awkward for me to go upstairs right now and find out what he's got planned for me to do today in my hunt for a husband.

It's already a little awkward. I'll just lie here on my bed for another minute and try to get all this toe curling out of my system before I have to face him again.

A low moan reaches my ears. It rises to a wail. Or is that a sob? Someone is crying, and strangely it's not me.

I sit up on my bed.

There it is again. It's female. "Gemma?"

I stand and wander out the door. The sound grows louder. I peek into her bedroom. Empty.

The sobs come like a machine gun now. Except muffled by rushing water. I raise my hand to knock on the bathroom door, but if Gemma is crying in the shower, I don't want to make her answer the door dripping wet. I'll wait until she gets out.

I hope she's okay. I wonder if Kai knows what happened.

I climb the stairs. He's lying on the couch as if everything is normal. Gemma's sobs follow me, so I know he must be able to hear them too.

"Do you hear that?" I ask to be sure.

His fungus feet propped on the armrest drop wide so he can see me from where his head rests on the other end. "Oh, yeah. I should have warned you."

"What happened?" I walk warily toward the love seat, because this whole moment feels horror-movieish.

"Gemma does this when she's plotting a new screenplay. She cries for her characters."

I stop. I hold my hands wide to show I need a bigger explanation. "She's not crying. She's sobbing."

"Yeah. I don't think she knows we can hear her. Charlie and I never told her."

I still don't get it. "She's crying for characters she made up? Imaginary friends?"

"They're real to her."

I point toward the bathroom. "And she does this a lot?"

"Yeah." Kai swings his feet to the ground and sits. "She'll come out of the bathroom in a few minutes and tell us about the sad story she's going to write."

I'm going to have to see it to believe it. I sink into the love seat. "Are you sure she doesn't have some degenerative disease she hasn't told anyone about?"

Kai leans forward toward his computer, resting his forearms on his knees. "Not unless being a writer is a disease."

It might be. "Speaking of disease, you could also try treating your foot fungus with baking soda."

"But then I couldn't gross you out with them."

I'm not grossed out anymore. His feet look normal. But treating him as if he has a fungus could help me keep my distance. "I have the weirdest roommates ever." Then it hits me. With Gemma sobbing in the shower, I'm breaking #23 on The List. I cover my mouth. "Oh no. I'm roommates with a wet rag."

Kai gives me his crooked grin. "We could ask Gemma to move out."

That would not be good. I'm not going to say it aloud, but the two of us need Gemma as a buffer. In case the foot fungus thing doesn't work.

"Or . . ." Kai spins his computer my way.

I don't look immediately. I want to see in his eyes what he means. There's a sparkle there that isn't going to explain itself.

"Or what?" I reluctantly glance at the screen to find an open email account. It's registered to a user named MeriMe. And it's full.

"*Or* you could respond to these thousands of men who have written to express their interest. Then you could marry one of them and be the one to move out."

I squint at the number on the screen. Literally thousands of emails. "Clearly I'm not the only desperate person in the world. When did you make this account?"

"Yesterday." He clicks the touch pad to open another page. This one looks like an advertisement. There's a close-up of me laughing. I've got my new sassy haircut, so it couldn't have been taken long ago. In big red letters the ad says:

#100. Get your personal ad in front of as many eligible bachelors as possible. Like on a billboard.

Meri Me on YouTube

We were joking about advertising on a billboard, but nobody would really do that. If Kai had the kind of money to pay for a billboard, he'd be better off buying a car. Or putting a down payment on a house.

Even if he spent his money on a billboard, how would he be able to make this happen so fast? Even I would have needed help from Charlie's ex . . .

I gasp. "You didn't."

"Oh, but I did."

I smash my face together between my palms and stare at the image that is, at this moment, displayed larger than life for the world to see. Okay, not the world, but my world. I could have college, high school, or even preschool classmates recognize this and call each other to say, *"Did you know Meri Newberg is still single? Poor dear."*

Kai spins and lies down the opposite direction with his feet closer to the love seat. "If you drive me to work, I can show you where the billboard is located."

Kai may be lazy, but he did not do this just to get free rides to work. "Why? Why would you do this when you could have used that money to buy yourself a car?"

He laces his fingers behind his head and grins. "It wasn't my money. Your adoring fans paid for this."

"I hate them." I drop onto my back and kick my legs toward the sofa side so that our feet point toward each other. "They are getting delight out of my singleness."

Kai nods toward the computer. "They're helping you get hitched. Don't you want to see what all those interested men have to say?"

I give his laptop a glance before returning to my pout. I'll read the emails later, when I'm alone. Right now I want to know what Kai has to say. "You don't care about them, do you? You're only trying to get interest from your director."

The glint in his eyes turns serious. "Win-win. This is what we both want, right?"

I study Kai's nonchalance and wonder what I really want. Mom said to pray to God about it, and He'd line up my desires with His. But I'm afraid to ask. I'm afraid I'm the person Jesus was talking about when He said some people wouldn't get married because they were never asked. "It must be nice to be the guy from Sunday's sermon who never gave marriage a thought."

Kai stills except for his gaze, which meets mine. "The Scripture said *seemingly* never gave marriage a thought."

Seemingly? Meaning his nonchalance is practiced? "You think about marriage?"

He looks to the ceiling and wiggles his feet a little. Is this part of the laid-back image he wants to project? "I don't think about it anymore."

I roll over to my side and prop my face up with a fist. Is he toying with me? Is this going to be all a joke? "When did you think about it? Kindergarten, when you had a crush on your teacher?"

He grins. "I did *not* have a crush on Mrs. Bietz."

"Bites? Your kindergarten teacher was a vampire?"

"Either that or a glutton."

I shake my head. "Are you trying to scar me with your traumatic childhood memories, or are you being purposefully vague?"

"You want me to tell you about the girl I proposed to?" he asks.

I slide my legs toward the floor and let their weight teeter-totter me up to a seated position. "You actually proposed?"

Did he get cold feet? Did she die? Did she turn him down because she was afraid he'd dent all her furniture with his butt?

"Don't act so shocked." His words are admonishing, but his tone is pleased. As if he'd hoped for this attention. As if he's teasing.

I should be embarrassed that I let him goad such a reaction out of me. His story is probably one of those pacts you make with a friend in college—where if neither of you are married by age thirty, you'll marry each other. He offered to follow through with his promise, but she knew he didn't mean it.

I need to relax. I should lie back down. But I'd rather be within reach to slap him if his story turns out to be as lame as I think it's going to be. "Who was she?"

"Alexis Long. She was on the track team at U of O with me. Pole vaulter."

She's real. Does that mean this is going to be a sad story? I won't slap Kai if it's sad. Maybe he's making light of it to prevent me from seeing how much it hurt him. I let the indignation seep from my body.

I glance at his bare feet to check for a scar from Achilles surgery, but with his heels planted on the armrest, it's hidden from view. "I know what happened with your scholarship," I offer.

"Yeah." He runs a hand through his hair. "After that, I moved back in with my parents and returned to my high school job at the cineplex."

That makes sense with what I know about him now. Late hours. Free popcorn. "Movies."

"Movies," he confirms. "Though, at the time, I just wanted to work my way into management so I could save enough money to get my girlfriend a ring. I thought we'd marry after she graduated, and she'd move up to Portland with me."

Oh man. Did I judge him unfairly? "What happened?"

"She fell for someone else on the track team after I left." He stretches overhead, making his long body look even longer. Perhaps like a pufferfish trying to appear tougher than he is. "She came up that next summer to break things off with me, but I didn't find out until after I'd proposed."

I study him in this new light. He's been through something I haven't. While I thought never getting asked to marry was bad, Kai asked and wasn't accepted.

He'd once been more committed to a woman than anything else in his life. And she hadn't felt the same way about him.

"I'm sorry."

"It was a long time ago." He shrugs. "I sold the ring and used the money to join another cinema employee at film school. They got me the internship at Channel 7, and Channel 7 offered me a job. See? It all worked out."

"It worked out?" I frown as I follow his connection. "You ruptured your Achilles, lost your scholarship, got dumped by your girlfriend, and you've been drifting through life ever since."

His eyes flash back and forth as if he can't see the same connection with the events in his life. "No, I'm not drifting."

"Really?" I hold my hands out wide. "Where are you headed? Where do you want to go?"

Kai sits up to face off with me. "I want the cameraman position."

I press my lips together. This really is none of my business. The guy just shared his sad story, so why am I so angry? Perhaps because he called me on my garbage but refuses to admit his own.

"You mean the cameraman position you still haven't applied for?"

He motions to the computer. "I'm doing something better than apply for it. I'm earning it."

I stand up. "You mean you're waiting for them to come to you?"

He stands taller. "Sure. Why not?"

It all makes so much sense now. He got up to bat three times in a row and struck out every time. So now he's sitting on the bench. Just hoping for the coach to put him in.

It's not that he doesn't want anything. He's *afraid* to want anything.

I motion to his computer. Not to the thousands of emails I've received, but to the online application he has yet to fill out. "They might prefer someone who expresses interest."

Kai's chest rises and falls inches from my face. It's as if his eyes dare me to make this about more than a cameraman position. "I'd rather they express interest in me, so I know I'm not wasting my time."

"Then you're wasting *their* time."

All along he's teased me about being desperate, about putting myself out there for public rejection, while he's done the opposite. Become lackadaisical. Apathetic.

That's why he looked at me as if he was going to kiss me at the waterfall, then stopped and asked what I wanted. That's why he's standing inches from me now.

Does he realize that, thanks to him, I'm not as desperate as I used to be?

I now know I deserve a man who believes I'm worth the risk. And Kai will never be that man.

I can't wait to drop him off at his dead-end job so I can go through these emails and find a guy both capable and willing to push the *send* button.

CHAPTER TWENTY-FOUR

Kai

*#56. Don't tell him about the fun you've had on
other dates. Men deserve and desire to be the center
of your attention.*

I stare angrily at the online application I've filled out for *Capers*. Lots
of people will apply for this position. Lots of hopefuls who will never
be chosen. Why would I click *send* and put myself into that pool?

Meri doesn't get it because she's so straightforward. If she sees
something she wants, she goes for it. But how's that been working for
her? Not so well. She's pretty much living the same life I am. Except
with a car.

I'm the creative one. I'm the trailblazer, using my connections and
resources to forge my own path.

See? I'm not drifting. I'm not Meri's red flip-flop she let cascade
over the edge of a waterfall.

I smile at the memory and click my computer screen to open our
YouTube page over the window with the job application. The knot
in my belly relaxes. This is a much better place for me to spend my
energy. And it's working. Since Meri's billboard went up, page views
have skyrocketed into six digits.

Meri wasn't as excited about that as I thought she would be. Her
overall interest in men has seemed to be dwindling. Of course, that
could be due to her recent disillusionment with the institution of marriage. It could also be due to a newfound confidence that has come

from my encouragement of doing things to please herself, like cutting her hair.

There is one other possibility that almost hurts to consider. The possibility that she'd rather be with me than someone who could give her the life she wants.

Our viewers don't seem to feel this pain. I scroll through their comments with a grimace. Meri and I may not be on the cover of a tabloid magazine, but these strangers surmise about our lives as if we are.

You're supposed to leave the falling to the falls, Kai.

She let her flip-flop go on purpose.

You idiot. She's begging you to kiss her.

She wasn't begging me to kiss her yesterday during our living room standoff. Though it would have been a nice way to shut her up.

For some reason, I expected her to have a little more compassion after I told her about my greatest heartbreak. But it was as if she thought I was just giving her excuses. As if she thought I was selling myself short.

I'm fine with my life. I'm content the way the apostle Paul tells us to be. The cameraman position will happen in God's timing. *Right, God?*

He doesn't respond by soothing my itch.

It makes me restless. Makes me wake up earlier than usual that afternoon so I won't miss the bus that will take me to Meri's office. I should probably get going soon. We've got filming to do.

#98. Wear a bandage in public and have a tale of daring to go with it.

I can't wait to see what responses Meri comes up with.

I swipe my phone screen to check the time. A little envelope icon at the top tells me I've received a message. It's either from Meri or my mom. I click the icon, wanting it to be from Meri.

Her name appears.

I sigh and tap the screen. Maybe she's apologizing for her blowup.

I can't film today. Luke saw the billboard last night and called. He's moving to town and asked if I would want to get together after work.

I read the message twice. *Who's Luke?*

Oh, yippee-Kai-yay. He's her cowboy. Everything every girl wants in a man.

I drop onto my bed. Numb. Ear-ringing numb.

It worked. The billboard worked. It got her the man she wants.

But did it get me all the views I need to get attention from the director of *Capers*? Because if she's dating Luke, she's not going to be filming with me anymore.

This is what I want, right? Distance between us. So I don't have to put myself out there and let her confirm I'm not enough.

I already know I'm not what she wants. She's made it clear from the very beginning. Even if we turned out to have amazing chemistry, she'd still be settling.

I'm not interested in marriage anyway. I want nothing to do with the rat race that requires one to climb higher and higher in order to build wealth only to retire and do nothing. I'll just live as if I'm already retired. Without the responsibilities of a spouse to please or children's mouths to feed.

So why does it feel like I'm the one settling?

I don't know if the cameraman job is all I want anymore. But I know this date with Luke is what Meri wanted.

Even though she never lassoed him. She lassoed me.

I shake my head to get rid of the memory. I'll replace it with other memories. Like the one yesterday, where she had just as much opportunity to "express interest" as I did.

If either of us were to do that first, it would have been her. But she didn't.

Instead she's going on a date with someone else.

I lift my phone to stare at her message. I should probably respond that I got it, so she's not afraid I'm going to show up at her office and demand she spend the evening with me the way I've done in the past.

I squint at the ceiling, imagining such a scenario. How would Luke react? How would she react? I'd get rejected for sure.

My belly cramps. Though it could be worse.

I could have kissed her. Then everyone online would know she's rejecting me.

Or would she have turned Luke down for me?

I'll never know.

I wave the white flag by typing: *Congrats.*

Meri: *Thanks.*

I growl at her quick response. It tells me nothing. What is she really thinking? Is she planning her wedding?

Okay, I'm getting ahead of myself. It's just a date. Dinner, maybe. She could be home before I even leave for work.

Where's he taking you?

Meri: *Oh no. I'm not telling you this time.*

I roll my eyes.

I'm not going to video you. But you should still practice #51. Prudence is a virtue.

Meri: *Thanks, Mom.*

My throat constricts. I may not be her mom. But I want to be here when she returns. No matter how late.

Joel agrees to cover my shift at work. It's going to be his job soon enough anyway.

I shove my resentfulness of Joel aside to be grateful because, if I'd had to work, I would have missed the sound of Meri's keys finally jingling in the lock a little after ten o'clock. This is what I'm truly resentful about.

The living room is dark except for the glow from my computer screen, which is probably lighting up my face in a way that will make it look as though I'm telling ghost stories when Meri walks in. Maybe I should have left another light on.

Except she's not walking in. She's lingering on the front step.

I want to go flick the porch light on and off a few times. She did call me *Mom* earlier.

I sit very still, listening. I can barely make out words being spoken. Though I'm relieved that's the only kind of "make out" going on.

The door swings open. Meri enters slowly, head down. She turns, waves, and closes the door. Then she's walking into the living area.

She hasn't seen me yet. Is she too busy reliving the evening's magical moments? Is she saying a prayer of thanksgiving? Is it too late for me to slide to the floor behind the coffee table cubes so she doesn't know I'm practically stalking her?

She takes another step forward and looks up. She screams so loudly that chills pop up on my neck.

What do you want to bet the neighbors call the cops again? "You okay there?" I ask.

"Kai." She grabs throw pillows from the love seat and does exactly that with them.

I use my elbows to block her attack, more worried about her breaking the screen off my MacBook than anything.

"Are you filming me?" she demands.

I hold up my empty hands just as I had for the police officer. "No."

"Then what are you doing here?"

That is a great question. How do I give her an answer when I don't even know? "I wanted to be here for you when you got home. See how it went."

Her shoulders sag. I'm not sure if that's from her frustration with me or disappointment in Luke. Hopefully Luke disappointed.

She marches behind the love seat and switches on the overhead lights.

I shade my eyes and watch her retrieve a pint of ice cream from the freezer. "Hey, I didn't know we had that."

She grabs two spoons, so she must not be that frustrated with me. "I'll share."

"Good. I want to know everything." That sounds like something a girlfriend would say, doesn't it? I might be putting myself in the friend zone here. But that's a safe place to be.

She sinks onto the sofa next to me and hands me a spoon. "I meant I'd share my ice cream, not share all the details."

I scoot my computer out of the way, so she can set the cold container down on the coffee table cube between us. And so we can lean in over it together.

She smells sweeter than the ice cream.

"You don't kiss and tell?" I ask, unsure whether to be upset or relieved.

She pops the top, scoops a spoonful, and slides it between her lips. "You want to know?"

Do I? She could be teasing me here. I hope she's teasing. "Only if you want to tell."

She twists her back toward me and looks over the strap of a flowery sundress. I can't keep from wondering if she knew about the date with Luke when she left for work this morning, and if so, did she take this dress to change into for him? Or might she have been planning to dress up to hang out with me?

She points to the mass of freckles on the back of her shoulder. "He kissed me here."

I look at the spot. It's so delicate. So feminine. So off limits.

My own skin begins to burn. They say you turn green with jealousy, but I'm pretty sure I'm turning red. I'm afraid to look up from the spot. Afraid Meri will see the heat in my eyes.

I clear my throat. "And that's when you told him about number fifty-one on The List?" I finally look up. But only because I want to read her response.

One corner of her lips curves. Though the usual spark in her eyes is missing. "That's when he asked me if I'd want to be roommates."

My eyebrows dance in confusion. Up. Down. Together. Apart. If I was a cartoon character, I'm sure they would have lifted all the way off my face.

I'd like to think this is a good turn of events. It's good for Meri to avoid such a disaster waiting to happen. At least, I hope she avoided it. "I didn't realize roommates were allowed to kiss each other on the shoulder."

She scoops another bite, and I follow suit.

Mint chocolate chip. This might help cool me off.

"They're not." She points her spoon at me. I'm so busted. "I think he wants someone to pay half his bills, and he was betting that I'm desperate enough to do it if he dangled the possibility of something more happening between us."

"That's so backward." But am I any better? I took a vacation day to sit on the couch and eat ice cream with Meri. She knows it too. She just doesn't want to ruin what we have by saying it out loud. So, I'll keep our moment going. "Who would want to fall for a roommate?"

She scoops another bite. "It would complicate everything."

"Everything."

We eat in silence. This may be as far as our relationship ever goes. Silent comradery and a shared carton of ice cream. But there's nowhere else I'd rather be. "I'm sorry it didn't work out with Luke."

She laughs around a mouthful. "No, you're not."

"You're right. I'm not." I get the dart of eyes and the inhale I was hoping for. Two can play this game. "I need you here to smuggle me ice cream after Gemma feeds me zucchini noodles for dinner."

"Zoodles? You poor thing. Here have the rest." She hands me the half-empty container. "I thought you were going to say you need me here to film more YouTube videos."

"Well, that too." I shrug and turn to face her as she turns to face me. "I'm sure I could get Gemma to wear a Band-Aid and make up stories to tell strangers about how she hurt herself, but she'd want it to be believable in the same way she does with her screenplays. She'd say she scratched herself with a fingernail. Or got a papercut."

Meri waves her hands as if to wipe away my fears. "Don't worry. I'll be completely outlandish."

We laugh over our plans for tomorrow. And in this moment, the itch in my chest is scratched.

CHAPTER TWENTY-FIVE

Meri

*#99. Create suspense like Alfred Hitchcock
by buying a convertible to go with your headscarf
and cat-eye glasses.*

I spray Dr. Snyder with purple Silly String.

"Surprise!" we all yell.

He pulls the chemical-scented goo from his face, smiles at the entire staff jammed inside the break room, and finally notices the cake with his name on it. "Oh, I'm going to miss you guys."

"We'll miss you too." I give him a side hug. This is appropriate for the workplace. Unlike shoulder kissing. And spoon fighting over ice cream at midnight.

"You know you can still apply for a job with the ministry, Meri. Nurses available to travel are in short supply." He's a kind man. I really don't think he's attracted to me. He simply wants me to be as fulfilled by life as he is.

I scrunch my nose. "Thanks for reminding me how unneeded I am here."

Roxy links elbows with me. "I need you."

Roxy doesn't need me. But if I can help at all, I want to be here for her.

The two of us take our plates of cake and squeeze through the crowd to enjoy the spaciousness of the waiting room. On the way, I grab a handful of Band-Aids to stuff in my pocket.

Roxy has perfected the art of widening her eyes at me as if I'm a psycho. "What's that for?"

I sit across from her and smile at my cake. Though I'm really smiling at the memories of my late-night plans. Roxy would think Kai's a psycho too.

In answer to her question, I set my cake down, pull a Band-Aid from my pocket, peel off the backing, and stick it to my forehead. "Shark bite."

She cuts her cake with the side of her fork and deadpans, "That's a bummer."

Kai saunters in, camera bag over his shoulder. "Hey, nice shark bite."

I grin like a teacher's pet with a gold star. "Thanks."

He points down the hallway. "Bathrooms this way?"

"At the end, on the left." I watch him stroll away, noticing things I haven't before. Like the thick strip of skin on the back of his ankle that must be the scar from his Achilles surgery.

There's also shadows under his calf muscles. I've never thought of calves as sexy before.

How could I ever have sat on his shoulders in a swimsuit and never noticed these things? Can I get a do-over? Can I get the whole summer back? Then I would cherish going to baseball games, singing together on public transit, and Kai being my other half so I don't feel as lonely when hanging out with Anne and Damian? September is coming way too quickly.

"Has Kai applied for the job yet?"

I snap back to face Roxy. And reality. "No, but he . . . uh . . . took last night off from work to eat ice cream with me."

"You mean he took last night off to wait for you to get home from your disastrous date with Luke?"

My chest warms. "Yes."

"That's . . ." Roxy clicks her tongue. "Kinda the exact opposite of what you want him to do."

I grab my plate and scoop spongy chocolate cake into my mouth innocently. "Why would I want him to do anything?"

Roxy licks frosting off her fork. "Because you're falling for him, and you don't want to end up like me."

Her words ring true—like a gong. My heart vibrates with the implications.

I'd deny it, but even if I could convince myself she was wrong, Roxy would know better. She's lived it.

I bite my lip until the pounding in my chest knocks the words loose. "I won't end up like you because Kai doesn't want to get married."

If only Kai and I could sit on the couch and eat ice cream together forever. And he would continue to look at me with the kind of intensity that makes him seem not lazy at all. And this fragile connection between us would continue to be as delicious as the spaghetti noodle from *Lady and the Tramp*. Only more fragile, because it would be made from a zucchini. "Did I tell you he once proposed to a girlfriend?"

"You mean Alexis Long? The U of O pole vaulter? Who fell for another teammate when he dropped out of college?" Her tone dips into a well of sarcasm. "No."

Okay, so I've mentioned it once or twice. Roxy's supposed to be sharing in my misery here. "You're fun."

"Sorry." The hard edge on her expression softens. "Here. Give me one of those Band-Aids. I've been injured too." She sets her fork on her plate and reaches toward me.

I pull a strip from my pocket.

She takes it, peels the backing, and sticks it on her scrubs as if she's reciting the Pledge of Allegiance. "Heartbreak."

The bandage represents how a relationship with Kai could cause more damage than a shark bite. "I'm sorry, Roxy."

She gives me a sad smile. "I'm sorry too."

I'm not sure if she's talking about being sorry for herself or for me, but when Kai returns from the bathroom, I'm not as excited about filming. What started out as fun now feels futile. Like dangling a carrot in front of a donkey.

Kai follows me out to my car as if he's working the plow I'm pulling. "You okay?"

I stand across the hood from him, stare into his warm brown eyes, and confess to myself that I'm not okay. I'm in love.

Forget *The Gong Show*. The pang around my heart lights up as if I just answered correctly on *Wheel of Fortune*. Which would be great except advancing to the final round means I only have one chance to solve the puzzle or else the prize will never be mine.

For decades I've wanted to fall in love, thinking it would solve all my problems. But it doesn't always work that way, does it? Love hurt Roxy. It hurt my mom. It's hurting me.

"You should get a car." Yeah, that's the first thing I say to Kai after I realize I'm in love with him.

Perhaps the game show analogy took over. Or perhaps I think that if I can get him to take baby steps, he will eventually walk down the aisle.

Kai scrunches his face. "What?"

"You could buy *my* car."

His gaze scans the tiny hood of my turquoise compact, then returns to meet mine with a crinkle of confusion. "No thanks."

Okay, I understand. I drive a chick vehicle. I picture Kai in a Jeep. Like the one we drove during vacation in Maui. I just need to get him to a car lot. "Hey, isn't there a suggestion on my list about buying a convertible?"

Kai stacks his forearms on the hood of my car and leans forward. "You want to buy a convertible? Tonight?"

I blink and open my eyes wide as I mentally calculate what a new car payment would cost and if I could afford it when I also have to get my own apartment.

There's still the chance I could move in with Roxy, but I don't want to count on that. I want Graham to step up.

"Yes." I can do it. I might have to moonlight as a hot dog vendor at the ballpark to make the numbers crunch, but hey, then I'd have both a convertible and free hot dogs.

Actually, I'd be okay. While most of my friends would have to wait to get their dream car until after their kids moved out, this is not a problem I have. Might as well make the most of my singleness for a change.

Kai scratches his head. "You remember we live in Portland, right? We are ranked pretty high in the nation for most rainy days per year. That makes us one of the worst places to own a convertible."

I give his little fun fact an overly bright smile. "Then I'll have *two* reasons to move to Nevada."

His eyes narrow, proving he remembers the first reason to be that Nevada has a larger male population. "You're only getting a convertible to attract a man?"

I stare at the man. "Yes."

"Meri." He shakes his head. "Are you sure you don't want to think about this? We can still film the Band-Aid thing tonight."

"Nope." I tug the driver's door open and drop behind my steering wheel for what might be the last time. I've had this car paid off for a couple of years now. I knew I would have to upgrade eventually.

Kai joins me, giving me the side-eye. "I don't want you to do something you'll regret."

I'm trying really hard not to, though I don't think he's talking about confessing my feelings. Can you imagine how that would go?

Kai, you aren't the man of my dreams, but I want you to be. So get out of your butt dent, and do something about it.

He'd probably run straight into the street and get hit by a bus. It would be all my fault. I'll have to be more tactful.

"I know what I'm doing." I start the engine and reverse from the parking lot with purpose.

Normally I would spend months browsing Craigslist for a great deal, but the best deals on convertibles will not be found during summer. Plus, I'll need a loan. I head toward the nearest car dealership.

Kai turns sideways, upper arm propped along the window to better watch me. "Have you read the emails from interested men?"

I roll my eyes. "I don't spend as much time on a computer as you."

He shakes his head. "I'm just saying you don't have to buy a new car to get male attention."

I glance at him without saying anything. His attention is all I want, but now I'm self-conscious about what he sees when he looks at me. He meets my gaze, and I'm exposed.

I turn my head to check my blind spot before changing lanes, but I can still feel the searing temperature of his stare. What if I don't tell him how I feel? What if I just show him? Just pull over, reach for his T-shirt, and tug his smirking lips to mine? Then he'd be too busy kissing me to run out into traffic and get killed.

No. This desire to kiss him isn't new. It's the one I've been fighting because I know it won't get me what I really want.

He has to buy a car. He has to apply for the job. He has to do something other than sit there watching me with wary eyes as I go nuts inside my mind.

I pull into a dealership with sparkly Mustangs lined up along the road. I've never thought of myself as a Mustang owner, but I never thought I'd fall for Kai either.

He's still studying me when I park. "You're serious about this."

He has no idea. I park in a spot by the building with giant windows designed to display car models so new that I've never even seen them before. "Get out your camera."

My favorite corner of his lips curves. "I've got a better idea." He reaches for his phone. "Let's do this live."

I pause, even as salesmen stealthily converge on us. Going live sounds a little scary for me, with my penchant for embarrassing moments, and I can't see how it would benefit him at all. "I thought the whole reason for the show is to display your photography and editing skills."

He taps on his phone screen. "It is. But if you're going to invest in a car, it would be good to get advice from people other than the car salesman."

My heart melts. Maybe I can trust it in his hands. "That's a sweet idea."

He leans toward me, and my pulse trips. But he's only getting close enough that we can both be on the screen, like in a selfie. He looks at his phone. "Hey, guys. Meri needs you. She decided to try number ninety-nine on our list tonight. She's buying a convertible. Live. So you can help her pick the best car and get the best deal."

"Yeah." I continue looking at Kai as I talk to the camera. "Kai doesn't know much about cars. Hey, maybe you can help him pick one out too."

Kai eyes light with mischief as he turns my way. So close. "Why do I need to buy a car when I can just ride around in your convertible?"

Sometimes I want to kiss him. Sometimes I want to knock sense into him. I narrow my eyes. A challenge. "Because I'm not going to be around forever."

The light in his gaze fades.

My collarbone tingles.

Something knocks against the window.

I jump.

A guy in his twenties stands on the other side of my car door looking like a model with his button-up and stylishly messy hair. He crosses his arms and nods as if that's all he has to do to get a sale.

And maybe it is. I do like his collared shirt.

Kai peers out the window, bringing his low voice close to my ear. "When did Zac Efron became a car salesman?"

"It's not Zac. It's proof God wants me to buy a convertible. He sent me a sales angel." I bet everybody feels the same way when they see this guy's baby-blue eyes.

"We're in trouble." Kai snorts. "I hope our audience can talk some sense into you, since I can't."

I open my door and stand. "Hi, I'm Meri." I extend my hand to shake, and almost expect the rest of the cast from *High School Musical* to pop out and sing about how we're all in this together.

"Nice to meet you. I'm Tommy Hayes." He shakes, rather anticlimactically.

I'd been prepared for him to swing me up into the rafters, like a trapeze artist at the circus. Though it's probably best for his silky, soft hands that we are still on the ground.

"What can I help you with today?"

I remind myself that I'm not here for the entertainment. "I want to trade my car for a convertible. And Kai wants to look at your Jeeps."

Kai circles the trunk and joins me in time to overhear my last line. He makes a face at his phone. "Since when do I want a Jeep?"

"Since I went to Hawaii and rented one. You're Hawaiian, so . . ." I wave my arms as if the rest of the sentence is obvious.

Kai smirks. "I rented a scooter in Hawaii. I also parasailed. Maybe I should buy a boat."

I nod thoughtfully. That's still a step forward. Not a very practical one, but neither is convertible shopping.

Tommy rubs his hands together. "What I'm hearing is that you want to buy a Jeep, Meri. Follow me."

I lift my eyebrows at Kai and trail after Tommy. "I did like driving the Wrangler in Maui." It will also fit in better at the golf club when Kai and I start playing foot golf. And it's possible my sales angel has one in turquoise.

Kai points his phone my way and follows. "Any viewers have feedback on buying Jeep Wranglers?"

Tommy pauses, his pretty eyes piercing us with questions. "Viewers?"

"Oh, yeah." I guess we should get his permission if we're going to film him live. "I have a YouTube show, and—"

"Meri?" Tommy turns completely toward us and takes a step my way. He looks me up and down then gives the camera his glistening smile. "Is buying a convertible on your list? Because it should be. Driving a nice car is a great way to attract interest from the opposite sex. To any viewers in the Portland area, my name is Tommy Hayes, and you can find me right here at Autoland."

"Wow. Okay." I scratch my head and glance at Kai for help.

Kai shoots me his smug smile, then nods to draw Tommy's attention. "In returning to our regularly scheduled program, you should know that our audience is going to be giving us live feedback on how to get the best deal for Meri. I've already had viewers chime in on the history of Jeeps, along with their most recent rankings against other four-wheel drives."

"Hmm." Tommy rubs his square jaw with the little cleft in the middle. He's probably weighing the pros and cons of selling a car with the world watching. His hesitation makes me question his integrity. Perhaps he's a fallen angel.

Kai's phone chimes. He looks down at the latest viewer comment. "Are you the Thomas Hayes who attended St. Ignatius and drove your first car through your parents' garage door?"

Tommy's baby face flushes, and I feel for him. "Uh, yeah."

How is it that I haven't been called out publicly for all the stupid things I've done in the past? Perhaps I have been, but it's just in the emails that I have yet to read. Or I could have been exposed in viewer comments. Maybe Kai knows all kinds of secrets about me, and he honestly does want to get married, just not to me.

He could be afraid our children would follow in my footsteps and get stuck in dumbwaiters at their best friend's house. Gwen's parents had to call the fire department to get me out, and I received all the blame even though Matt McIntosh had been the one to talk me into trying to ride in it like an elevator. Come to think of it, Gwen's parents had also called an ambulance for me when we were having a snowball fight in her back yard, and I unknowingly ran right onto the top of their pool cover and sank into the freezing water. I shiver, just thinking of it.

Kai's hand rubs my spine, warm and inviting. "You cold?"

Goosebumps pop up on my arms from his touch. Can I say yes to get him to put his arm around me? I might have, if he didn't have his camera pointed my way. "No."

Phooey on Gwen's parents for being rich enough to have both a dumbwaiter and a swimming pool. If not for them, Kai might put his arms around me on his own.

Oh, wait. There would still be the biology class where we dissected frogs, and when Wes Preston joked that it was my boyfriend, I'd picked it up and kissed it.

Is that why Kai hasn't kissed me? Because I have a history of kissing frogs? With anyone else, that would just be a figure of speech.

Tommy clears his throat. "Anyway, I have both new and used Jeeps. Did you want a soft shell or hard shell?"

Kai's phone dings. "Lainey in Spokane suggests hard shell since it rains so much here."

"Thanks, Lainey." I nod at Tommy. "Hard shell."

He blows his baby cheeks out. "Two- or four-door?"

Kai's phone starts chiming like an annoying neighbor ringing the doorbell. He studies his screen for a while. "Viewers are arguing. Some prefer the two-door for being the original and sportier model, while others think the four-door is more practical and looks tougher."

I twist my lips. My instinct is to go with four-door because it would be easier with a family, but we can probably all agree that's a nonfactor at the moment. I'm in love with a guy who will never grow up. What do I do? "Is there a price difference?"

Tommy stuffs his hands in his pocket and turns with purpose. He leads us toward a row of colorful 4x4s. "If you're wanting to save money, the two-door model is less expensive."

I follow with just as much purpose. While I may not have the power to change my love life, I do have the power to pick out any car on the lot. My history of financial responsibility and self-discipline will unlock these doors for me. So, I'm going to climb into the driver's seat and prove to Kai that he's missing out.

The new vehicles are displayed in a rainbow of color. Red, of course. Silver—boring. Yellow? Ooh . . .

"The green one is you," Kai tells me.

Green? It's fresh like Easter. It's lush like Portland. It's the school color for the Oregon Ducks. But . . . "How's it me?"

Kai glances up from his phone, eyes warm and adoring.

My stomach flips.

"You wore a green dress when you moved in. I remember because you fell asleep in it, and I had to cover you up to keep you from indecent exposure."

I should be embarrassed. The bridesmaid dress was unflattering to begin with, and I was wearing the world's ugliest Spanx underneath. But instead of caring about what horrendous image Kai might have seen, I'm touched that he'd made the effort to protect my virtue. "I thought Charlie covered me."

Kai gives a half shrug as if he doesn't care, but he's still smiling the tiniest of smiles. "I'm sure he would have."

Does this mean Kai is capable of growth? Could his act of protection be the first bloom of spring? The fact that he remembers the color of my dress has to mean something, right?

The dinging of Kai's phone brings me back to reality. The world now knows about my green dress and could very well be imagining a wardrobe malfunction. I have to do something to get that visual out of their minds. I lean forward to give them all a close-up of my face. "What do you guys think? Should I go with green?"

Our viewers chime in their agreement, so we take the green Jeep for a test drive. It's different than my little car, but the main difference is the open roof. I whiz along the Terwilliger curves and lift a hand into the chilly wind toward the golden sky of sunset. I love summer nights, and this Jeep will help me love them even more.

I'm confident I got a good deal on the vehicle. Vic in Toledo made sure of that, posting prices from Kelley Blue Book and haggling with Tommy for us. I'm finally driving Kai to work through the dark in my new Jeep with the mental and emotional satisfaction of winning a marathon.

I park in the empty parking lot of Channel 7 News and sigh in contentment. I'm the proud owner of a Wrangler. "I think I'll name her Julia."

Kai shoves his camcorder in his bag. "Your Jeep?"

"Yes." Julia the Jeep gives me hope just like Julia Roberts in *My Best Friend's Wedding*. It also gives me hope that Kai hasn't gotten out yet. I push the button that turns off Julia's engine. The automatic headlights dim as well. So fancy. It has to at least make Kai want a car a little. "What would you name your vehicle?"

"My old Honda was named . . ." Kai pauses. "Oh, that's right, I don't name my cars."

At least he used to own a car. But then again, he used to go to college and compete in track. He's capable. Just not willing.

His humor simmers in response to my contemplativeness. "I'm glad you got a good deal on Julia."

"Thanks." We're alone. In the dark. And a pang in my chest reminds me a new vehicle is not enough.

"Hey," he says huskily. Affectionately. The silhouette of his finger crooks to invite me closer.

My pulse picks up speed. My eyes zip to his, trying to read his intent through the dark, but he's a shadow. There's only one reason I can think why he would want me to lean toward him. It's something we've been avoiding.

My toes curl. My stomach warms. I take a deep breath, like when jumping off the high dive, and I lean forward.

Not being able to see Kai's face heightens my other senses. The sounds of the city. The cool night breeze seeping in my pores. Kai's exotic scent mixed with the plastic new-car smell.

I hesitate. If we do this, there's no going back. And there probably won't be any going forward either. Will this moment be enough? Or will it turn out to be as impulsive and regrettable as a Jeep purchase come Portland's rainy season?

He lifts his hand toward my face.

My lips tingle. It's too late to be rational now. When I realized I was in love with him, I should have canceled our plans for this evening completely. I should have taken the time to build a wall against my vulnerability. Instead, I opened the gate to my heart.

His warm fingers slide along my forehead to brush my hair to one side. I want to rub my face against his palm like a cat, but I wait to see what he'll do next. Where his smooth touch will travel. How he'll draw me in. I've been waiting for this moment from even before I knew I wanted it.

His fingers lift. They return to my forehead. Then dig slightly into my skin and peel something away.

The Band-Aid.

I freeze in confusion as my brain attempts to register this unexpected interaction. (1) Kai wasn't trying to kiss me. (2) I'm not going to get kissed. (3) He can't see me, so hopefully he doesn't realize his touch has melted me like candle wax. (4) I should be glad I've escaped the burn of being kissed by Kai while knowing nothing will ever come from it. (5) I'd rather be burned. (6) He left the Band-Aid on my head for the entire car purchase.

I point. "You left that on my head during the whole video?"

His white teeth flash in the dim streetlight as he smiles. "I thought you'd see it when I turned my phone into selfie mode, but you were too caught up in buying a car. After that, I figured it would just be awkward to pull the bandage off your head mid video when there's no wound underneath."

Right when I start to hope that he cares about my well-being from the blanket revelation, he goes and neglects me like this. Then when he does take the bandage off, it's by motioning me toward him and touching me softly. I want to cry in a Lucille Ball kind of way.

Instead, my spine stiffens. "The Band-Aid idea was to get men to ask questions. Did nobody on your live video feed ask what happened to my forehead?"

"Oh, they did. I told them it was a shark bite."

"Get out."

Kai hands me the bandage and reaches for the door handle. "You know, if you wanted to talk to those guys yourself, you could read the thousands of emails in the account I made you."

"I will." I huff. He probably made that account to get me to talk to other men because he knows he's the only guy I want to talk to. And whether or not he wants to kiss me as much as I want to kiss him, he doesn't want to marry me. No big news there. Which makes it stupid that I let the rejection hurt so much.

He stands and faces me, all tall, dark, and lazy. "Thanks for the ride."

I'm glad I'm not driving him home. Then he would be there to hear me cry in the shower like I'm Gemma or something. "You're welcome."

His shadow nods before closing the door and heading inside.

I stare for a long while, wishing so many different things that nothing makes sense anymore. Then with the kind of ache Roxy must live with daily, I place the Band-Aid over my throbbing heart.

CHAPTER TWENTY-SIX

Kai

*#11. If you learn to drink your coffee black,
you'll attract a higher quality man.*

I clock in, then lean against the door and drop my camera equipment to the floor. I'd thought Meri would fight when I motioned her toward me. I expected her to slap me or demand a reason for why I'd wanted her to lean forward. I thought she'd at least get all defensive, like when I'd told her about Alexis.

She did *after* I pulled the Band-Aid off her head. But not before. Not when I brushed her hair away from her face.

It had been too dark to see if she'd closed her eyes or not. But I'd heard the intake of breath. I felt her tilt her face slightly toward my touch. And even now my fingers throb to continue the caress.

What if I hadn't removed the bandage? What if I'd traced from her temple down to her jawline? Lifted her chin?

She would have let me.

And then what?

It's much easier to imagine the physical connection than the emotional. It always has been. Because emotionally, I'm kind of a parasite. And for the first time in a long time, I want to be more.

I don't only want to kiss her. I want to be the man she's looking for, but I know I'm not. I also know what I have to do to change.

Okay, honestly, I still prefer the path of least resistance. Who doesn't? But at this point, there's nothing in the world I can think of that would be harder than not kissing Meri.

Kissing her tonight would have been a mistake. I've got to keep myself under control long enough to apply for the job that will provide for a family.

Yeah. I said it. I'm going to provide for a family.

A gentleman always chooses what he wants most over what he wants in the moment.

I laugh at myself—or whoever this gentleman is that I'm becoming. Maybe he's just the guy I used to be before I gave up on my dreams.

This must be what it's like to fall in love. It's basically the same thing as going crazy. But the idea of a future with Meri is so fun that I don't even care.

Everybody on our YouTube channel was right about us. They'll be thrilled to find out that I almost kissed her. Maybe I should film our first kiss just for them.

I roll the idea around in my mind. I bet if I did film it, our views would go through the roof. The clicks. The shares on social media. The press attention.

The director for *Capers* wouldn't be able to ignore it.

No. Meri put on a show for all those other guys. I want what she has with me to be real.

Also, she might be kind of embarrassed about how I didn't kiss her in the Jeep just now. I'll probably have to fast-talk my way into a relationship with her. Whisper sweet nothings in her ear. Perhaps nibble on said ear. And other intimate but honorable stuff I don't want the world to know.

A car engine guns to life outside. Meri.

As much as I wanted to kiss her tonight, I know I can't do what Luke did to her. I can't be the roommate who hints at the possibility of something physical without working toward a future together.

I have to offer the possibility.

Tomorrow I'll apply for the job on *Capers*. With Gemma and Riley offering to put in a good word for me, my chances have to be high.

A slamming door wakes me up, though I'm pretty sure I've barely slept. This is one of the many reasons I've preferred not to set goals over the past decade. Goals keep you awake at night. Or during the day, if that's when you usually sleep.

I roll onto my back and stare at the fan spinning lazily from the vaulted ceiling. It's still pretty dark in here, but if someone downstairs is awake and slamming doors, the dim light must be the result of a cloudy sky, not early morning hours.

Is Meri the one slamming doors? Is she upset about something? Is she trying to wake me?

Now that I'm awake and wondering, I can't possibly go back to sleep. I climb out of bed, pull on a T-shirt that in no way matches my pajama pants, and half-heartedly smooth my hair. I'm almost all the way down the stairs before I consider the fact that if I'm going to romance Meri, I might want to put a little extra work into my appearance. In the same way she's been learning to live life for herself, I'm going to have to learn to care for someone else's wants and needs. It's a weird but good thought.

For example, right now I really want to know what Meri is angry about. I hope it's me. And I hope kissing her is the solution.

Shoot, I should have brushed my teeth before leaving my room. My whole mindset is going to have to change.

Gemma stands in front of the refrigerator, but I don't see Meri anywhere.

I pad onto the hardwood. "Hey, Gemma. Where's Meri?"

Gemma pulls out the half-empty ice cream carton. "She's not up yet."

I rub my eyes then squint at the little blue digital numbers of the microwave clock. It's only ten in the morning. Even if it were ten *at night*, it wouldn't make sense for Gemma to be slamming doors or eating ice cream. "Aren't you lactose intolerant?"

Gemma slams the fridge and tugs open the silverware drawer so hard the utensils jingle. "So?"

I scratch my head. "What's going on?"

"I got fired from *Capers*."

There goes my referral. I'd known this day would come, but why today? Hopefully she didn't leave on bad terms. If she did, then just being roommates with her could cast a shadow over my career. "What happened?"

She scoops ice cream into her mouth and cringes as if she's already got brain freeze. "This is cold."

"It's ice cream." Has she seriously been eating turkey and sweet potatoes for so long that she's forgotten how ice cream is made? And, more importantly, is it going to distract her from explaining the effect of her situation on my future? I grab a coffee pod and slide it into the Keurig to help her out. "Why did you get fired?"

Gemma tries a second bite and nods as if now the temperature makes sense. "I wouldn't sleep with Riley."

Well, this conversation just took a mighty personal turn. "You mean in the script? You didn't agree that your character should sleep with Riley's character?"

"That too."

"Oh man."

She stares off into the distance and chews. The girl really doesn't understand how ice cream works.

I grab a mug from the shelf and hit the button to brew. While I applaud Gemma's moral compass, I can't help wishing the script hadn't called for a sex scene until after I'd been hired. Though, would I really want to get paid to film it?

Can I still justify *Capers* as my dream job? Would that make me a bad friend? A bad Christian? The moment I finally decide to work again toward something, it becomes something that I shouldn't work for. *What now, God?*

I place the full mug in front of Gemma.

She scoops another spoonful of ice cream, pauses, then stirs it into the steaming mug of coffee. Hey, that's not a bad idea. She's basically turning the warm beverage into a peppermint mocha.

She lifts the mug and faces me. "The love scene isn't organic to the story. They tried it back in the second *Superman*. Clark Kent had to give up his powers, which almost destroyed our planet."

"Okay?" So maybe this isn't about sex as much as it is about comic books plots. If Gemma can justify working for such a show, I can too. "Would you have done the love scene if it was appropriate to the story?"

"It's network television, so it couldn't be graphic or anything." She leans against the counter and frowns. "But I don't know. Is that embracing art or selling my soul?"

She just defined my dilemma. And the dilemma of anyone in Hollywood. Well, maybe not Charlie's dilemma, but Charlie's not dealing with Hollywood. He never does. Even when he's in the same hemisphere.

The stairs creak. Meri emerges from the dungeon, wearing sweats, my visor to hold her morning frizz out of her face, and an expression moody enough to tell me I should grab another coffee pod and mug. Her eyes flash my way, daring me to try to charm her so she can attack with all the sarcasm she's probably wishing she'd unleashed last night.

I can't help but grin. Despite my lack of sleep and this new glitch in my plan, there's pleasure bubbling in my chest where the itch used to be. I could get used to waking up to Meri's freckled face.

Her eyes narrow suspiciously. "What are you guys talking about?"

Gemma huffs. "Sex."

Meri stops. Purses her lips in that judgmental way she must have learned from her mom. Pivots toward the stairs.

This is the only time Gemma and I have ever talked about sex, and we're not even really talking about it. We're talking about our careers. "Gemma, explain."

Gemma sets her mug down without taking a sip. "I lost my role on *Capers* because neither I nor my character, Elenore Evergreen, would sleep with Riley. Why is it that men only want sex?"

Meri makes a U-turn around the end of the couch, plops onto a cushion, and tucks her knees into her chest. "Maybe from you. Not from me." She doesn't look at me when she says this, but that some-how makes her remark feel more pointed.

This seems unfair. Would she rather I have made a move on her last night before I'd decided I wanted something more than physical intimacy? I'm pretty sure she has higher standards than that.

I grab a clean spoon and make my own peppermint mocha. I'm the one who deserves coffee for having to deal with the emotions of two women.

Gemma, however, abandons her coffee, grabs the carton of ice cream, and joins Meri on the couch. "Want some?"

Meri eyes me with concern before addressing Gemma. "You're going to make yourself sick."

"I'm already sick."

Meri squishes up her face. "I have a story that will make you feel better. While you were working a summer job, earning extra money, I spent the money I should have been saving on a Jeep. I can't even take the top off today because it's raining."

I shake my head. I told her she'd regret it.

Gemma pauses with her spoon in her mouth, then pulls it out slowly. "That green Jeep outside is yours?"

"Yep." Meri's lips make a popping sound on the *P*. "Number ninety-nine: *Create suspense like Alfred Hitchcock by buying a convertible to go with your headscarf and cat-eye glasses.*"

Gemma twists my way and points her spoon at me. "You let her do that?"

My mouth drops open. I should not have to defend myself here.

Meri lifts a finger to speak for me.

Good girl.

"He let me do it with a Band-Aid on my forehead."

What? My arms spread wide. "Okay, the Band-Aid is on me, but I honestly tried to talk her out of buying a new car."

Meri shrugs. "He did."

I snort and sip my coffee. The sweet melted ice cream overcomes the bitterness of the beans, so it's only Gemma's conversation with Meri that leaves a bad aftertaste. Gemma had once defended me to our newest roommate. Now they're ganging up on me.

At least Gemma's eyes soften after that first glare. Not that she had anything to be glaring about. "Well, what's with the Band-Aid? Was that from your list, as well?"

"Yeah." Meri eyes the second cup of coffee on the counter. "Are you going to drink that, Gemma?"

Gemma drops her spoon into the container and sets it on a coffee table cube. "No. My stomach feels nauseous."

I wonder why.

Meri stands and heads my way. My stomach feels nauseated as well. Have I suddenly become lactose intolerant?

"What are you guys filming today?" Gemma asks.

Meri pads in, glances my way but not in question. More as if she's gauging my mood.

What does she see? Can she read my new indifference to her list? My loss of desire to ever film her trying to attract attention from someone else? The vulnerability of a man who is ready to admit his feelings?

If ever there was a moment *not* to kiss a woman, this is it. Coffee breath. Pajamas. Roommate on the sofa.

How do I get us to the right moment? We've had lots of right moments—I just wasn't in the right place mentally. Now that I am, it feels impossible to recreate those situations. This is why I prefer the whole hang-loose mentality. The trying thing is way too hard.

Meri picks up the coffee Gemma abandoned and takes a sip. "This is really good. What's in it?"

"Ice cream," I answer for Gemma. I want Meri all to myself. In the kitchen with me. Talking to me. Looking at me.

She looks up. Open yet wary. Lonely yet independent. "I like ice cream."

"I know." I know? Gah. Who do I think I am? Han Solo responding to Princess Leia in *The Empire Strikes Back*?

I am so not Han Solo. I'm not even a Luke. My only weapon is a spoon.

"I don't feel up for making a video today," she says.

"Okay."

I don't want to make any more videos either. Not only because I don't want her trying to attract other men, but because my whole goal had been to get noticed by the director of *Capers*. Now that goal is shot.

Or is it?

If I don't get this cameraman position, I'm going to be working for peanuts at a job I hate. I'm not going to be the kind of man Meri deserves. I could kiss her. Actually, I could even propose, but why would she say yes? She's not *that* desperate.

I'd have to start from square one. Look for another position where I might fit the requirements.

Capers is an opportunity right now. It would be a big leap forward. One that I've almost made. I know it's bad that they killed off Gemma's character, but that means it will probably be a while before the plot can get to another potential sex scene. By then, I'd have earned more money and a name for myself. I'd be a viable candidate for better positions. Perhaps even for lead operator.

If I'm going to join this rat race, I have to get started. I'm way behind and can use every opportunity I'm given. I know Gemma can't put in a good word for me anymore, but I could still film my kiss with Meri to get our show trending on YouTube.

I rub a hand over my mouth.

"What?" she asks. "You're not going to try to talk me into doing something crazy for film?"

I study her, but what I see is a "dummy reel" of memories we've made together. What's one last video? Our fans deserve a happily-ever-after. She deserves a happily-ever-after. And this is the only way I see it possibly happening.

I'm sure she'll understand. As long as I don't film us kissing when she's wearing her sweats and my visor. What do I need to do to create that perfect moment?

I shrug. "We don't have to leave the apartment for you to check something off your list." I scroll through The List in my mind. "I could teach you to play poker. Or help you write poems to send someone anonymously. Or advertise for a man to share ownership of your boat."

She nods slowly. Her eyes glance down, then back up, and I'm lost in their depths. "You mentioned at the car dealership that you want a boat."

That's not all I want. I set my coffee down, this tug on my heart so strong that I might as well be a fish she's reeling in from the boat we'll someday share. I'll kiss her for the camera later. Right now—

The trash compactor slams open across from us. Gemma groans and drops her ice cream carton inside. "I should not have done that. As long as I'm miserable, I'm going to watch romance movies and bawl my eyes out about how I'm so alone. Wanna join me, Meri?"

Meri's eyes meet mine, questioning. I'm not able to answer with a kiss, but the tiny hint of a smile at the corner of her lips tells me she doesn't feel as lonely as she used to. "Sure, I'll join you, Gemma. Then Kai will teach us to play poker, so we can someday attract men who want to be with us."

Her someday has just arrived.

CHAPTER TWENTY-SEVEN

Meri

*#72. Your first kiss should last four seconds.
Long enough to make him want more but not long
enough to come across as well practiced.*

We laugh. We cry. We paint our toenails and do each other's hair. I'm pretty sure Gemma puked, but other than that, it's been a great girls' day.

What makes it even better is this hope swelling like a balloon in my soul that ensures something big is about to happen with Kai. It has to. The balloon inside is stretching so thin that either it needs to be deflated or it's going to explode. One might reason that if the balloon explodes, there's no more balloon, and I'm really trying to consider that argument. On the other hand, I don't want to take the time to deflate and wait for someone else to fill me up.

I draw a full house in poker. My laughter makes Kai shake his head, which makes my hope expand even more.

He folds.

I motion to his hand on the coffee table cube across from where I'm sitting on the floor. "You're giving up?" This fits his MO, and it should be as much of a warning sign as the balloon analogy, but it makes me laugh even harder. Because I won.

He tries to frown, but there's a glimmer of admiration in his dark eyes. "You can't giggle in poker."

"Where's the fun in that?"

"Where's the fun in letting everyone know you have a winning hand?"

I continue to hold my cards close to my chest. "Maybe I'm bluffing."

His gaze doesn't waver. "I know you too well to buy that."

"He's right." Gemma stands from her spot on the love seat and picks up the empty pizza box from the other cube. "You showed me your cards while cackling, Meri. You're holding the best hand of the night, and you just wasted it."

"Hey, you'd already folded," I call after her as she carries the pizza box to the trash compactor. "I showed you so you'd laugh with me."

She tosses one of the braids I'd given her over a shoulder and smiles her gorgeous smile. While I've always been a little jealous of her beauty and never thought of her as lonely before, I realized today that it's her beauty that keeps her alone. Maybe that's why she tries so hard to prove herself through her writing. She wants people to see her as more than just another pretty face.

We have something in common. Not the pretty face thing, but the loneliness thing. I never would have imagined.

"I don't think poker is the game for you," she says.

"Yeah," Kai agrees. "You need something where you can make a lot of noise when you're doing well."

Speaking of noise, Gemma gags and covers her mouth. She runs across the room and down the stairs.

I wrinkle my nose in concern. "Poor Gemma."

Kai shakes his head. "I told her not to eat that pizza."

I can relate to her. We all can, can't we? We make choices based on how we will feel immediately rather than down the road. Thus, I defend our roommate. "I'm glad I'm not lactose intolerant. I'd be puking every night."

"Me too." He smiles, and I feel it to my toes. "So what do we do now?"

I twist my lips in thought. "According to number seventy-nine, I'm supposed to use this house party to show that I'm not a bore, but we've already played games and had refreshments. What else is there?" I know most parties look different today, but I'm thinking of The List. "Poker is out. Writing poetry is out too, because I'll need Gemma's help on that one."

I don't bring up the buying a boat thing again.

After the way Kai set his coffee cup down this morning, joking about buying a boat together would basically be begging him to kiss me. Which would lead to begging him to marry me.

"Golf is out," he adds. Thankfully.

"I've struck out, then. Where am I ever going to find a man?" Is that too close to begging? Let's call it flirting—playing at love. He doesn't have to find out I'm really in love with him.

"I know where you can find a man." He stands and reaches down to grab my hand.

My mind whirls. I tell myself he's just going to pull me up. That keeps me from going stiff and numb as I clasp his warm palm. But with the way my heart twitches in my chest, something inside knows it's more.

He tugs me up as if I don't weigh anything. "Bingo," he says.

I'm so close. We're still holding hands. I lift my eyes to read his because I can't decipher his last word. "Bingo?"

"You know. Bingo. The game." One corner of his lips lift. "It's a game you would be good at because you get to be loud when you're winning. You could meet a man playing Bingo."

He's teasing me again. Like last night with the Band-Aid. I want to shove him, but I also want to pull him closer. I laugh instead. "That's a great idea for where to meet a man. When I'm eighty . . ." I turn to leave and take a step. I'll pick up the cards then go check on Gemma. I can't just stand here talking but saying nothing.

Kai doesn't let go of my hand. He uses it to swing me around toward him for more teasing. I'm secretly thrilled. He may not be able to admit his affection, but he can't let me go either. I laugh until I'm pulled right against Kai's chest and his other arm circles behind my back.

Heat floods through my limbs. My chest heaves, holding my breath. Is this real?

If I saw any other woman in a man's arms like this, I would absolutely know what was happening. But I thought I knew last night, then Kai took a Band-Aid off my head.

Maybe tonight I sat on a piece of pizza, and he's going to remove it from where it's plastered to my pants.

I have to know. And I have to find out without making a fool of myself again.

I force myself to breathe. To lift my gaze to his. "What are you doing?"

He lets go of my hand, and I prepare for disappointment. But his eyes are dark without their mischievous glint. They drop to focus on my mouth as the warm pad of his thumb brushes my bottom lip. "This."

The tingles he ignites in my lip spread through the rest of my body. I savor the feeling, afraid he might remember that "this" is not enough for me and be scared away by my desire for marriage.

In this moment, I don't care about marriage. Because if I can't find a husband who creates this kind of longing by just a brush of his thumb, then I don't want a husband.

I want this achingly slow slide of Kai's fingers into my hair and the confident tilt of his head as he lowers his lips toward mine. I want this intense eye contact that offers to pull away if I ask him to but promises to give me so much more if I don't.

I can't wait any longer. I lift my heels and nuzzle his nose. My eyes close, and I breathe in his scent of bamboo and summer rain. Then his mouth is on mine.

Each lazy kiss stretches every moment to its fullest. It's sipped. Satisfying.

I'm never complaining about Kai being lazy again. I need more lazy in my life.

His fingers don't move from my hair or my back as if he's afraid of popping our bubble. But rather than just let my arms dangle all Scarlett O'Hara like, I bring my hands up to his biceps and stop. His arms are solid underneath my touch. The reward of T-Rex syndrome.

Perhaps his biceps are proof that he can be taught. He went to the gym in exchange for Gemma's cooking. Maybe he just needs the right incentive. Maybe I can be the right incentive.

We take our time. Perhaps because we've waited so long for this moment. Perhaps because it's better than we expected. Or perhaps because we don't want to know what will happen next.

This. This is what matters now.

His lips press against mine once more before pulling away. The space between us feels cold and empty. He returns to nibble again. And again. But gradually the pauses between kisses fills with unexpressed words. I won't know what they are until I speak them. I swallow the emotion in my throat to let them escape.

"This wasn't supposed to happen." I catch my breath. I'm not trying to push him away. I'm clarifying what has kept us apart for so long.

He loosens his grip around my waist, but his gaze holds mine. "Maybe it was."

Okay. That's reassuring. He's not apologizing for making a mistake. He's not saying it was good we got this out of our system. But I need more. "Will this happen again?"

He grins his contagious grin. "I hope so."

My chest squeezes tight as if there are more balloons being blown up in there. It's a whole party for my heart. But I can't let this party get out of hand. "I think I better move out."

His grin droops for a second, but then his eyes dip to my lips and he nods. "That's probably a good idea."

I step backward. My hands slide down his arms. His hand slips from my waist. I miss him already.

I'm going to miss seeing him every night after work. Every weekend. I'll still see him at church. I can probably still see him mornings at the gym, though I might have to pay for my membership now. "I'll go pack."

He reaches out and grasps air because I'm already retreating toward the stairs. "Right now?"

It would be too easy to step back into his arms. I've waited thirty-one years for this. Would it be so wrong to spend the whole night making out and cuddling? And falling asleep together on the sofa? And waking up and kissing some more. And . . .

Yeah, I better set some boundaries before it's too late. Besides being mentioned in the Bible, I think it's also on The List. I remind him. "Number fifty-one: *Prudence is a virtue.*"

He follows me to the top of the stairs. "In that case, I'll wait up here."

As much as I'd rather him follow me down, his presence would be a distraction from what I have to do. I call Roxy and make sure she's okay with my barging in late at night like this.

She's fine with it as long as I'm quiet, so I don't wake Angel. There won't be a guest bed, and my real bed is in Anne's garage, so I'll be on Roxy's couch. It's not as if I've never done that before.

The last time I slept on a couch was when Kai covered me up. It seems like so long ago. I've spent almost every spare minute with him since then, but it doesn't feel like enough. How will things change when we live miles apart? Will he still take a bus to see me? We won't be making the YouTube channel together anymore, so he might not have the motivation. I just don't know.

I finish filling my suitcases with everything I have here, but I'm not ready to go upstairs yet. I'm not ready to say goodbye when I don't know that it's not goodbye forever. Those were some good kisses, but they only make us kissing friends. Nothing more. Why would he continue to pursue me when he doesn't want to get married? Is this what my brother was trying to warn me about?

I walk across the hall and knock on Gemma's door—that used to be Kai's before I moved in. It's slightly open and there's dim golden light coming from a lamp. It's so quiet, she may have gone to sleep.

She moans. "Come in."

I find her curled on her side in Kai's old bed, hugging a stuffed unicorn. I assume the unicorn is hers, not also a remnant from Kai's room.

"Why did I eat that pizza?" she asks.

I sit at the foot of the bed and rub her bare calf. Of course, it's hair free and as soft as Angel's cheeks. She's gorgeous *and* she has perfect skin. She's pretty blessed that way, though I'm not sure I'd trade my tolerance of lactose and gluten for her looks. "You ate pizza for the same reason I just kissed Kai."

She closes her eyes as if my deep thoughts give her a headache. "Because it's not fair that everyone else gets to enjoy cheese when you can't?"

"He *can* be pretty cheesy."

Her chuckle morphs into a groan. "I know what you're saying," she mumbles after a moment. "You want something you know isn't good for you."

I wish she hadn't understood so well and explained so clearly. I'd been complicating matters by describing what I saw through rose-colored glasses. "Yeah. So, I'm going to move out."

"Oh . . ." She reaches for my hand. "When?"

"Right now."

She squeezes. "Why right now? We just had our first girly day."

"I know. I'm sorry. I wish we'd had more girly days. You're a beautiful person, and I don't only mean your appearance. But now that I've kissed Kai, I don't think—"

"Wait." She peeks with one eye open. "You mean you kissed Kai for the first time tonight?"

I roll my eyes around trying to figure out what she'd thought I'd meant when I said I kissed Kai. I'd compared it to her eating pizza, so maybe because she'd eaten pizza before, she thought I'd meant that I'd kissed Kai before as well. "First time."

"Huh." She closes her eyes again. "Since a lot of the things on your list were done for him, I figured there was more going on between you two."

What did she mean the things on my list were done *for* him? I'd never called him Dreamboat, and he'd certainly never called me Angel Face, as we were supposed to if going steady. "You mean because Luke helped me lasso Kai?"

"That and other stuff." She curls her knees in tighter. "This morning you wore the visor he bought you."

#54. Make a show of wearing any jewelry or accessory he gives you. "He didn't actually buy that for me."

She opens her eyes only wide enough to scowl like a mother who knows you're trying to hide the truth. "And you guys have a song."

What is she talking about? I know it's on The List. *#63. The two of you should claim a song as your own so whenever he hears it, he thinks of you.* But Kai and I have very different taste in music, so Gemma must be hallucinating from eating cheese. If that's possible. "We don't—"

"'Count on Me' by Bruno Mars. I saw the video of you guys singing it on the train, and I've heard you both play it since."

And I'd thought Gemma was disconnected from reality. Maybe she's only attuned to romance, since she writes it. But this isn't a romance. It's a friendship. As the song says. "If that's all you've got—"

"You've double dated with him, his mom gave you an apple pie recipe, and I've even heard you point out to him that married men live longer than single men."

Ooh . . . I don't even know if that statistic is accurate anymore, but it *is* on The List. #75.

"You've got me." I was never consciously trying to land Kai, but I guess this list isn't as crazy as I thought. Women do a lot of these things without even realizing it. Or I did, anyway.

Am I now subconsciously trying to do #17? *Treat a bad guy like the hero you want him to be.*

I'd ridiculed that when I first read it. It's unhealthy, for sure. But even as I've seen the wreck that Roxy's life has turned into because she ignored the warning signs, I'm headed down the same track.

Gemma sighs and smiles sleepily. I'm thinking she probably took some pain killer that is making her drowsy because this realization is nothing to smile about. "You two are good friends, sweetie. Just give the relationship time. What feels like lactose intolerance could very well be gastroenteritis . . ." Her voice trails off, ending the grossest analogy of all time.

But as I would with a good antacid, I let it sink in. Maybe my kissing Kai isn't the same as Gemma's eating cheese. Maybe his laziness is not a disease, just a virus. And he only needs time to heal.

But how much time? What if I wait, and he doesn't make the choices to grow?

Will I keep enjoying cheese?

CHAPTER TWENTY-EIGHT

Kai

#69. For a proper courtship, have a chaperone.

Meri is taking forever in the basement. With as good as our first kiss was, I'd think she'd simply stuff everything in her suitcase so she could rush back up here for more.

Was it really as good as I remember it, or had the anticipation that had been building over the weeks heightened my experience? Like a starving man gobbling down the first thing set in front of him?

I check the stairs for her again before grabbing my camera and connecting it to my computer to download footage. Meri had known I was filming our poker game, so she won't be shocked to realize our first kiss has been recorded. Though she might be surprised to know I'd tugged her to the exact spot I needed her to stand for the shot to be centered. And I'd purposely reined in my emotions, so it didn't look as if I was mauling her in the YouTube video. But neither of those things made a difference in our connection.

Oh man, that connection. It's the reason wars have been fought over women. It's the reason I'm willing to fight for her now. Okay, I'm not exactly fighting, but, you know, I'm willing to apply for another job.

I tap the mouse to play the moment when our lips met. I watch her smile up at me on the screen. I watch her grin fade. I watch her still as I pull her toward me and graze her lip with my thumb. The pad of my thumb still tickles from that touch.

My chest aches all over again as she asks what I'm doing, and I give her a chance to pull away. She doesn't because she's mine. Meant for me. And this knowledge ignites the itch inside as much as watching myself kiss her. I may be biased, but I can't help believing that people all over the world will watch this kiss because it's everything they've ever wanted.

The soft thud of a suitcase bumping against the stairs jolts me to action. I slap my computer closed and stand to help Meri with her luggage.

Her eyes meet mine, and I'm both a nervous kindergartner and a cocky frat boy. I close the space between us and meet her at the top of the stairs, but there's just enough hesitation in her last step that I take the handle of her luggage instead of her hand.

"Thanks." She releases her grip and waits for me to move so we can head outside.

It's Saturday. I'll see her again tomorrow at church, but that seems a long time from now. Will she join me in the audiovisual booth again? Will I be able to stay on top of changing the worship slides? Will I get to join her and her family for lunch?

These questions assault me as I lead the way toward the front door that I'd once refused to answer when she knocked. I hold it open, being the gentleman she wants and step aside to let her pass first into the damp night.

Her eyes flash with pleasure, erasing all gentlemanly thoughts.

She clicks a button on her key fob, and I use my long strides to beat her to the rear gate of her Jeep. The sooner I can get rid of this suitcase, the more time I'll have to say goodbye.

Suitcase in. Gate slammed.

She flicks her gaze my way, then steps forward as if she's going to slide right past me without the reminder of why she's leaving in the first place.

I block her with a hand to the chilly, raindrop-covered window, and I don't pause this time before crushing my mouth to hers.

She responds with a small whimper before her fingers run through my hair on their way to anchoring around my neck and pulling me closer.

I hug her to me, sliding my hands up and down her spine before circling her waist. How did I ever think I could live the rest of my life without her?

Her hands slip down to my chest and firmly press me away. #51. *Prudence is a virtue.*

I grin and nip her lips a couple of more times before letting her slow me down.

Her hands rise and fall with my chest as I take deep breaths.

"Sorry," I say, but her smile draws me in again. I cup her freckled face in my palms and brush her lips with mine. "Oops. I didn't mean to . . ." I kiss her a little longer. "I just can't . . ."

Meri melts and her arms slide back up around my neck, but she pulls away to create enough distance that she can study my eyes. Hers are as misty and as dreamy as the fog on our trip to the Oregon Coast. "No need to apologize," she says. "I was hoping you'd kiss me."

It's good to know I'm not the only one who's been thinking about this. "We're not in the fifties anymore. You don't have to wait for me." In fact, I like the idea of getting ambushed by her. I'm a little taller, so she'd have to grab my shark tooth necklace to pull me down, or jump into my arms, or crawl across the couch into my lap.

She bites her lip and studies me. "I'm not sure how this works. Can I just kiss you whenever I want?"

Hasn't she ever been in a serious relationship? Maybe it just feels different with me. I certainly feel different with her. I arch my eyebrows in suggestion. "Try it."

She studies me for a moment, and my pulse flutters in anticipation. As if drawn by the throb against my throat, she leans in until her lips graze my neck.

Whereas she'd once lassoed me, she's now branded me, and my heartbeat reacts like a bucking bronco.

A gentleman always chooses what he wants most over what he wants in the moment.

Gulp . . . This moment is what I want most.

My lips move toward her earlobe to nibble and whisper, "I don't want you to go."

She lifts her head but clings to me, breath warm and ragged. Is she considering staying?

My words weren't supposed to be an invitation. More of an admission. But if she wants to stay . . .

Her hands slide to my chest once again. "That's why I have to go."

"Right." She's right.

I know she's right.

I'm going to let her go. I will. Eventually. We're not hurting anything right now.

She's still in my arms, but the openness in her eyes starts to close as if she's distancing herself. "It's not as if I'm going to marry you and move into my brother's master suite together."

"Ouch." There's a nice little reminder that I don't have much to offer, and I'm not what she's been looking for. I didn't want to hurt her, but apparently she's okay with hurting me.

She shrugs, allowing her hands to slide down my arms. "You're a really, really good kisser, but how's this going to work?"

I'm still holding her, but she's slipping away. I let my hands drop from her waist so I can use one to lift her chin and force her to face my sincerity. "Hey. I know what you want. I wouldn't let myself kiss you until I was willing to consider the prospect of . . . a future."

Her eyes narrow to study me through slits.

Does she not believe I'm serious? Does she not believe I'm capable of growing into the largeness of marriage? Does she not believe I can get a better paying job? Because I can. I will. Tonight.

"My dream of . . ." Her voice quavers. "My dream of marriage and family doesn't scare you away?"

Truth be told, I'm terrified. I like doing my own thing. I like not being burdened with a mortgage or dealing with the expectations of others. But I don't want to lose her. "I have a plan."

Her eyes twinkle amber, and she sighs with relief. "A plan, huh?"

My heart beats again. "Yes. It starts with letting you go tonight." I lift her chin higher so I can kiss her goodbye. I resist the urge to slide my fingers into her hair because we both know what happens then. Except even with just holding her chin, we keep kissing.

At least this time it's with promise. She's not kissing me out of fear it will be our last. And I've pretty much committed to moving forward in a relationship even though we haven't even gone on a real date.

I'm going to have to change that soon. Like tomorrow. And the next day. And every day after that.

She pulls away slightly, and by slightly, I mean her lips are almost brushing mine when she says, "Your plan isn't working very well."

I hover. "It's because I'm Hawaiian. In Hawaii, we say 'Aloha,' which means both hello and goodbye. Goodbye kisses confuse me."

She grins. I know this by the crinkles at the corners of her eyes, since she's still too close for me to see her mouth. "Goodbye, Kai."

"Aloha." I lift my hands and step back. She stares at me in wonder, and I think of a list from the Bible that better sums up our relationship than her list from *Sophia Magazine*. Proverbs 30:18 and 19. "There are three things are too amazing for me, four that I do not understand . . ." Number four is "the way of a man with a young woman." "You better hurry and leave before I get confused again."

She does a little bounce, grins, and spins to open the door of her Jeep. "I'll see you tomorrow at church."

I can't wait. But I have a lot to do before then. Mainly, blow up the internet with the greatest love story that's ever been told.

CHAPTER TWENTY-NINE

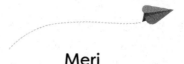

Meri

#91. Rent an apartment in a rich area of town.
You'll meet men of greater means.

I'm awake when the phone rings at four in the morning. And not only because there have been jets roaring overhead all night long. I barely even noticed the jets. I've been too busy smiling at the popcorn ceiling above Roxy's couch.

Roxy had been skeptical when I showed up last night. "Kai said he has plans for your future?" She dug through the linen closet only to come up with an old Care Bears quilt. "What does that mean?"

I took the quilt and spun it around me like a cape, though I was imagining it to be the mermaid-style wedding gown with a V-neck and three-quarter lace sleeves that I'd tried to get Anne to buy for her big day. "Maybe he's going to propose."

"You don't want him to propose too soon," said Roxy.

I paused mid spin. "Why not?" That's pretty much exactly what I'd wanted since I was a five-year-old flower girl.

Roxy returned to the closet for a penguin Pillow Pet. "Because anybody can make a grand gesture, claiming to have changed, but you want to see his day-to-day choices. You want to know his growth will last."

I dropped onto the couch with a sneaking suspicion that her husband had pulled such a bait and switch on her. "Is that how Graham got you?"

She pursed her lips and nodded. "We'd broken up over all the little things, then he surprised me with a steamboat cruise and brought me flowers, and as the sun set on the Columbia Gorge, he promised to treat me like a princess forever, and I felt like I deserved that."

I remembered because I'd felt that she deserved it too. And I'd wanted to believe I deserved it as well. Since she was the first of our college friends to experience such a swoonworthy proposal, the rest of us had all been a little jealous. I'd even thought it was romantic that they'd eloped to Vegas so they could consummate their marriage sooner, but now I can see how there are other reasons why he might have rushed her. He knew the sooner he could get that ring on her finger, the sooner he could sponge off her.

I grimaced at the new perspective on this memory. #89 from The List plays through my mind. *"Earn the proposal. Get him to see that matrimony is key to his personal fulfillment."*

"Is it though?" she asked rhetorically. "It hasn't personally fulfilled me, but I hope it works out for you." She gave me a sad hug before heading down the tiny hall toward her room.

I prayed for Roxy then. It had to hurt for her to watch a friend fall in love when her own marriage was falling apart. Kind of like it hurt me to meet Mom's boyfriend when I was desperate and dateless.

But I wasn't worried about Kai and me anymore. Yeah, there had been that moment where I thought he was going to pressure me for sex, and I'd been tempted to give in because I was afraid it would be the extent of our relationship. I love Kai, and God forgives, right?

It sounded so good and felt so good that I could almost justify it. But since God is love, anything I do against His direction isn't loving.

This was even better than spending the night with Kai. I mean, he didn't say that he loves me yet, but he's making plans for our future.

Gemma had been right about how he just needed time to heal from the wounds of his past. He wasn't always a lazy person. He'd only given up on his dreams, and now he's dreaming again. For me.

This was my dream come true. So rather than fall asleep and dream, I stayed awake, making plans of my own.

I was deciding between gray or navy kitchen cabinets when my phone rang. Charlie. It had been a while since I'd heard from him. Maybe he'd seen a video of the billboard Kai posted and wanted to know if Nicole had been involved in its purchase.

I swipe my thumb across the screen and sink back into the furry pillow. "Hey, Charlie."

"I warned you not to get into a relationship with Kai."

Uh . . . How does he know? Had Kai called him? Is Kai asking my brother for my hand in marriage since he can't ask my dad? Obviously, he didn't explain the full extent of his affection. Or his plan. "Good morning to you too."

"Meri, are you okay? Do you need me to come home and kick Kai out?"

"What? No." I frown at the ceiling. What is Charlie so upset about? Maybe Mom had really ingrained the whole appearance-of-evil thing, and he was just being protective. "I'm staying at Roxy's. I moved out after Kai kissed me. But how do you even know about . . . ? That we . . . ?"

Gemma? She's the only other person I've told. But she writes drama, she doesn't create it.

"I saw the kiss. Kai posted it on the YouTube channel."

The words ring in my ears, but they don't compute. There has to be some other way Charlie found out about the kiss.

Because why would Kai do that?

I suck in a breath as all the puzzle pieces fall into place. This isn't the image I wanted to see.

I close my eyes but can't keep from remembering. Kai filmed us playing poker, so the camera was still rolling when he kissed me inside the house. Now that I think about it, I realize he'd pulled me back in front of the camera when he kissed me. He'd kept *that* kiss soft and sweet. What a show.

Anger simmers inside, infusing itself into every other emotion. Betrayal. Pain. Fear. Love. I keep it all under control, as I do my tone when I ask, "How many views are there on the video?"

"Over a hundred thousand already."

The balloon in my chest deflates. While I'd wanted marriage, this had been what Kai wanted the whole time.

Was posting our video the plan he'd been talking about last night?

While I'd been wrestling with the temptation to give up my dreams and even my morals for him, he'd been plotting to put them on display for the world to see. It fits what I know about him. I'd just wanted to believe he was better than this.

Maybe he's fallen for me, maybe he hasn't. But, either way, he's used my dreams to pursue his own.

"You can report the video and get YouTube to take it down," Charlie consoles in his factual way.

I roll onto my side, remembering the way Kai closed his computer as I was coming up the stairs last night. Had he already been working on editing while I was packing to move out? I'd been so worried that would be the end for us, but I'd never thought I'd be the one to end it.

I'm in love with a man who chose a television show over me. My heart stings with unshed tears. This is worse than having nobody to love.

"I'm going to go watch the video," I say. "Thanks for calling, Charlie. And thanks for trying to warn me."

"Meri . . ." His pause says he hurts for me, and I take comfort in the fact that I'm loved even if it's not from the man I want to love me.

I could use one of Charlie's boa constrictor hugs right about now. "Yeah?"

"In the video . . . you look as if you've really fallen for Kai."

I fiddle with a strand of yarn on the quilt, wrapping it around my ring finger. "I have."

"He looks as if he might have fallen for you too."

I have to see this video. "Then why would he do this?" He should have talked to me before he ever posted the video.

The first day he kissed me will also be the last. Aloha.

I hang up, then roll to a seated position so I can concentrate on opening up my YouTube app more quickly. My fingers tremble. I have to type *Meri Me* three times before I spell my own name correctly.

An icon of me in Kai's arms appears on the screen. My heart lodges directly in my throat and my finger hangs over the *play* button. This was a special moment. An intimate moment. I study what I can see of Kai's expression, comparing it to how I remember him.

His gaze seems to be only on me, but how much of that was an act? He'd been so slow and deliberate. While I thought he'd been savoring our first kiss, he'd really been prolonging the performance for our audience. I don't even want to think about who all is in the audience. My mom? Dr. Snyder? Luke? Okay, Luke could use the kissing lessons, but Kai isn't any better a person.

I tap *play* before I chicken out.

The video opens with Kai wiping a smile off his face before he talks to the camera. "You guys told me to kiss Meri, and that was some really good advice."

After only one look at him, the ache in my chest melts.

I sit up straighter to stiffen my resolve and hold onto my anger. Without it, my heart has no protection.

The scene flashes to me giggling with my poker hand. I've watched myself do a lot of crazy things on these videos, but this one is surreal.

My stomach heats as the images get closer to what I know is coming.

Back to Kai's confession. He scratches his head and shrugs. "I've wanted to kiss her for a while."

No. He doesn't get to break down my defenses like that. I'm angry, and I have a right to be.

Little Meri is on the screen again. "Where am I ever going to find a man?"

I cover my mouth as I watch. Did I really ask that?

Cut to another close-up of Kai. He's doing his huge smile that makes his eyes disappear, and I love him so much.

"I didn't think I was interested in the kind of commitment Meri was looking for," says the Kai on-screen.

My pulse threatens to drown out his words. I really want to believe him. But my brother saw this, and he was still concerned. Just as Roxy should have been at her marriage proposal.

"Then this happened . . ." says Kai.

The image of me in Kai's arms. Little Meri laughs at first, but she soon stills. "What are you doing?" she asks.

He lifts a hand to her lips, and I feel it all over again.

"This," says little Kai.

Tears drip down onto my phone screen as I watch Kai cover Meri's mouth with his. That kiss had been perfect. Before it became propaganda.

"This wasn't supposed to happen," Meri says.

"Maybe it was," says Kai.

I narrow my eyes. Is he talking about a kiss or instant stardom?

"Is this going to happen again?"

"I hope so."

This. *This.*

Should I have expected *this*? Is *this* what I get for agreeing to do a "reality" show? Does the entire country now have the right to invade my privacy? Not to mention Ecuador and the rest of the world, which makes it an international invasion.

Angel runs into the dim room wearing only a diaper. It's still close to four in the morning, but I guess toddlers live on Ecuadoran time.

She waddles to me and slaps my leg as if she wants up. I don't have the energy to lift her. I force a smile and take her hand to wiggle her tiny little fingers.

Roxy follows at a much slower pace. She trudges through the living room to wash her hands in the oddly modern kitchen sink.

When she returns, she looks from Angel to me. Her shoulders slouch and her head tilts in compassion at whatever it is she sees on my face. It could probably be a mirror to how she's been feeling lately.

She lowers next to me and places a hand on my leg. "What's wrong?"

I lift the phone and push the button for replay.

Her tears mingle with mine on the screen, blurring the image before it ends.

"Chemistry isn't everything," she says.

I wish she was wrong. "I like him," I say in my defense. Can that be enough?

"I do too. He's very likable." She also likes Graham. I need more.

I fiddle with the yarn on the quilt and come up empty-handed. "He didn't do this because he cares about me. He did this as a shortcut. Because he's lazy."

Why couldn't he just apply for the job like a healthy human being? Why couldn't he prove he was capable of growing into the largeness of marriage?

Roxy scoops Angel into her arms and stands. "You should talk to him."

I don't want to talk to him. I want to type a comment on the YouTube page in all capital letters, asking WHAT IS *THIS*? But that would probably be opposite of proving that *I'm* capable of growing into the largeness of marriage.

Maybe part of growing into the largeness of marriage is letting go of the fear that makes me want to choose bad love over no love at all.

CHAPTER THIRTY

Kai

#86. Parental approval is of utmost importance.

I'm a little worried when Meri doesn't respond to my good morning text, but since she's not driving me to church today, she doesn't have to get up as early. She might still be in bed. Especially if she had as much trouble falling asleep as I did.

Of course, I was up until one in the morning editing the latest episode of *Meri Me* and reliving all those kisses, so I probably had more trouble than she did. I should be tired right now, but I'm too jazzed by all the YouTube comments.

The reaction of viewers was everything I'd hoped it would be, and we're trending now, which will make views go even higher. I also pressed send on the job application, so if the director of *Capers* doesn't hear of me through industry buzz, he'll find my name in his inbox, hopefully Google me, and see the success I've had.

Meri Me has definitely been a success. For both Meri and me. I can't wait to show her the video and relive our first kiss together. The kiss heard 'round the world.

I'm checking the stats of all our other *Meri Me* episodes when the worship pastor strums his guitar. I look up, startled. I didn't realize it was this late because I'd expected Meri to join me in the booth long before the service started. Maybe she's as afraid of being distracted by me as I am by her.

I click to the right slide on the computer, then lean over the balcony to find her. My pulse trips with excitement at the idea of just getting a glimpse.

I find her mom right away. She's hard to miss in today's yellow blazer. Douglas sits on her right side, though the spot on her left is empty.

Maybe Meri wanted to sit with Gemma and make sure her old roommate is feeling better. Gemma is also easy to spot with her long, icy-blonde hair. Unfortunately, not a single parishioner within ten feet of her is female.

I double-check the slides and realize I'm two behind. *Sorry, Lord.* I click to correct my mistake and refocus.

But where's Meri? Is she sick? Is she going to Roxy's church with her today? No, she would have texted to tell me. The last thing she'd said to me was that she'd see me at church.

The worship band slows for the bridge, and I scramble to flip the slide again. I don't feel like worshipping. I feel like cussing.

The only reason I can possibly think for why Meri isn't here and hasn't texted is that she saw the YouTube video and thinks I only kissed her for show. My heart sinks with the weight of misunderstanding. I'd love to find her and clear it up, but I'm currently attached to my seat by the chain of responsibility.

This is why I don't like being responsible. It keeps me from doing what I want to do. *No offense, God.*

I continue to click away at the stupid slides. Finally, the sermon starts. If we had a guest speaker, I could leave, but Pastor Mick always prepares fill-in-the-blank notes for me to flash on the screen. If there was anybody else up on the balcony, I'd show them how to do this, and tell them I need to take off for an emergency, but I'm all alone. I consider turning off the projector and shrugging at Mick as if I don't know what's wrong with it.

Then he says this: "'So whoever knows the right thing to do and fails to do it, for him it is sin.' James four, verse seventeen."

The hair on the back of my neck stands on end. There's the lightning I expected to be struck with when Meri was up here last time. Oh, how it burns.

I change slides, and the click of my mouse sounds like the boom of thunder that follows lightning. On the screen, in black and white, are the pastor's words I've somehow avoided up until this point in my life.

There are a lot of right things I don't do. The sins scroll through my mind like Meri's list. I've always been able to ignore them because the Bible doesn't literally say things like: "Thou shall not pretend the church projector broke so you can leave service early." But that doesn't make it right.

I've read the Ten Commandments. I'm good at the *thou shalt not*s. Which, I figured, gave me permission to avoid taking responsibility for all the *should*s.

I *should* have opened the door when Meri rang the doorbell.

I *should* have avoided peeking before covering her with the blanket.

I *should* have helped clean the kitchen once in a while.

I *should* tithe. I planned to—I just put it off for so long I'm not sure how much to give.

I *should* read my Bible or at least pray every day.

I *should* have kissed Meri as if I wanted to love her for a lifetime, not only as though I wanted to make love to her.

The feeling that I'm not good enough for Meri is not a new thing. That's probably why the whole idea of being a gentleman pricked me with guilt.

But this is more than guilt. This is conviction.

What I'm supposed to want most in life is to please God. I'm supposed to choose His ways over everything I desire in the moment.

His way is to lay my life down for others. I know this because Jesus demonstrated the act of love by dying on the cross.

Though I thought I was in love with Meri, I have not been treating her with love.

I don't rush out as soon as the service ends because I don't want to run into Mrs. Newberg downstairs. What if she saw me kiss Meri? She'd been against that from the beginning, and I don't blame her.

I should delete the final episode of *Meri Me*. Meri's heart is more important than the entertainment of strangers. Or the advancement of a career.

In case Meri has commented on the video as a means of communication, I scroll through the comments first. It's a mix of excited fans and disappointed men who'd apparently emailed Meri without getting responses. Many of them confirm in great detail how I'm not good enough for her. I won't mind deleting those statements before Meri reads them. If she hasn't already.

My phone rings.

I jump. Without even waiting to see who's calling, I swipe and answer. "Meri?"

"Uh . . . no. This is Zach Price, the director for *Capers*."

God has a funny sense of humor. I'm not laughing though. I'm disappointed. "Hello, Mr. Price."

"I take it you're waiting to hear from Meri of *Meri Me?*"

Yeah, I'm waiting. That's what I do. I sit around and wait for life to happen. And that's not right. It's a sin. "Not anymore. I'm going to be the spiritual leader she deserves as a husband."

"Well . . . okay then. Good for you." Small pause as if he's reconsidering his next words. "I'm calling because I'd like to interview you for the cameraman position tomorrow morning at nine. Does that work?"

I press my lips together in disbelief. I've wanted this job all summer. Many people would call this success, but is it the right thing? It may require compromising my beliefs, though it could also create opportunities for me to share those beliefs with others. How will I know what's right unless I ask God? "Sir, I'm going to have to pray about it and get back with you."

"You didn't do that before you applied?" His tone is mocking, and I get the impression he doesn't like to consider any authority higher than his own.

But that's between him and God. The same way my life is between me and God. "I should have, sir. I apologize."

"Well . . ." He huffs as if he doesn't know how to respond. "If I don't hear back from you before nine o'clock tonight, I'll take it that your God told you *no*."

I blink in surprise that I'm having this conversation and that I'm okay with it. "That's fair."

My phone buzzes.

I pull it away from my face to see Meri's name light up. My heart thrums in my chest. "Meri's on the other line. I've got to go."

I click to disconnect with him and answer Meri's call. "Meri, I'm so sorry. I'm taking the video down now."

The other end is silent long enough to make me wonder if I didn't actually disconnect, and I'm still talking to the director. Hearing me say I'd take down a trending video would probably make him even more wary of working with me.

"Really?" asks a sweet voice. It's her.

I sink into my chair. "Yes. I told myself I was doing it for you, but if that was true, I would have talked to you about it before posting."

"If you take it down, it could keep you from getting the job you want."

"The director already contacted me. I just got off the phone with him."

Another pause. What? Did I expect her to be thrilled that my scheme worked? That I'm being rewarded for my insensitivity?

"So that's why you're okay with taking it down now?" she asks.

Oh shoot. She thinks I'm only offering because I got my way. "Not at all. I was taking it down when he called me. I was going to take it down for you."

"I don't understand."

I don't understand anymore either. What had I been thinking? "I posted the video because I knew you wanted a stable man, and I didn't think I could be that man without a better job. Basically, I thought I was catching two birds with one stone. Being resourceful. A good steward, if you will. But when you didn't come to church today, I realized I was wrong."

More silence. Maybe she'd be good at the game of poker after all. "I feel used."

Her words trump mine, like a royal flush. "I made a mistake. Can we please meet to talk about this in person? I just want to see your face."

Her deep breath echoes over the phone. "I want to see you too, but I'm going to take this day for myself. When I'm with you, it's too easy to get swept away by emotion."

My stomach clenches. I'd rather she get swept away than drift away. She's with Roxy, who could very well convince her that being single is better than marrying a man who isn't really there for her.

I want to be there for her more than anything. That has to be more important than what I want in this moment.

CHAPTER THIRTY-ONE

Meri

#59. Saying "I love you" is a relationship milestone.
Let him be the first to take that step.

For some reason, Kai wants to talk at a Portland Pickles game. I'm supposed to meet him at the stadium, since it's not as if he can pick me up on the way. Unlike the night I bought my Jeep, I find this annoying fact endearing now.

I think it's cute that he walks everywhere. I think it's cute he carries his camera equipment in a backpack and stays up all hours of the night like a perpetual college student. I think it's cute that he's always watching life around him as if it's a sitcom, designed to amuse. I love it, and it works for the life he's chosen to live.

The thing is that it won't work for a future together. I'd be the breadwinner as well as the housekeeper, chef, nanny, and chauffeur. All those things I love about him, I'd start to resent. And as much as I want to marry him, I don't want to be a resentful wife.

This doesn't have to mean it's over. It means he needs time to choose which life he really wants to live for himself. He can't only change for me so we can kiss and stuff. That would make him a resentful husband.

He sounded so desperate on the phone. It's as if we've traded places. I'm the one hanging loose for a change. Though, seeing the bleachers where we'd once filmed brings back a rush of memories, a tightness in my chest, and the prickle of tears behind my eyelids. If I'd known then what I know now, what would I have done differently?

"Hey." Kai's deep voice turns me his direction. He's gotten a hair-cut, and it's styled in a way that tells me Gemma was involved. He's also wearing a white button-up shirt. It's not tucked in and the sleeves are rolled, of course, but this is the most dressed up I've ever seen him.

"Hey." My breath gets trapped in my lungs, not only because he looks like the kind of guy I've always been attracted to, but because I know he's putting in the effort for me. "You look nice."

His teeth flash bright against his dark skin, and his eyes search mine. "I tried."

These two words intoxicate my soul, and my earlier resolve melts away. It would be so easy to step into his arms and pretend every-thing's all right.

Instead, I hold up the green foam hand I bought. It matches the ball cap on my head. "I tried too." Though I obviously erred on the side of dressing for the occasion rather than dressing for him. Not sure how this compares to having my clothes pressed and mended per The List.

He smiles at my getup. "You've always looked good in green."

I shake my head but can't help grinning. "Are you telling me that you even liked the bridesmaid dress you compared to a napkin?"

He steps close enough that I can smell his clean yet exotic scent. It's even better than the meaty aroma from the nearby hot dog stand. "I *really* liked that dress."

My heart shimmies in my chest, and I look up to meet his gaze. I lift the foam hand between us to prevent any more connection than that. "Do you like it as much as you like my foam finger?"

"It's a toss-up," Kai jokes, but his eyes don't shine with their usual humor. They penetrate mine, looking for all the things I'm not saying.

Why am I not saying them? I came here to say them.

I know why. Because I'd rather be kissing him. Because I like his compliments. Because I don't want to hurt him.

I should just go enjoy the game. We can cheer for the Pickles, eat peanuts, laugh at silly things that nobody else in the world finds funny, and maybe Kai will put his arm around me as if we're a real couple. Then, after I walk him to the MAX and he climbs on his train, when the doors are about to close, I'll yell out the thing about not dating until he's ready.

"Ready?" He tips his head toward the front side of the bleachers where we can find our seats.

"Yes." I turn so that we're side by side, and part of me is really wishing my hand closest to his was not the one wearing a foam finger. We've never held hands before.

He's given me a piggyback ride, I've sat on his shoulders, and we've made out like teenagers, but we've never laced our fingers together. It feels like a loss.

He checks his ticket and motions to the bleachers on our left.

I climb the steps in front of him, and he puts his hand on the small of my back as if for support, though we both know that's not why he had his hands there the last time. The skin beneath his touch buzzes to life. I should use the foam finger to swat his hand away before I'm stung.

I continue wavering like this through the starting lineup, the national anthem, and the first inning. It's the whole willing-spirit/weak-flesh thing. I'm sure I send as many mixed messages as a blinking red light. But as usual, Kai is not making the first move to break the ice. Apparently, he only does that in front of a camera when it will get him national acclaim.

This confirms my choice, but it also makes me want to punch him for letting me down again. How long can this go on? It's stupid.

I look at my watch. Baseball games are not known for being short. "You might have to leave before the game is over to get to work."

"I . . . uh . . ." He rubs his jaw, then hesitantly meets my gaze. "I'm going to be working days starting this week."

The noise around me fades away. While Kai is one step closer to becoming the man of my dreams, he took advantage of my dream to get here.

I plaster a smile to my face. "You got the job." My voice comes out high and squeaky. "Why didn't you tell me?"

He shakes his head. "I didn't take the cameraman position, because it would require sacrificing my morals. I'm going to be working in promotions at the news department until I find a better job to apply for."

Frustration surges through me like white water on the Deschutes. I'm tumbled by the current until I don't even know which way is up. Am I angry that he's found another excuse? Am I hurt that he exploited me for nothing? Am I sad that I wasn't included on this decision? "What?" I ask between gritted teeth.

He holds a hand out as if this news can be shrugged off. "The job isn't what matters anymore."

"It did Saturday night." My tone doesn't squeak anymore. I don't like it. I'm supposed to be the mature one here.

He twists on the metal bleacher to face me. "Meri, if I could go back and do that all again, I would. I'm in love with you."

My emotions simmer. My body stills. Everything from my skin to my breath to my pulse. This is the moment I've waited for all my life. It sounds so wonderful, and at the beginning of the summer it would have been enough.

He continues. "I know I'm not what you dreamed of. But you make me want to be the kind of man you deserve. I didn't take the job, because I want to do the right thing. At work. At church. With you."

I want to believe, but it sounds too good to be true.

He grabs my hand and twists me toward him. His eyes aren't lazy or laughing, like usual, or even lustful. They are daring and driven. As if he's ready for the challenge that is me.

But how do I know it will last?

I don't. Which is what makes this so hard.

I take a deep breath. "I'm in love with you too, Kai."

His lips part. He sucks in a deep breath. "I was afraid I'd never hear you say that. I was afraid I'd messed up too badly."

I smile sadly and look down. I wish I could say more things that he wants to hear. But love doesn't do what the other person wants. It does what's best for them. "The thing is that I'm going to mess up too. I'm going to let you down. I'm not perfect either."

"You are." He nods with the energy of a puppy dog's tail. "You're cute and fun and sassy and smart and hardworking and caring and . . ." His quirks an eyebrow. "Tastier than ice cream."

That last one makes me smile. I force myself to finish what I had to say before we get too distracted. "I'm glad you think so, though I could tell you a ton of things that are not that great about me. And if we decide to eventually commit to one another, you're going to find out every one of them. In which case, you might regret changing your plans just for me."

"I would never regret—"

"You might." I wrinkle my nose. "That's why you can't change for me. You *shouldn't* change for me."

His chin lifts. His eyes lose their glint. "I don't know what you're saying."

"I'm saying that number ninety on The List is horrible advice." *Wait until marriage to make him over. Once you're his wife, you can worry about what kind of husband he'll be.* "I don't want you to change at all. I want you to heal from your past hurts. I want you to grow healthier in every way. I want you to pursue your own dreams and figure out what you want most out of life before committing to anyone else. I want you to get married someday only if you want to get married."

He looks away. Glares and squints at nothing in particular before facing me again. "How do I do that when I just want to be with you?"

The question punches my heart like a fastball in the catcher's glove. Kai's offering exactly what I want in this moment, and I have to turn it down to wait for what I want most in life.

"There's nobody else I want to be with." My gaze caresses his face. His full lips. His high cheekbones. His smooth skin. I want to memorize it all. "But I don't only want to get married as my final goal. I want a marriage that lasts. And since you haven't wanted marriage at all, I think if we're going to build such a foundation, it's going to take time."

His eyes plead for more than I can give. "Will I still get to see you? Can we still date?"

Here's the hard part. The part that most people would call crazy—

that I would have called crazy only a couple of months ago. The part that might break us. "I took a job as a nurse manager at a hospital in Kenya. I won't be here."

His eyes grow wider and his face paler than I've ever seen them. "With the doctor who wanted to ask you out?"

He would remember that part. Though this has nothing to do with Dr. Snyder. "No. He'll be working here in the States. He only told me about the openings overseas, which I honestly never would have applied for without you. You helped me grow enough to go for it."

His head rolls back so that it looks as if he's talking to God in heaven. "This was not how I pictured today going."

I squeeze his hands. "Hey. I'm here right now."

He looks down and gives me one of those smug grins that make my toes tingle. "I should have known falling for you would be an adventure."

I give him my cutest smile. Hopefully it makes his toes tingle too. Hopefully this connection lasts a lot longer than tingly toes. "There are worse things."

He jolts upright at my words and gazes across the field toward the announcer's booth. "It's gonna get worse. I need to . . ."

"What?" I follow his gaze to try to see what he might possibly need to do in the middle of our serious conversation.

He stands and tries to squeeze past me toward the stairs, but the giant pickle mascot blocks his path.

"Oh no." He jumps on the bleachers, facing the announcer's booth and waving both arms overhead.

And he made it sound as if I was the strange one. "You okay?"

"Ladies and gentlemen!" The announcer's voice booms through the speaker system that I've been ignoring up until now.

Kai drops back down beside me and grabs my hands. "Meri, I made another mistake."

What could he have possibly done that's worse than sharing our first kiss with the entire world?

A hand in a green plastic glove drops on my shoulder, and I look over it to find Dillon, the mascot. With his other hand he passes Kai a microphone.

The announcer's voice continues to boom. "Please direct your attention to where Dillon is with a couple of fans in section 104."

That's our section. I know Kai is friends with the audiovisual guy, so maybe he agreed to help out with something, and he feels bad that he's abandoning me in the middle of such an intense discussion. That's probably why he wanted to meet here for Tuesday's game. I focus on Kai to see what he's up to.

He drops onto one knee like a guy would do if he was going to—

My hands fly to cover my mouth. Kai wouldn't be proposing. He couldn't be. Just because he's in love with me, and he knows I want to get married . . .

This is the grand gesture Roxy warned me about.

I look around at all the faces turned our way. My image is even on the JumboTron.

"In case you haven't noticed," the announcer says. "This is Kai and Meri from the famous *Meri Me* YouTube show, and Kai has something he wants to ask Meri."

My heart clatters like a cowbell. This is really happening.

"Meri." Kai looks up at me with a mix of purpose and fate. "For the first time, I understand that working to buy an engagement ring is only the beginning of the work a marriage requires. I fully expect you to run out of here tonight and make me *that* guy, but I will continue to pursue you because you've taught me how a dream is worth pursuing even after you fail."

My dream has turned into a nightmare.

The crowd cheers so loudly the bleachers rumble beneath me. Or maybe I'm trembling.

Kai takes out a little red ring box from his jeans pocket. This isn't the ring he bought for Alexis Long, is it? No, he sold that and used the money for film school.

"Will you marry me?" he asks.

No joke. There's a man who wants to marry me, and he's looking me straight in the eye with a crazy kind of confidence. The kind willing to sacrifice himself for love.

He knows I'm going to say no, right? After what I just told him, he must. But, before that, did he really think I'd say yes?

The crowd chants, "Mar-ry me. Mar-ry me."

His last proposal was the worst moment of his life. That rejection knocked him down to the point that he's just now barely getting up. And I'm going to knock him down again.

His eyes are clear and understanding and oh so loving as he waits patiently for my response.

What if I just say yes for show?

Except we really do have a show. This will be news. Everyone will know if I say yes, then take off for a job across the country. Would that be any better?

He gives me his crooked smile. I could just kiss those lips right here. I could back out of my commitment with the hospital in Africa. I want to in this moment.

But then what? Will we become another divorce statistic because we didn't take Jesus's advice? We both have to learn to be capable of growing into the largeness of marriage before we try to make it work. It's too important not to.

I'm still standing here with my hands over my mouth while even the players in their dugouts wait for my response. Who else is watching? What if Alexis Long happens to be here in the audience?

The questions swirl inside me like angry hornets, and static crackles over the PA system as the announcer comes back on to kick their nest. "Well, folks, it looks as if you're about to witness YouTube history. I've only ever seen these kinds of rejections on the internet. Maybe Kai and Meri's online love story wasn't any more real than reality TV."

I didn't even want our first kiss to be public, and now this. I have to get away. I whirl and push past the giant pickle. "I'm so sorry. I'm so sorry."

CHAPTER THIRTY-TWO

Kai

#81. To get your MRS degree, you have to let him think he's more intelligent than you. Brilliant women never marry.

If I'd wanted YouTube views, I've got them now. Hopefully Meri and I can laugh about this someday.

I knew before I even pulled out the ring that she would say no, I just wish she would have done it a little quicker . . . before my knee started to ache from the cement and the announcer made that quip about my love life. Completely heartless. But not as bad as the fans turning on me.

"She-said-no. She-said-no," they chant.

I hand Dillon his microphone back, wiggle my thumb and pinkie in the hang loose sign, and thunder down the stairs to find the woman who is not my fiancée.

What would I have done if she'd said yes? She's right about me not being ready for that. I don't even remember what it's like to have a normal sleep schedule. I'd probably have been one of those husbands who zonked out on the couch and snored before even eating dinner. Nobody wants that.

How backward is it that I feel more loved that she said no than if she'd said yes? It's as if she thinks I'm worth waiting for. And I really hope I am.

I jog between the bleachers, not seeing anything amiss except for a few strangers pointing my way and whispering. If Meri had run out here, wouldn't they all be pointing at her?

She could be in a bathroom, but then I'd never find her. My eyes slide toward the back end of the bleachers where I'd hid my camera when we filmed here. A giant green foam hand peeks out from behind a metal column.

I sigh with relief at the same time my chest tightens in guilt. It's my fault she's run out here to hide.

Again, I'd thought I was doing the right thing. I thought I was giving her what she wanted, but that had been my own selfish attempt to manipulate the situation. The loving thing would have been to give her what she needed—a man willing to get out of his butt dent to be there for her every day.

I duck under some bars and weave through the metal structure.

Meri's eyes meet mine and she rubs at the wet trails on her cheeks.

Oh man, I'd made her cry. I'd rather make her laugh. "Are you letting me see you cry because I have the power to cheer you up?"

She sniffs and looks down, but one corner of her lips curves up. "I think you've mistaken me for a single woman in the fifties."

I don't slow until I'm close enough to cup her face with my hands and smooth my thumbs across the sticky spots where her tears had been. "Maybe. I've heard those fifties women had tricks for attracting men, and you've definitely attracted me."

She lifts her damp lashes, revealing an innocence and openness that I wish I'd protected from the beginning. "Do you really want to marry me?"

"I don't want to lose you." My core clenches tight. How unfair of me to propose before I was ready. She deserves so much more than that. "And I want to become a man worth marrying."

She grips my wrists on either side of her head. "I wasn't trying to reject you. I know that when you were rejected before—"

"Hey." I lower my face to be on eye level. "I'm glad I was rejected before."

My throat clogs with this realization. If I hadn't had my heart broken by Alexis, I wouldn't have met Meri. I wouldn't be here now. I wouldn't know what real love is.

A laugh bursts from her mouth, warm on my thumb, so I slide my hands down to her shoulders to give her the freedom to shake with mirth and share her joke.

"We are quite the pair," she says. "You're afraid of getting married, yet you propose. And I'm afraid of being single, yet I say no."

"If I want a nurse, I must be patient." I grin with her, glad it didn't take as long for her to laugh about this as I'd expected. I add, "Which is something I should have thought of before proposing in front of a live audience."

Meri rolls her eyes at what's destined to become another YouTube video she'll never live down, but when they meet mine again, they hold and darken. "I'm glad we're not in front of a live audience right now."

So am I, but I keep my hands on her shoulders anyway as I lean forward. I pause a breath away and lift my eyes to hers. "Since we're not engaged and you're leaving, I'm not sure how this works. Can I just kiss you whenever I want?"

She grabs my lapel and pulls me in the rest of the way, and I decide, among other things, to start wearing more collared shirts.

CHAPTER THIRTY-THREE

Meri

*#101. Make matrimony your career and
live happily ever after.*

Mom, Douglas, Charlie, Gemma, and Kai all take me to the airport. I'm not so bothered by Douglas anymore. If he wasn't in Mom's life, she'd be really lonely this year with both me and Charlie traveling all over the world.

Charlie does claim to be staying in town indefinitely, which may have something to do with his recent visit to a certain advertising executive. He said it was a business meeting, but he's the one who offered to get the billboard with my face on it taken down. And, hello, Nicole is calling him again now, so he disappears into a coffee shop for another "business" conversation.

As for Gemma, she just hugged me goodbye, then ran off across the airport's iconic funky carpet because she spotted the cop who'd come to the town house when she was all tied up. She said something about wanting to sign up for citizen's police academy as research for her next screenplay, but she could have talked to any law enforcement officer if that was her only intention.

Perhaps the moment I caught the bouquet at Anne's wedding, we were all doomed/destined to find love. I really messed up the whole Bermuda-Triangle-of-relationships thing they had going.

I'm left with Kai, Mom, and Douglas. I'd like to say goodbye to Kai alone, but I doubt that either Mom or Douglas are going to take off to answer mysterious phone calls or chase down law enforcement officers.

Case in point, Mom reaches for me and pulls me into a warm hug. She smells like tea and roses, but she hangs on as if she's Charlie. "I'm so proud of you, Meredith."

"For what?" Moms have to say this kind of thing, and I'm really not sure what I've done that she's proud of. I made a spectacle of myself this summer, which is something she'd always warned me not to do.

"For following your heart and taking your head along with you."

Okay. That is something to be proud of. As I found out, it's way too easy to let my feelings overcome my good sense.

Douglas pats my shoulder. Still awkward, but he's trying. And trying is something I've come to really respect. "You're doing something good, kid. Mission work makes a difference."

He called me kid, but I'll try not to hold it against him. "Thanks, Douglas."

Mom releases me to take Douglas's hand. They look cute together. As if they'll become one of those little old couples who have loved each other for fifty years. They might not make it to half a century, due to getting together later in life, but I bet they'll appreciate each other even more because they'd spent so much time alone. Kind of like me and Kai.

I catch Kai's eye over Douglas's shoulder. Kai's got his hands stuffed in the pockets of his cargo shorts, and he's wearing flip-flops even though it's raining. He smiles the kind of smile that I can feel from far away, and I know that even from Africa, I'm going to feel it.

"Oh, honey," Mom says, and I look at her only to realize she's speaking to Douglas. She points in the window of the airport bookstore. "They have that book we've been wanting to get for our premarital counseling."

I follow the direction of her finger. Yes, I'd turned down Kai's proposal, but that doesn't mean I'm never going to get married. It means I *need* to read books about relationships because there's no such thing as a foolproof list of ways to find a husband. A proposal can't be earned the way it claimed. Love is only given, not taken.

Douglas lets go of Mom's hand and heads toward the shop. "I'll go get us a copy."

Mom peeks at me. "I better go with him. He's kind of a nerd and could get lost in there."

I hug her once more because I agree with Douglas being a nerd, but also because I know what she's really doing. "Thanks, Mom."

I take a deep breath and face Kai. Despite living in separate houses this past month, we've become even better friends. I'm going to miss him.

He steps closer, blocking out all the travelers, TSA, and intercom announcements that surround us. He takes my hand in a loving way, but his dark eyes sparkle with mischief. "Mind if I make one more video of us?"

I can't tell if he's joking or not. "Since not everyone in the world has seen us kiss yet?"

He pulls out his phone, switches to selfie mode, and lifts it high. I smile up at our on-screen images. The benefit to dating a cameraman is that he knows the best angle to make me look good.

"I'll stop filming before I kiss you this time, but I have something to tell you along with our followers."

My stomach flip-flops. "You better not be proposing again, because I'd like that to be private, as well."

Kai looks down his nose at me, big smile on his lips. "No. As you so publicly pointed out, I'm not ready for marriage yet. Which is why I made a list of things I need to do to become a gentleman."

My heart gallops with giddiness. "You made a list?"

"I did."

I grin at how far we've come. "Did you put down 'get rid of foot fungus with iodine and peroxide'?"

"I'll have to add it." He smirks, then lets go of my hand and digs into his pocket to retrieve a folded piece of printer paper. "This copy is for you. I'll be posting mine online so our viewers can help keep me accountable. Though I'm going to have to change the spelling of my show to *M-A-R-R-Y Me*."

I take the paper and unfold it. I already know he's planning to make my Jeep payment and take care of Julia while I'm gone. What else does he have up his sleeve? "You better not lasso yourself a date while I'm in Africa."

"Of course not. Who in their right mind would do something so absurd?"

"Hey." I laugh and give him a little shove before reading.

#1. Volunteer at church outside the video booth.

This isn't a list of things that I want him to do. This is a list of things that will make him a better person. And that's what touches me most. It shows me his growth is real. This is between him and God, as it should be.

I can't wait to see how he performs these tasks. Is he going to take Gemma's place in the Easter bunny costume during the next Easter egg hunt? I might have to come back for that.

"I hope you'll still work in the video production booth. I like sitting up there with you."

"Oh, I like it too." He tilts his head as if he's ready to kiss me, but then turns his face toward the phone. "And that's all for you guys." He clicks it off and stuffs it in one of his many pockets.

I clap, since I'm his biggest fan. "Yay. You can kiss me goodbye now."

He steps closer and cups my face. "I don't say goodbye, remember? I say aloha."

Then he gives me a kiss I'll never forget. I'm almost regretting my decision to leave.

The intercom buzzes. "Attention in the terminal. Flight number nineteen-oh-one to Las Vegas is now boarding at gate B5."

That's me. And I haven't even made it through security yet. I pull away and open my eyes to stare into Kai's. "I have to go."

He slides his fingers down my neck and shoulders to release his hold. "Go change the world."

His expectations might be a little high, but I'll do my best. I adjust the bag on my shoulder, grab the handle of my rolling suitcase, and stare down at The List in my hand. "Déjà vu."

He stuffs his hands back in his pockets and grins. "You know, there's one thing on your list you never accomplished, so I did it for you."

I walk backward, rolling the suitcase with me. There's more than one thing on The List I didn't do. I fell in love before finishing. And also, some of the suggestions were even more outrageous than trying to lasso a date. Is Kai going to stow away on a cruise ship? Take a bicycle trip through Canada? Sit on a park bench and feed ducks? "What's that?"

He follows me as far as he can before we reach the TSA checkpoint. "Look out the plane window as you fly over Roxy's house, and you'll see."

My mouth falls open. "You didn't."

He shakes his thumb and pinkie finger at me, then turns to saunter away. I'm really glad his new growth hasn't affected his saunter.

I get through security and to my seat right as the gate agent closes the plane door. If not for the view I'm looking forward to on takeoff, I might be bummed I made my flight. I wouldn't have minded spending another day here in Portland with the man who loves me.

Though there's something freeing about our love. About not needing each other in order to be happy.

I press my forehead to the smooth window, hoping I can make out which roof is Roxy's. The plane engines rev, sounding a little like barking dogs. The runway turns into a blur. Then my belly drops as we rise off the ground.

I needn't have worried about spotting Roxy's house since she's so close to the airport. And since Kai didn't actually use Christmas lights but covered her roof with a blue tarp.

Rather than just a phone number, he painted, I'LL GIVE YOU A RING, MERI.

And I don't think he means on the phone.

I smile, then my breath catches. I touch my fingers to the glass and strain my neck to see Roxy's house as the plane soars higher and hides it from view.

It's too late to double-check, but I'm pretty sure there was a brown truck that looked like Graham's parked in front of Roxy's house. And the man who climbed out held something red in his hands. Maybe roses.

Here's hoping I might soon be attending another best friend's wedding.

101 WAYS TO FIND A HUSBAND

Meet Him

1. Volunteer with shelter dogs.
2. Fake a flat tire or pretend engine trouble.
3. Offer to take your dad's new car for an oil change. Have the cutest mechanic check your odometer, so he knows you're not the type of girl who gets around.
4. Move to a state with more men than women. We recommend Nevada.
5. Attend funerals to check out widowers.
6. Sit in front of him at church. You're not trying to distract him from the good Lord. You just want to show him how bountiful God's blessing can be.
7. Learn to golf. It's a great place to meet a man and also important to play with your man so you know he's not playing around.
8. Check out his grocery cart. If you like what he buys, you might like him as a person.
9. Buy a lawn mower or power tool you don't need just so you can ask his advice about the best one to get.
10. Pretend to trip or fall in front of him so he has to help you up.
11. If you learn to drink your coffee black, you'll attract a higher quality man.
12. Make friends with beautiful women. They usually have a cast of unwanted suitors.
13. Ask your friends' husbands to set you up with eligible bachelors they know.
14. Join the local historical society.

15. Plan an outdoor trip. That way if you get angry at him and accidentally tell him to "take a hike," you won't have to apologize.
16. Work as a waitress or nurse. Men love being taken care of.
17. Treat a bad guy like the hero you want him to be.
18. Blind dates can be the best way to open a man's eyes.
19. Throw nothing but gutter balls at the local bowling alley the night the men's league is playing. Soon, one of them will be sure to come by to offer helpful hints.
20. Go to your local fishing pier and feign squeamishness about baiting your own hook. Chances are some handsome angler will happily skewer that worm for you, never realizing that you were the bait all along.
21. Ask a man to take your photograph. Chances are, he'll want his own copy.
22. Work at a hardware store.
23. Don't be roommates with a wet rag.
24. Get a job in a male-dominated field. You'll stand out, gain respect, and up your odds.

Attract Him

25. Change up your look. Try eyeglasses.
26. Look over your whole ensemble in a mirror before ever answering the door for a date.
27. Practice blowing kisses in front of a mirror to perfect your pout.
28. Root for his baseball team. As you know, diamonds are a girl's best friend.
29. Let the sun kiss your skin for a rich and healthy glow.
30. Advertise for a man to share ownership of a boat.
31. Be sure to laugh at his jokes, but allow a light, airy chuckle. Nothing boisterous.
32. Act in a play with him. Preferably as Romeo and Juliet, but if he turns out to be brainless like the Scarecrow in *The Wonderful Wizard of Oz*, play the part of a tree and throw apples at him.
33. Go to a rodeo. Rescue the Lone Ranger from himself.
34. Wear dresses. If you dress casually, he'll treat you casually.

35. Be dangerous. Be well-read.
36. Why stop with a hat, when you could carry a hatbox? Be both charming and intriguing.
37. If you have large feet, buy shoes one size too small. Beauty requires discomfort sometimes.
38. A man should never see you without makeup.
39. Never accept an invitation less than twenty-four hours in advance or he will think you're undesirable to other men.
40. Never outshine your man in any athletic activity. Men have sensitive egos and usurping their sportsmanlike prowess will lead to the demise of your relationship.
41. Be the model of a glamorous housewife. Do calisthenics to keep your figure.
42. Keep your hair perfectly coiffed, even if he's completely bald. Bald men are more eager to please.
43. Holiday at an adventurous location.
44. Hang out near the entrance to the men's room.
45. Wear red shoes. They make you walk faster, and if you have pretty legs, people will notice.
46. Become famous. Hollywood is golden, like a wedding ring.
47. If he's riding a train, he's going places. Sit next to him and find out where.
48. Don't forget to wear gloves on your first date!
49. Sit on a park bench and feed ducks.

Get Him to Commit

50. Bake his favorite dessert. Bad cooking will drive your man to seedy saloons.
51. Prudence is a virtue.
52. Double date with a married couple so he can see what he'd be missing if he doesn't marry you.
53. If you are going out to dinner, eat beforehand so you can order something small. This will do two things: show him you don't have a large appetite and save him money.
54. Make a show of wearing any jewelry or accessory he gives you.

55. Only let him see you cry if he has the power to cheer you up. Otherwise, you're wasting your tears.

56. Don't tell him about the fun you've had on other dates. Men deserve and desire to be the center of your attention.

57. Don't let him see your age on your driver's license. You are whatever age he wants you to be.

58. Let your date do the ordering. Never directly ask the waiter for anything.

59. Saying "I love you" is a relationship milestone. Let him be the first to take that step.

60. Compliment his car. How he takes care of it will symbolize how he will take care of you.

61. Be the glamorous single girl at your high school reunion. Show your old beau what he's missing out on.

62. Listen to your mother. Adam and Eve's issues may have stemmed from the lack of a mother's wisdom.

63. The two of you should claim a song as your own so whenever he hears it, he thinks of you.

64. Send anonymous roses to his house with poems. He may suspect they are from you, but keeping it anonymous will keep you from looking too forward.

65. Breathe as little as possible around him and make them shallow breaths. No man wants to see the full girth of a woman's rib cage.

66. Send a note to his pastor explaining why you're a good candidate for marriage.

67. Buy new furniture so he can help you move it.

68. Keep him guessing. Learn the art of a poker face.

69. For a proper courtship, have a chaperone.

70. Find out what books, movies, and music he likes, then make them your favorite too.

71. If he's not friends with your brother, then become friends with his sisters. They can spy on him and tell you his secrets so you know how to best fulfill his every need.

72. Your first kiss should last four seconds. Long enough to make

him want more but not long enough to come across as well practiced.

73. Have your father offer him extra season tickets to the local theater.

74. Share recipes with his mother. If she knows her son will be well-fed, she'll be more apt to encourage the romance.

75. Educate him on the fact that married men live longer than single men.

76. Never argue politics. Instead, ask him who to vote for to show how much you trust his judgment.

77. If he asks what you want as a gift, tell him perfume. Then you'll know you're wearing a scent he likes.

78. Have a nickname for your steady. He can be your Dreamboat, and you can be his Angel Face.

79. Throw a house party to show him you're not a bore and possess the skills required to plan a successful engagement event.

80. Don't be catty. Unless you're purring like a kitten.

81. To get your MRS degree, you have to let him think he's more intelligent than you. Brilliant women never marry.

82. If he wants to never grow up, like Peter Pan, don't make him face his consequences the way Tinker Bell did. Be his mom, like Wendy.

83. Don't talk about having children.

84. The wrong wife can break the right man. Let him be right, so he knows he won't go wrong with you.

85. Take dance classes together, so you'll become a natural at following his lead.

86. Parental approval is of utmost importance.

87. Having your clothes pressed and mended and your shoes shined not only makes you look good, they show him that you know how to make him look good too.

88. Always sit like royalty, with your legs crossed at the ankle. It worked for Grace Kelly, and it can work for you.

89. Earn the proposal. Get him to see that matrimony is key to his personal fulfillment.

90. Wait until marriage to make him over. Once you're his wife, you can worry about what kind of husband he'll be.

Go for the Gold

91. Rent an apartment in a rich area of town. You'll meet men of greater means.
92. Stow away on a cruise ship.
93. Take a bicycle trip through Canada.
94. Learn how to use a lasso and rope the cowboy of your dreams.
95. Faint in front of him. Seeing a woman's weakness awakens a man's nature to take care of her.
96. Using Christmas lights, decorate your roof with your phone number for curious pilots.
97. There's nothing more romantic than a view. Ask a Ferris wheel operator to leave you at the top of the ride for longer than usual.
98. Wear a bandage in public and have a tale of daring to go with it.
99. Create suspense like Alfred Hitchcock by buying a convertible to go with your headscarf and cat-eye glasses.
100. Get your personal ad in front of as many eligible bachelors as possible. Like on a billboard.
101. Make matrimony your career and live happily ever after.

ACKNOWLEDGMENTS

This book will always be special to me because I wrote it before my breast cancer diagnosis, I sold it during treatment, and the dream of one day having you read these words kept me going. Anyone who helped me with this book also helped me win a battle.

First came my IDAhope Writers. They sat around the conference table with me, suggesting modern-day scene ideas for using dating advice from the fifties. Peter Leavell, in particular, was so entranced by the idea of a hatbox that I had to put him in my book. He trusted me enough to give permission, even though he still hasn't read this. Not to mention it's his character in real life that fit my story pieces together.

My critique partners Heather Woodhaven, Hilarey Johnson, and Kimberly Rose Johnson read the manuscript and honed the message. My agent, Sarah Freese, was awesome too, and not only because she died her hair pink with me for breast cancer awareness. She is my Jerry Maguire.

Then came a few editors who championed the book with their publishers. Though they weren't able to make offers on this novel, their belief in me inspired my real-life story.

It was at the ACFW conference in San Antonio where my bathroom buddy, Melissa Ferguson, introduced me to Janyre Tromp. Though Kregel hadn't published romantic comedy before, Janyre persuaded them to take a risk. And when we had our first video conference, her enthusiasm for *Husband Auditions* told me it was in good hands. Thank you to the whole team.

I also have to thank my amazing readers group. When I found out that I couldn't use the original list I'd based this story upon, my online readers helped me create a whole new list. What began as an overwhelming task turned into a fun game. They are brilliant, and I hope they see their fingerprints in all my work.

The cherry on top of this sundae is my dear friend and editor Christina Tarabochia. I met her at my very first conference fifteen years ago. We had grand dreams, but never in our very wild imaginations considered the possibility that she would one day get paid to make my books better. She's taught me as much about life as she has about writing. And that's a lot.

As for all the family and friends whom I haven't mentioned, they carried me when I couldn't walk. Their prayers and support dug a hole through the roof and lowered me to the feet of Jesus. I can only tell of God's love because I've been changed by it, and they are part of that miracle.

In the same way that everyone who helped me publish this novel helped me fight my battle with cancer, the reverse is true as well. Everyone who helped me survive this past year also helped me create this book. I am forever grateful for the meals, socks, bracelets, journals, lotions, blankets, and flowers. Thank you.

ABOUT THE AUTHOR

Angela Ruth Strong sold her first Christian romance novel in 2009, then quit writing romance when her first marriage fell apart. Twelve years later, God has shown her the true meaning of love, and there's nothing else she'd rather write about. Her books have since earned top pick from the *Romantic Times*, won the Cascade Award, and been Amazon best sellers. Her book *Finding Love in Big Sky* was converted into a screenplay; the movie, also titled *Finding Love in Big Sky*, recently filmed on location in Montana.

To help aspiring authors, Angela started IDAhope Writers in Idaho, where she lives, and she teaches as an expert online at *Write That Book* and blogs for *Learn How to Write a Novel*. She also writes nonfiction for *SpiritLed Woman*. Besides writing, Angela teaches exercise classes, works for an airline, and enjoys Harley rides with her husband and camping with her three kids. Find out more at www.angelaruthstrong.com.